FROM THE FILMS OF

Harry Potter™

Watercolor Magic

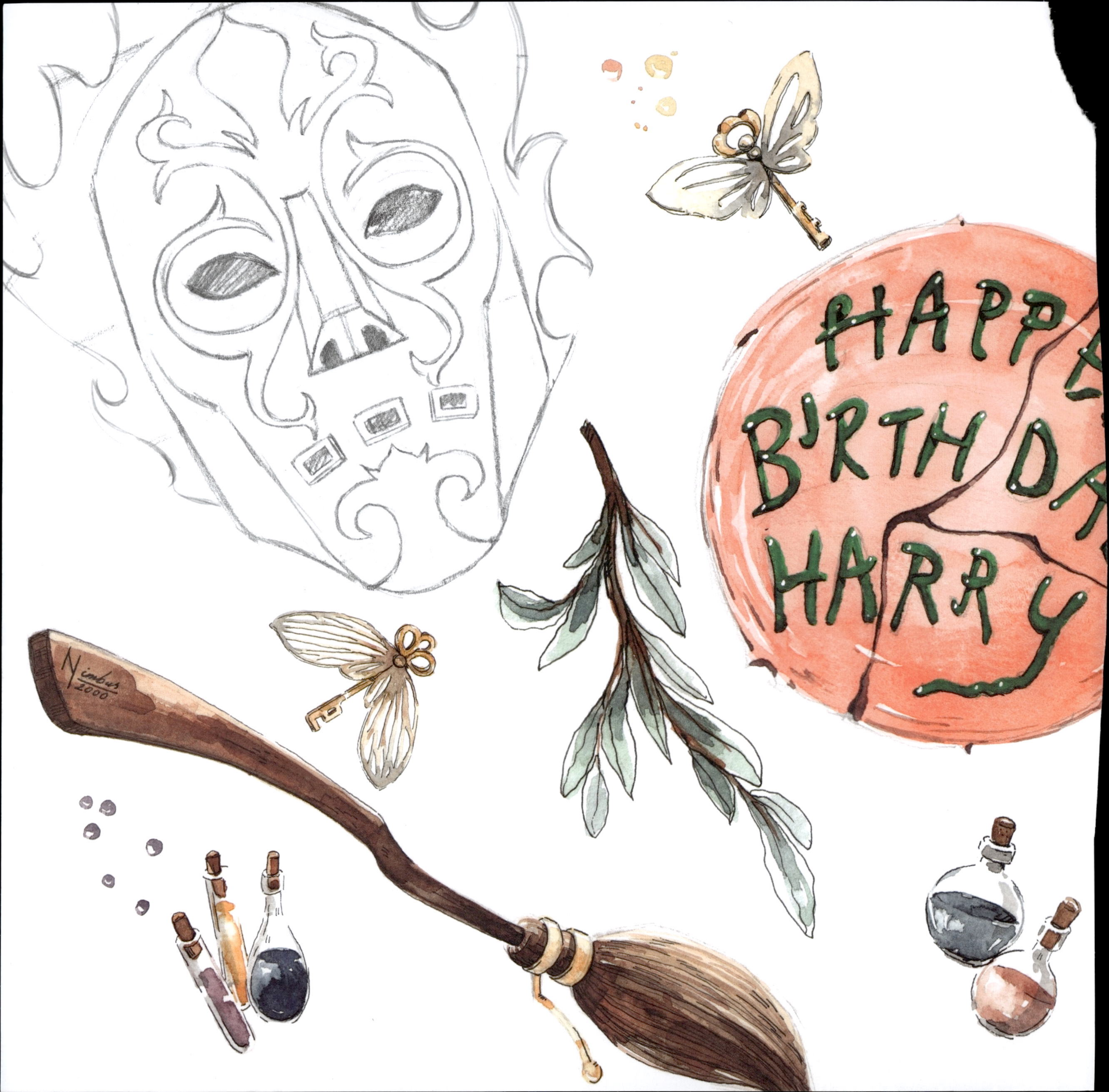
HAPPE
BIRTHDA
HARRY
Nimbus
2000

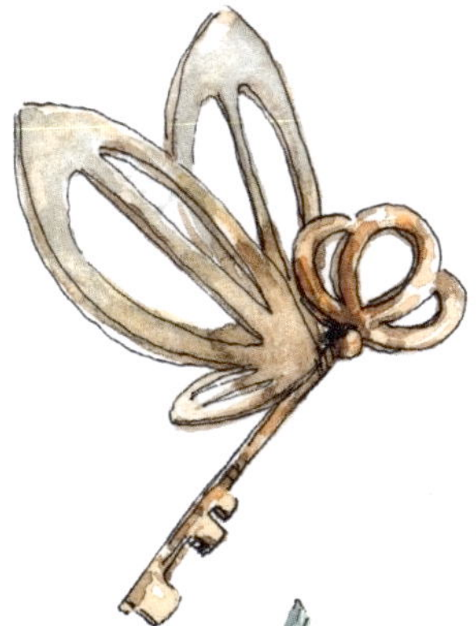

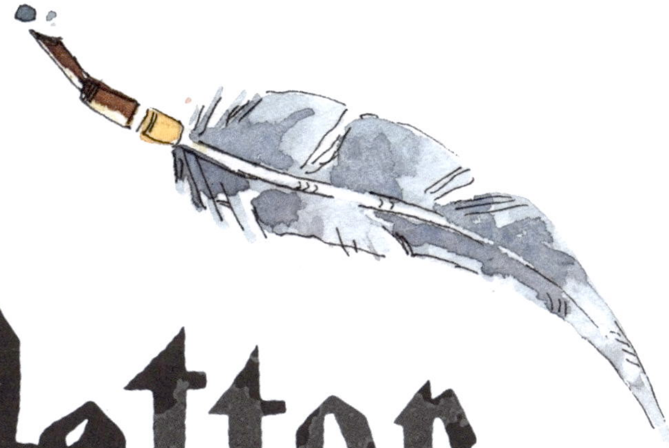

FROM THE FILMS OF

Harry Potter™

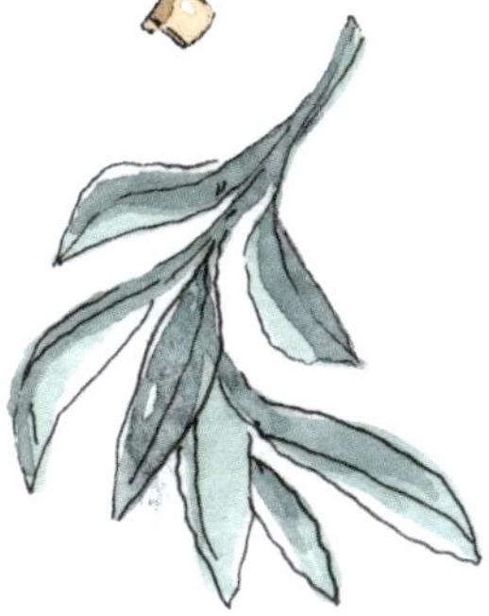

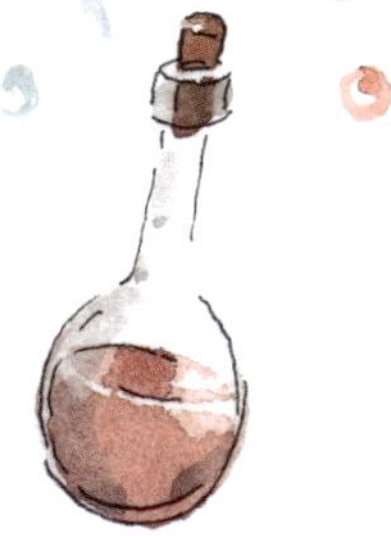

Watercolor Magic

32 STEP-BY-STEP ENCHANTING PROJECTS

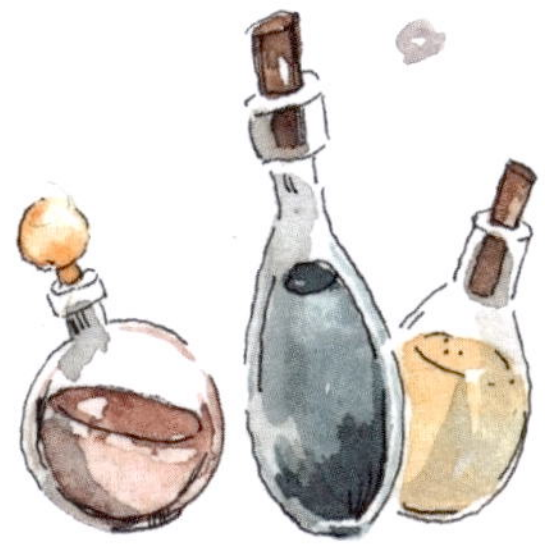

Tugce Audoire

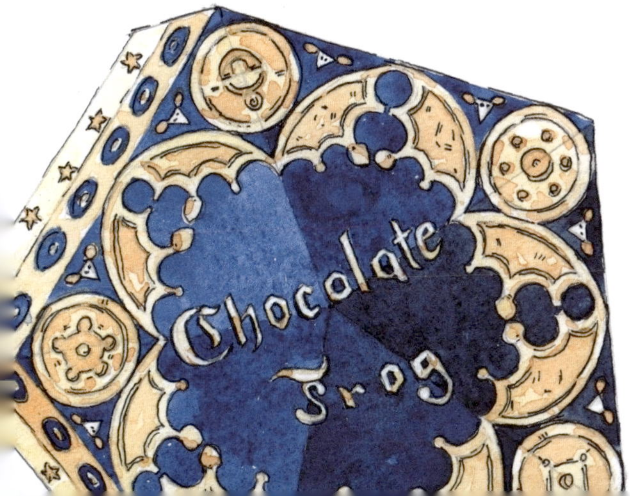

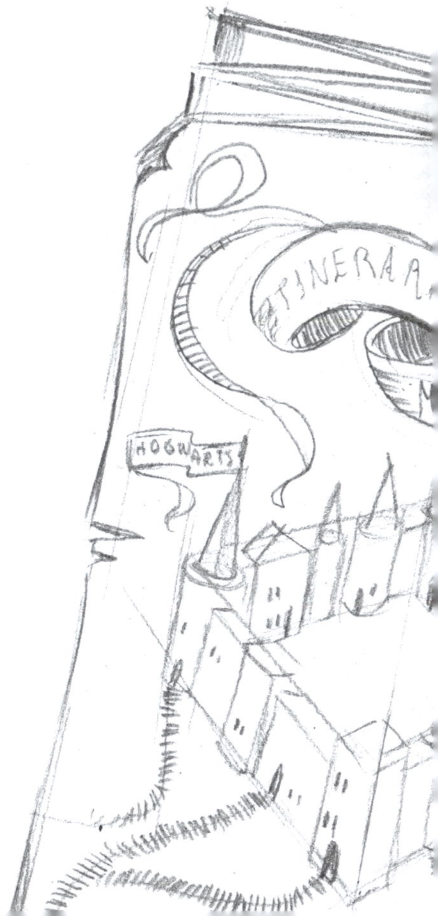

INSIGHT EDITIONS

SAN RAFAEL • LOS ANGELES • LONDON

Contents

Each piece has been assigned a difficulty rating:

Simple ⚡ Intermediate ⚡⚡ Advanced ⚡⚡⚡

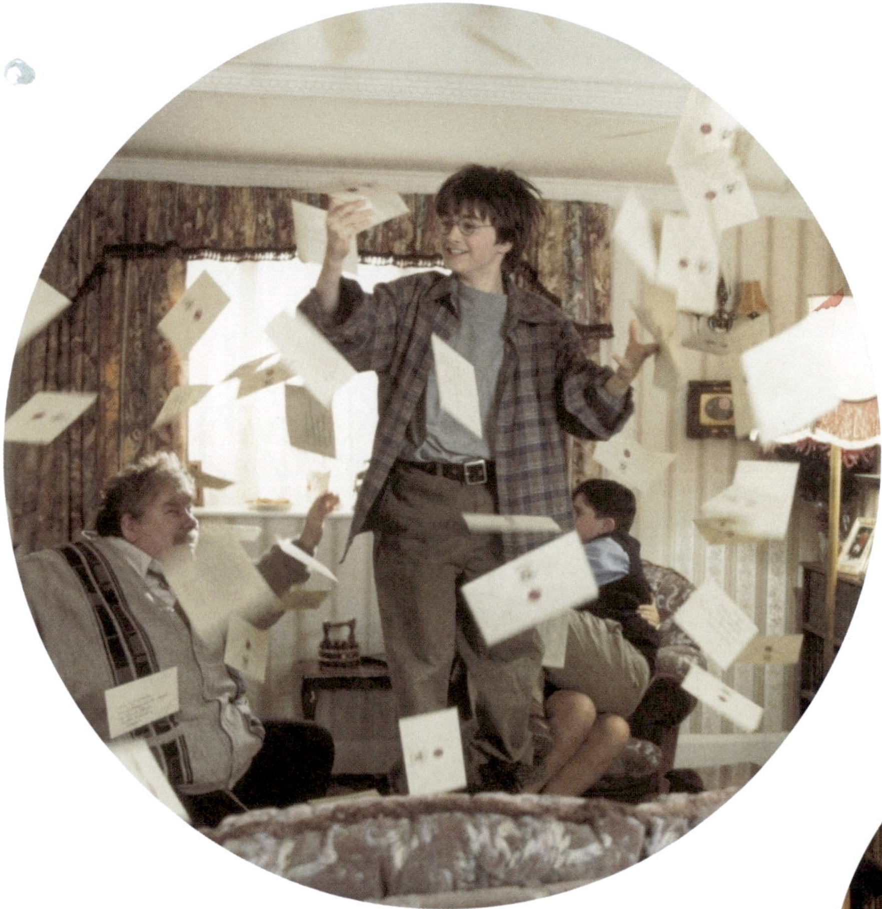

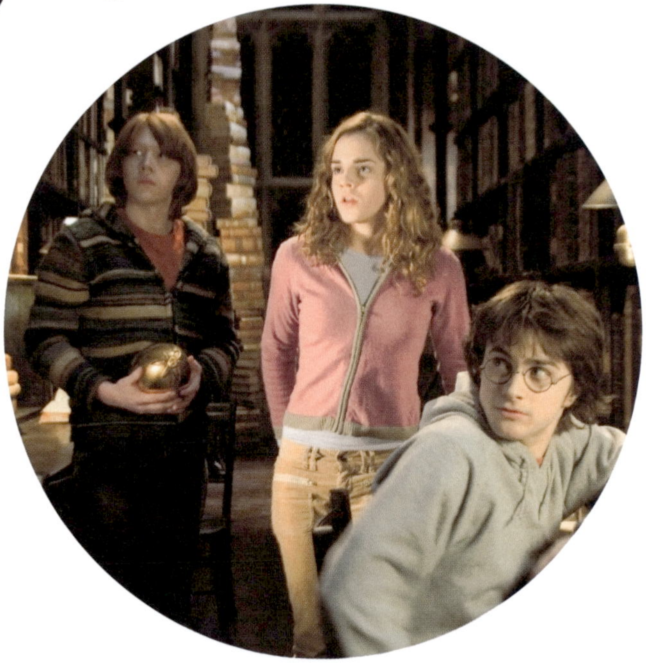

Introduction

The world of the Harry Potter films is filled with magic, mystery, and delight. And the whimsical nature of watercolor makes it the perfect medium for fans of all ages and skill sets to enjoy painting some of the most iconic places, people, creatures, and items from the beloved series.

Whether you're new to watercolor or a fan of the Wizarding World, this book will give you the practice and confidence to create your own beautiful and unique watercolor pieces.

For each piece, we provide a full-color image and step-by-step instructions, as well as the suggested color palette and supplies. The back of the book contains thirty-two corresponding sketches printed on premium watercolor paper. The removable pages make it easy to tear out the sketches, place on your workspace, and practice your watercolor skills! When you're done, your creation can easily be hung or framed.

If you're new to watercolor, it may be best to start with simple pieces. This allows you to become accustomed to applying paint in various ways, as well as to blending shades to create smooth transitions on designs that are more forgiving. The intermediate and advanced pieces provide instruction and practice on more advanced techniques, helping you create more detailed pieces for your collection.

Grab your paint and brushes. It's time to create some Watercolor Magic!

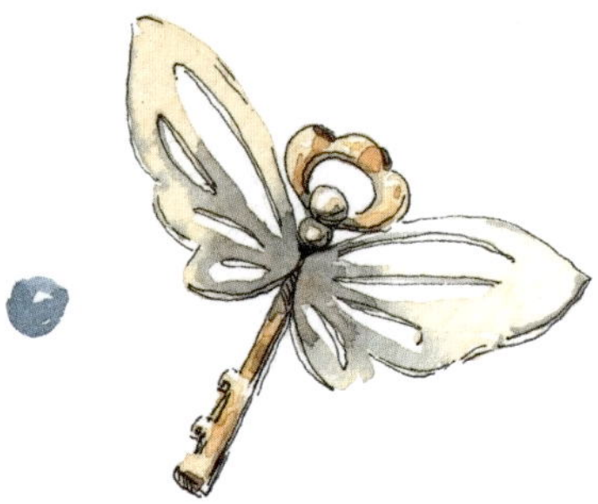

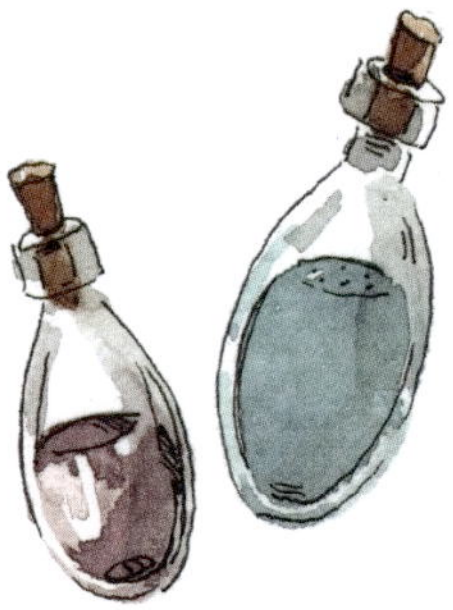

Master Color Chart

The colors listed here are mostly taken from the Winsor & Newton Cotman Half Pan Studio Set 45, but comparable colors from other brands will work well, too.

We've listed the base colors here, along with a few colors that are mixed from others. As you paint your own creations throughout the book, you may notice that the project palettes often list something as "Light." When you see that, it means that you should dilute the color listed to create a lighter shade.

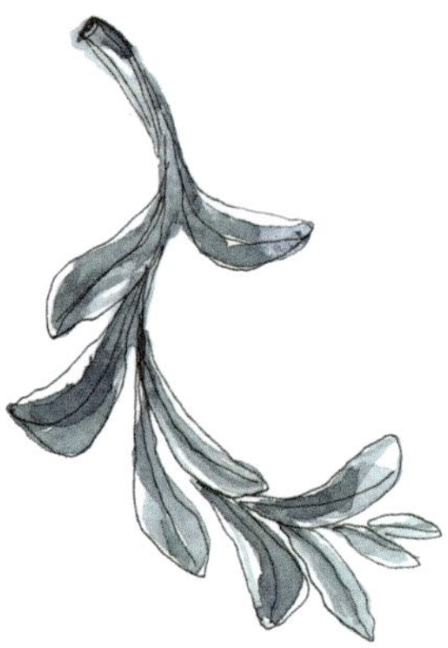

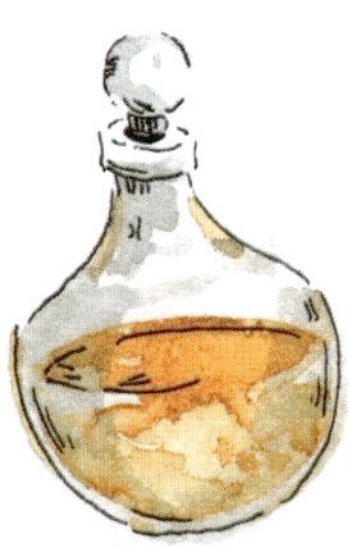

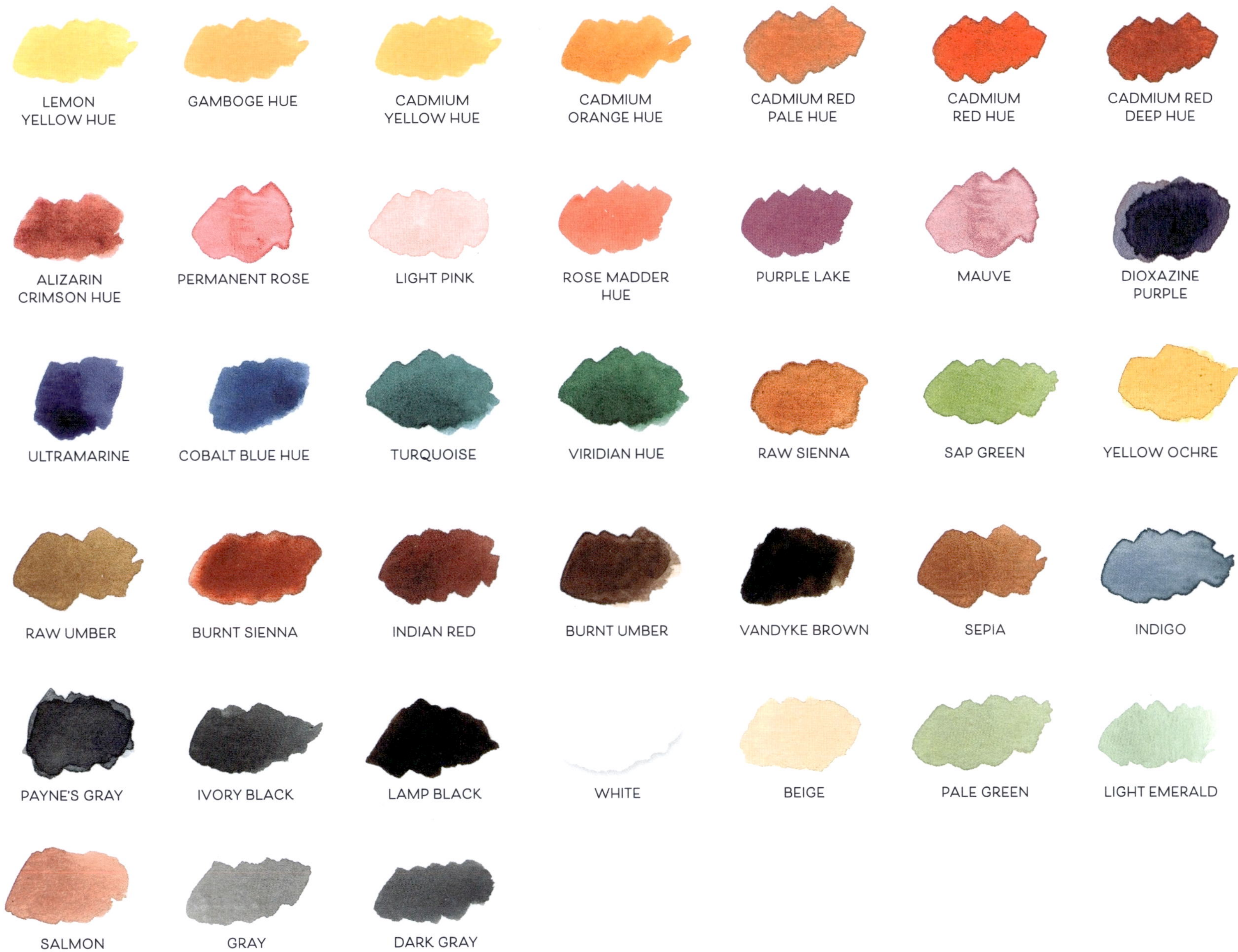
LEMON YELLOW HUE
GAMBOGE HUE
CADMIUM YELLOW HUE
CADMIUM ORANGE HUE
CADMIUM RED PALE HUE
CADMIUM RED HUE
CADMIUM RED DEEP HUE
ALIZARIN CRIMSON HUE
PERMANENT ROSE
LIGHT PINK
ROSE MADDER HUE
PURPLE LAKE
MAUVE
DIOXAZINE PURPLE
ULTRAMARINE
COBALT BLUE HUE
TURQUOISE
VIRIDIAN HUE
RAW SIENNA
SAP GREEN
YELLOW OCHRE
RAW UMBER
BURNT SIENNA
INDIAN RED
BURNT UMBER
VANDYKE BROWN
SEPIA
INDIGO
PAYNE'S GRAY
IVORY BLACK
LAMP BLACK
WHITE
BEIGE
PALE GREEN
LIGHT EMERALD
SALMON
GRAY
DARK GRAY

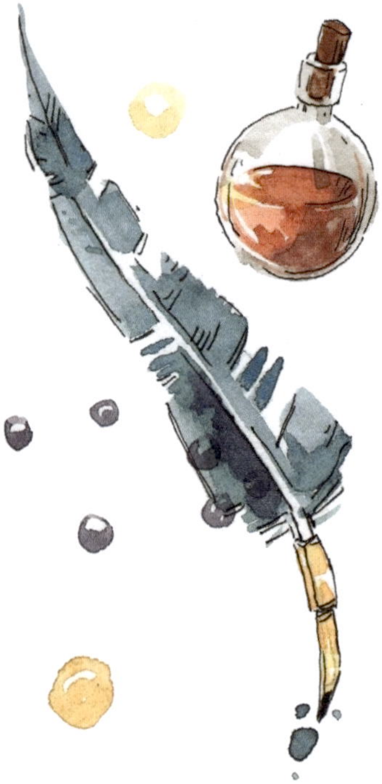

Supply List

While the brushes listed here are all Winsor & Newton Cotman Brand, other good quality brushes will serve you well, too. Daler Rownery, Raphael, and Mont Mante all provide solid brushes to get you started.

COTMAN BRUSH SERIES 111

These round brushes are great for all-purpose watercolor use. They work well for applying broad strokes of color but can also create sharp points for careful work.

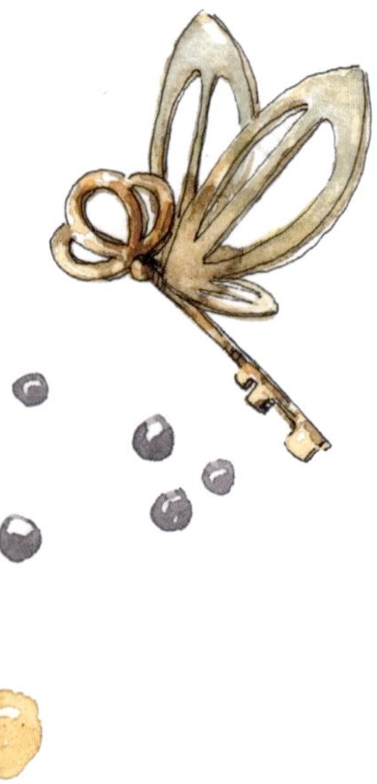

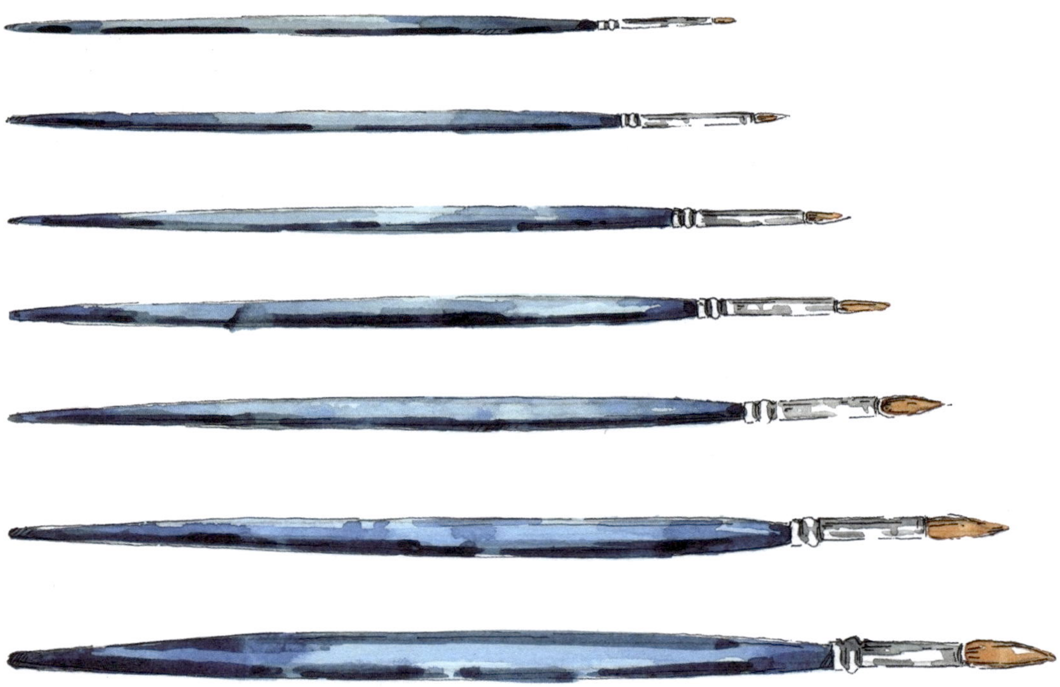

Size 000 brush

Size 01 brush

Size 02 brush

Size 04 brush

Size 06 brush

Size 08 brush

Size 10 brush

COTMAN BRUSH SERIES 666

These flat wash brushes are perfect for creating sharp edges and bold shapes.

Size 3mm brush 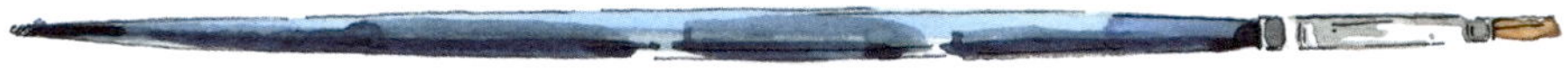

Size 6mm brush 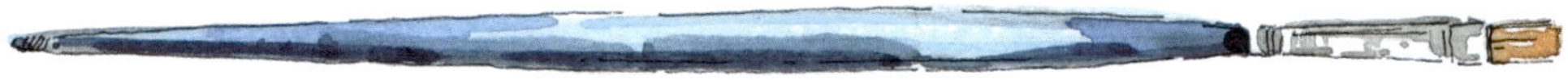

Size 10mm brush 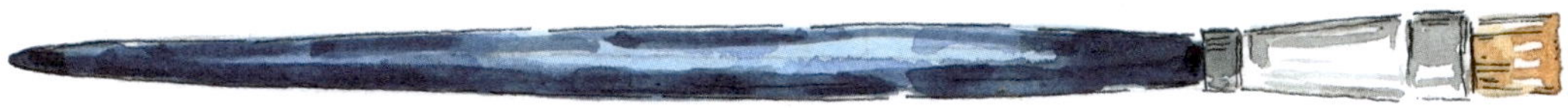

PILOT G-TEC BLACK GEL PEN
UNI-BALL SIGNO WHITE GEL PEN

Gel pens, in both black and white, are also extremely useful for adding fine details.

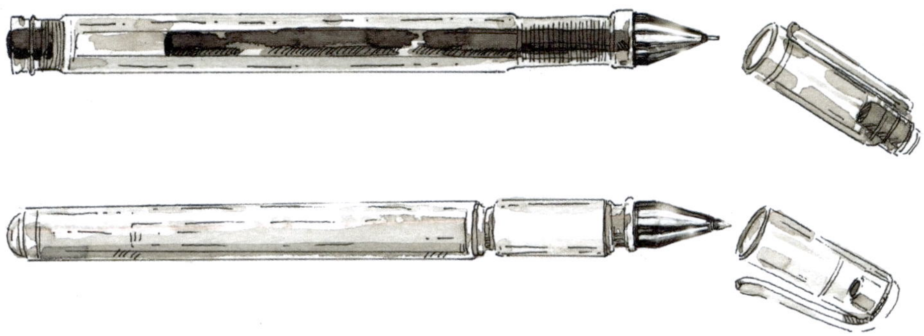

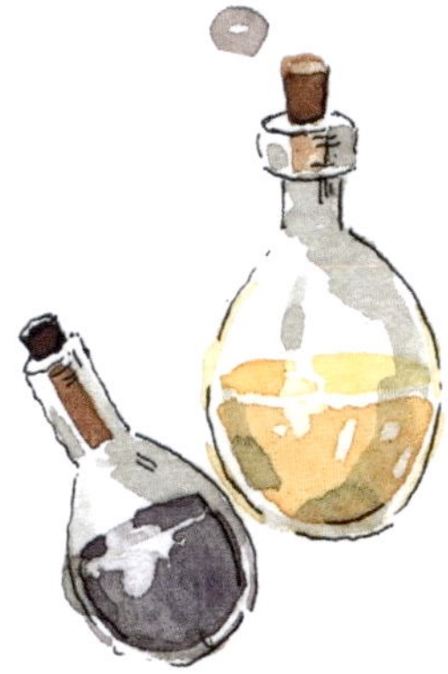

DIFFICULTY: ⚡

The Sorting Hat

"Hmmm difficult, very difficult. Plenty of courage I see; not a bad mind either. There's talent, oh yes, and a thirst to prove yourself. But where to put you? Not Slytherin, eh? Are you sure? You could be great, you know? It's all here in your head, and Slytherin will help you on the way to greatness, there's no doubt about that. No? Well, if you're sure . . . better be . . . Gryffindor!"
—The Sorting Hat, *Harry Potter and the Sorcerer's Stone*

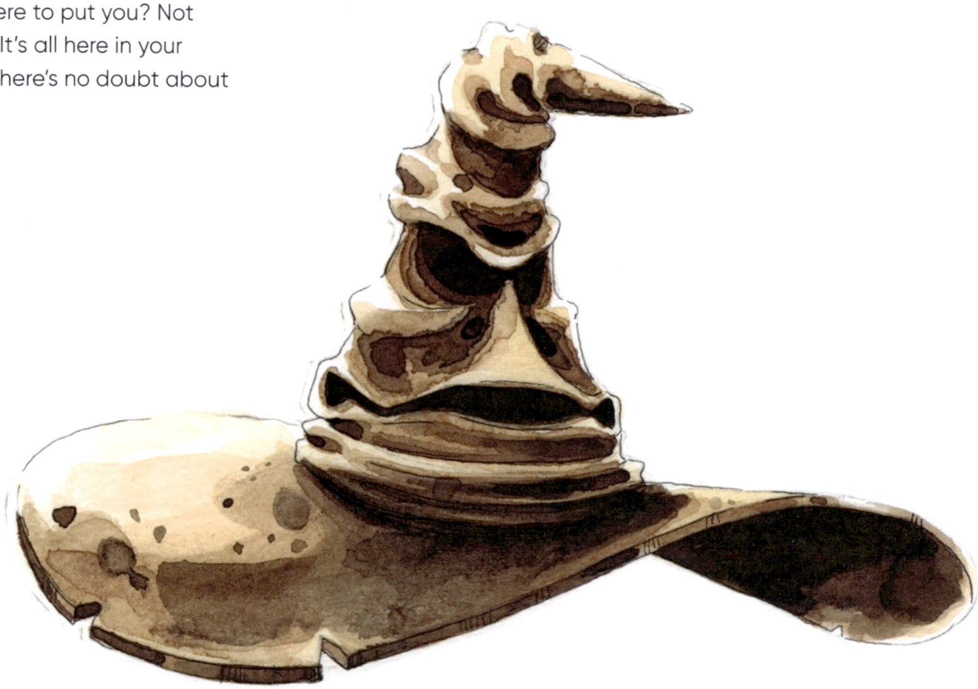

COLORS

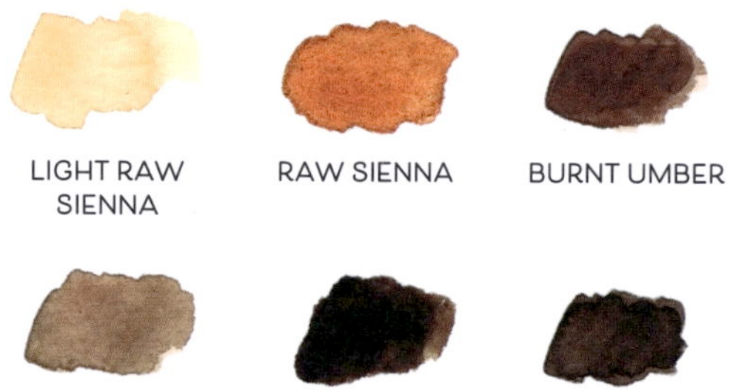

LIGHT RAW SIENNA

RAW SIENNA

BURNT UMBER

LIGHT VANDYKE BROWN

VANDYKE BROWN

DARK VANDYKE BROWN

RECOMMENDED SUPPLIES

Size 06 brush

Black gel pen

1. Use your brush to add plenty of water to the light raw sienna in your palette. However, avoid using too much water, as it can cause your paper to become warped. Using a size 06 brush, paint the entire hat with this color. Let it dry for a couple of minutes.
2. Build up the shading on the right side of the hat by layering the other colors, starting with the raw sienna. It's always best to start with the lightest color, before moving to the next darkest, and so forth. Tilt your brush and start adding this color starting from the tip of the hat. Resist the urge to cover the entire hat. Leave some areas, especially on the left of the hat, with the lighter colors showing through. This will help the hat look three-dimensional and give the effect of a light source shining from the left.
3. Repeat the same process with the burnt umber and light Vandyke brown, shading in the folds and wrinkles of the hat. It's an organic object, so avoid having sharp edges, but instead use soft, round lines. For a better result, move your arm from your elbow, avoiding wrist movements. Do not fill in the eyes and mouth yet. When you're happy with your shading, let the paint dry completely.
4. Once it is 100 percent dry, fill in the eyes and mouth with the Vandyke brown. Let it dry, then dip a clean brush into water and use it to smooth some shades into the eyes and mouth. Because the paint is water based, you can manipulate it even after it is dry by adding a touch of water.
5. Add some dirt marks on the hat to make it look old and damaged. You can randomly splash a bit of paint on it or use the tip of your brush to create round dirt marks.
6. After it is completely dry, add some dark Vandyke brown (mix a small amount of black into your Vandyke brown) to sharpen the shadows in the eyes, mouth, and the underside of the hat.
7. When that is dry, use your gel pen to add final details, such as borderlines, texture, and wrinkles.

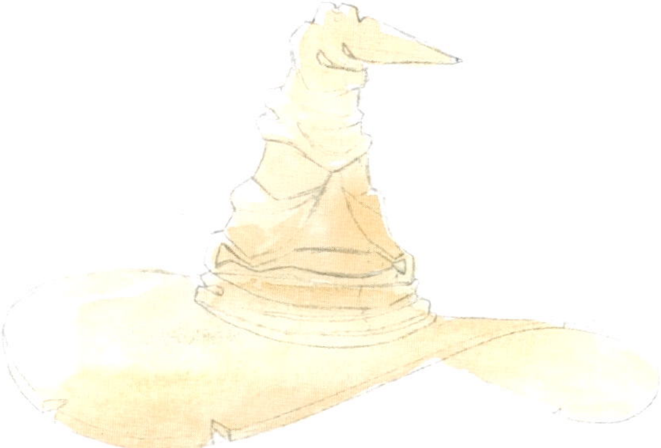

1

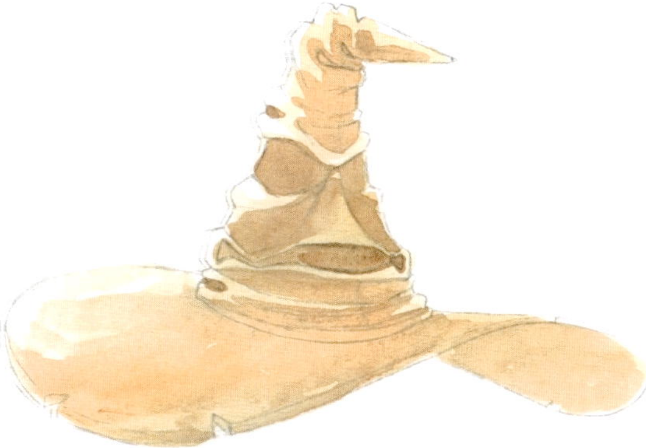

2

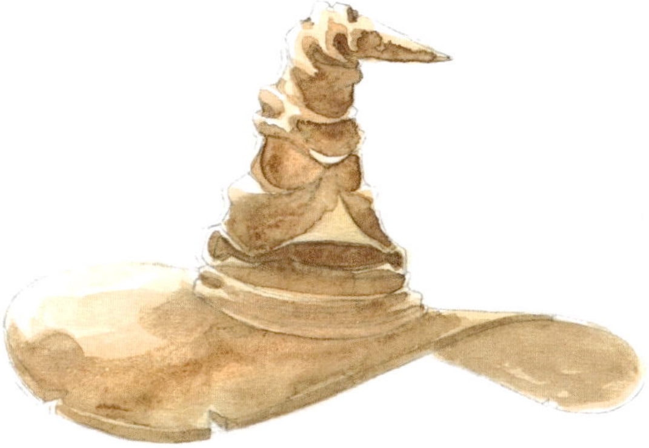

3

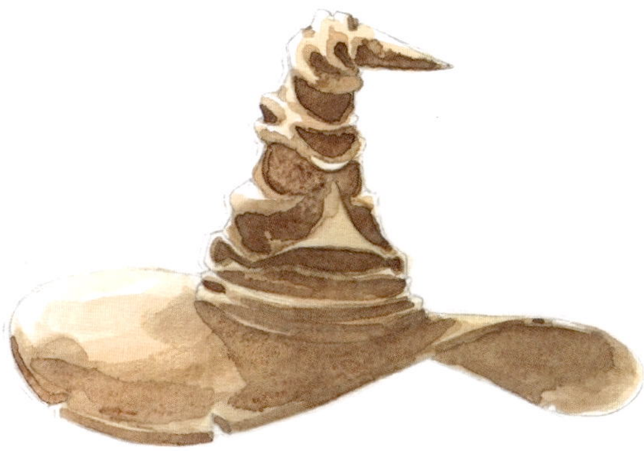

4

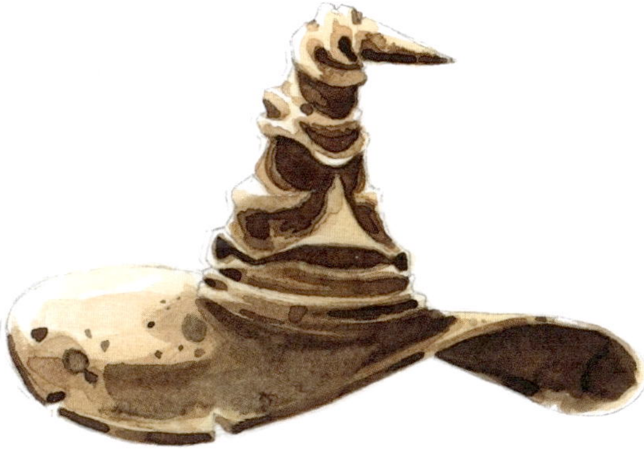

5

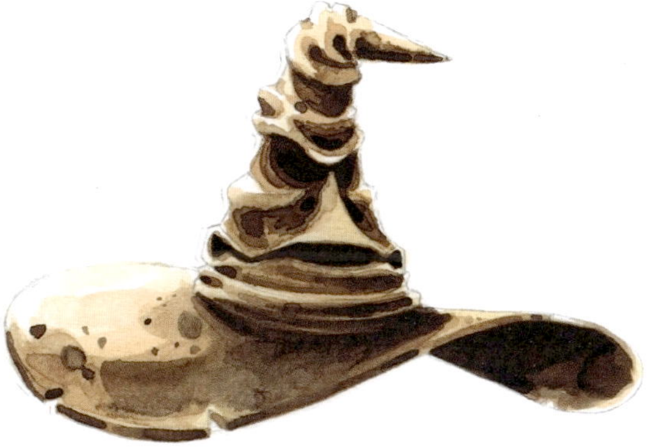

6

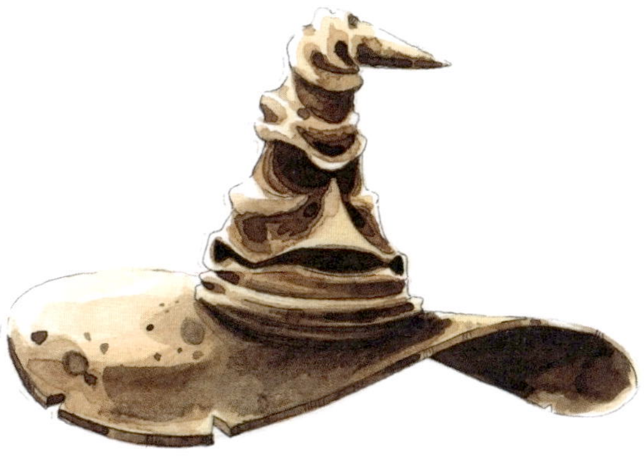

7

DIFFICULTY: ϟ

Happee Birthdae Cake

"Got something for you. 'Fraid I may have sat on it at some point, but I imagine it will taste fine just the same. Ah, baked it myself, words and all. . . . It's not every day your young man turns eleven now is it, eh?"
—Rubeus Hagrid, *Harry Potter and the Sorcerer's Stone*

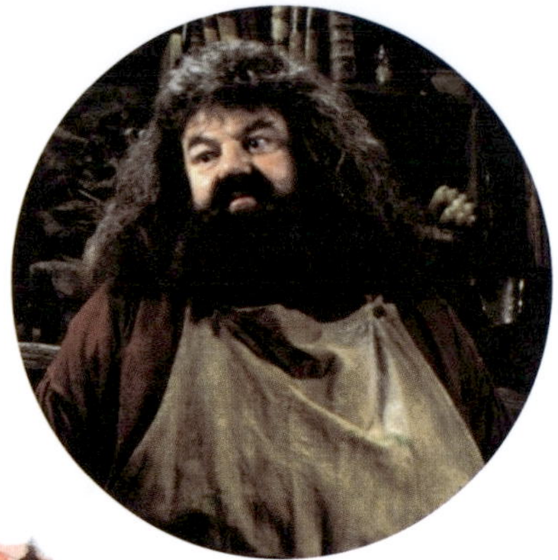

COLORS

LIGHT PINK

ROSE MADDER

ALIZARIN CRIMSON HUE

VIRIDIAN HUE

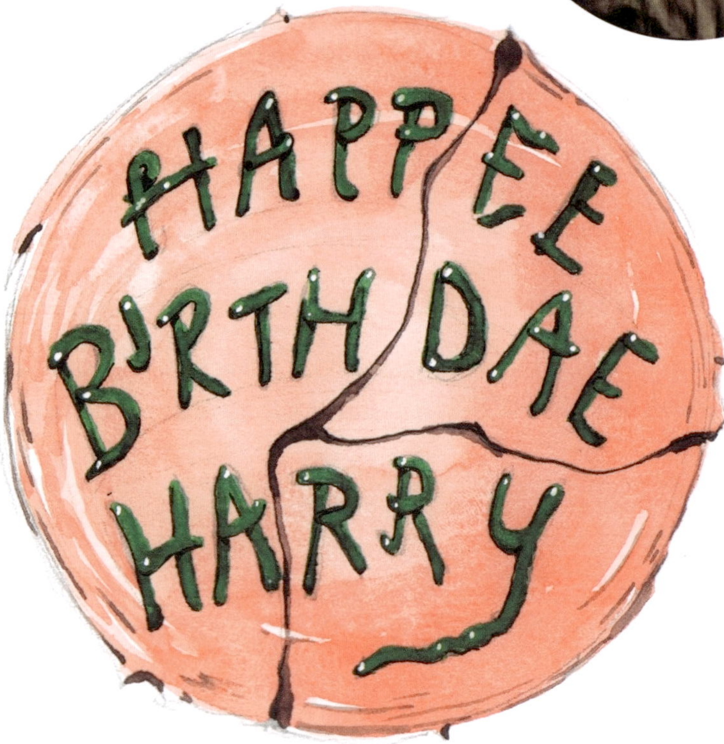

RECOMMENDED SUPPLIES

- Size 10 brush
- Size 01 brush
- Black gel pen
- White gel pen

1. Take your size 10 brush and apply a layer of light pink over the entire cake, painting in circles to create round brush lines.
2. While this layer is still wet, apply rose madder to the edges, blending with the light pink. Leave the light pink to show through the center to give the cake dimension.
3. When dry, use your 01 size brush to apply the alizarin crimson hue to carefully create the cracks in the cake.
4. Once the cake is completely dry, use your size 01 brush to grab a small amount of the concentrated viridian hue and use the tip of your brush to create the lettering.
5. When the lettering is dry, use your black gel pen to add details, like shading under the letters.
6. Use a white gel pen to add highlights to the letters as well.

DIFFICULTY: ϟ

Platform 9¾ Sign

"But Hagrid, there must be a mistake. This says platform nine and three-quarters. There's no such thing. Is there?"
—Harry Potter, *Harry Potter and the Sorcerer's Stone*

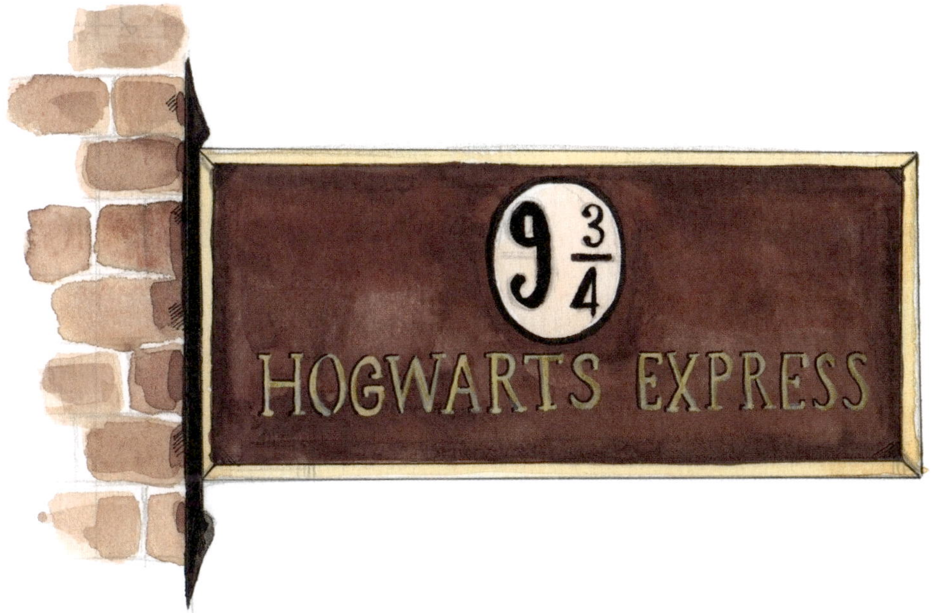

COLORS

- LIGHT BURNT SIENNA
- LIGHT LEMON YELLOW
- RAW SIENNA
- BURNT SIENNA
- INDIAN RED
- LAMP BLACK

RECOMMENDED SUPPLIES

Size 10 brush

Size 06 brush

Size 000 brush

1. Using your size 10 brush, apply the Indian red to fill the main rectangular part of the sign, leaving the oval for the "9¾" white. Tilt your brush to achieve straight, clean edges.
2. When the red base is fully dry, add the light burnt sienna to the oval.
3. Once the light burnt sienna is dry, use the tip of a size 000 brush to write "9¾" in lamp black.
4. Use the light lemon yellow to paint the outer frame, blending in a bit of raw sienna to the lower right of the frame.
5. Once the frame is dry, use your size 000 brush to apply the lamp black to the post attaching the sign to the bricks.
6. Use your size 06 brush to paint the bricks with light burnt sienna. Add water to create a variety of shades to avoid having the same solid color on all of the bricks.
7. While still wet, dilute some of the burnt sienna, and apply it to the bricks, followed by a darker shade of burnt sienna, making sure each brick is slightly different. Blend the layers together to create a smooth effect.
8. Use a 000 brush with light lemon yellow to apply the text to the sign.

DIFFICULTY: ϟ

Cauldron

Every witch or wizard eventually needs a cauldron. Useful for brewing potions, cauldrons can be placed over a fire or stove to achieve the proper temperature needed for whatever magical concoction is brewing inside.

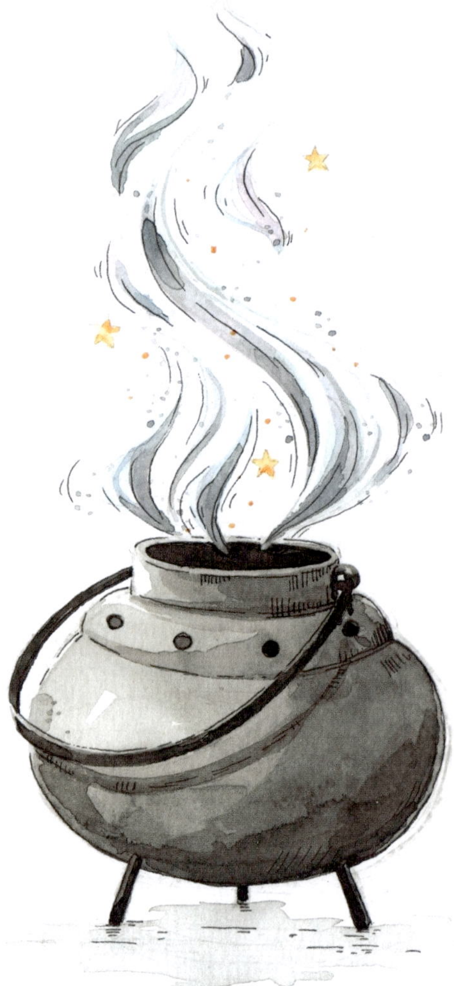

COLORS

LIGHT GRAY

DARK GRAY

IVORY BLACK

LEMON YELLOW

PERMANENT ROSE

INDIGO

LIGHT INDIGO

RECOMMENDED SUPPLIES

Size 06 brush

Size 02 brush

Black gel pen

1. Using your size 06 brush, apply light gray over the entire body of the cauldron, leaving a few white spaces to simulate where the light falls on the upper-left portions of the cauldron.
2. While it is still wet, add a bit of water to some of the dark gray on your palette, and apply it to the cauldron, leaving the upper left light gray and getting darker as you move to the lower right to convey its round shape.
3. Once it is dry, apply a darker shade of the dark gray to the lower parts of the cauldron, the handle, and to the shadow cast by the handle, as well as to the circular details near the opening.
4. When this is dry, use the ivory black to add shadows to the underside of the cauldron and to color the inside of the cauldron and the legs.
5. With your clean size 02 brush, use light indigo to begin painting the smoke. Tilt your brush and start at the top, moving down by making "S" shapes with your wrist. Be sure to raise your brush up as you reach the end to create a fine point.
6. Add a bit of diluted permanent rose, blending with the light indigo, to create some variations in the smoke color.
7. Once this layer is dry, use indigo to add shadows and dimension to the smoke.
8. Use the lemon yellow to create stars and apply small dots of the various colors to add a magical touch.
9. With your gel pen, apply any final small details needed.

DIFFICULTY: ϟ

Hedwig Holding a Letter

Hedwig's snowy white feathers make her stand out even among the other owls of the wizarding world. Harry's stalwart companion is extremely intelligent, proud, and loyal.

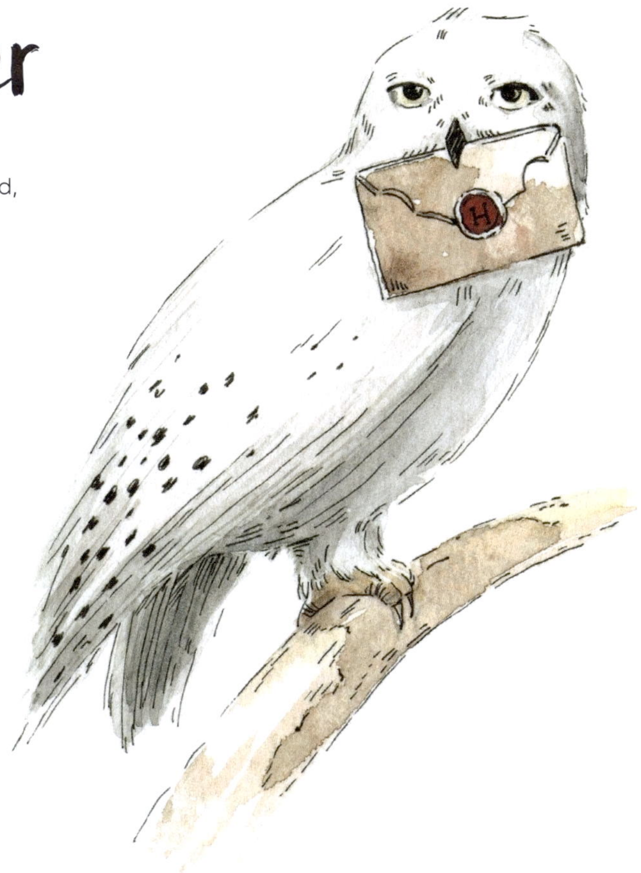

COLORS

- LIGHT PINK
- LIGHT GRAY
- DARK GRAY
- LIGHT BURNT UMBER
- BURNT UMBER
- BURNT SIENNA

RECOMMENDED SUPPLIES

Size 06 brush

Black gel pen

1. Using a size 06 brush, start by applying the light gray to Hedwig's underside and to the bottom edge of some of her feathers, leaving some white gaps on the left side to simulate light coming from this side. Avoid using dark shades, since Hedwig is snowy white.
2. Working quickly while the light gray is still wet, apply the dark gray in small strokes, starting with the darkest part on her belly and the underside of her body, including her tailfeathers, as well as very lightly to the right side of her face. Applying this coat while the light gray is still wet allows you to blend the shades for a smooth effect.
3. Apply the light pink to the very top of Hedwig's head, coming down slightly to the very top part of her wing, which helps to give her feathers a smooth look.
4. With the light pink still on your brush, paint the right and left edges of the branch.
5. When Hedwig's body is dry, use your brush to add plenty of water to the light burnt umber in your palette. Paint the envelope, being careful to avoid paint reaching Hedwig's feathers.
6. While the light burnt umber is still wet, apply the burnt umber, starting with the lower portion of the envelope and blending upward so that the color is most concentrated in the lower portion, leaving the upper part of the envelope white.
7. With the burnt umber still on your brush, apply a thin coat over the branch, being careful to leave the pink at the ends visible.
8. Using the light pink, apply it to the top of the envelope. Then, apply the light pink to Hedwig's feet.
9. Once the paint on the envelope is fully dry, use the burnt sienna to color the seal.
10. Let the remaining paint dry before using the gel pen to add the final touches, such as the symbol on the seal and the black marks on Hedwig's wings, her beak, and the perfect haughty look in her eyes!

DIFFICULTY: ⚡⚡

Hogwarts Crest

The crest of Hogwarts School of Witchcraft and Wizardry incorporates the four houses, along with the motto "Draco Dormiens Nunquam Titillandus"—never tickle a sleeping dragon.

COLORS

LIGHT GRAY

DARK GRAY

LIGHT LEMON YELLOW

YELLOW OCHRE

VIRIDIAN HUE

BURNT SIENNA

ULTRAMARINE

LEMON YELLOW

LAMP BLACK

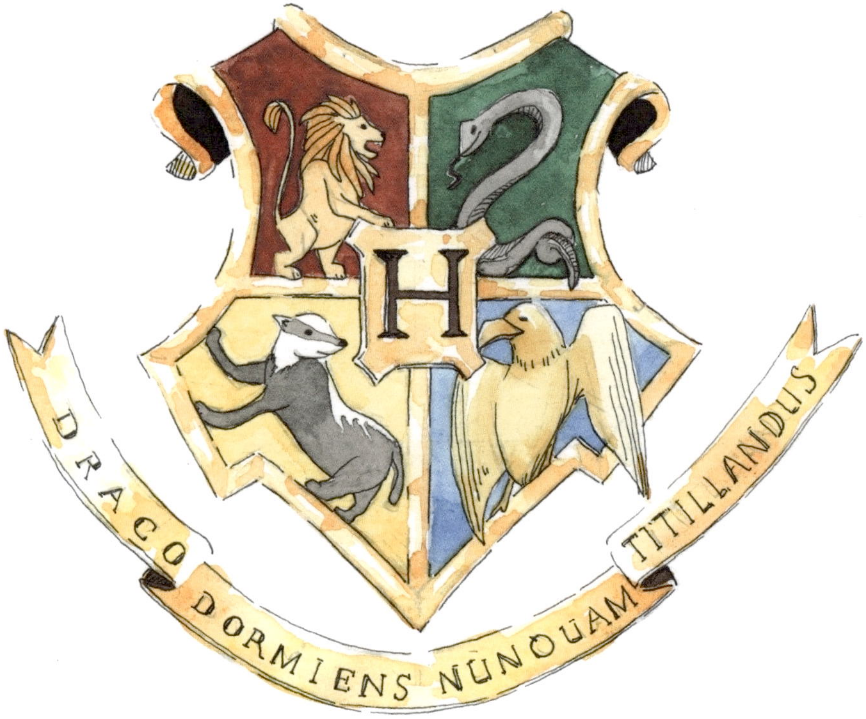

RECOMMENDED SUPPLIES

Size 04 brush

Size 10mm brush

Size 02 brush

Black gel pen

1. Begin by using your size 04 brush to color the mascots, using two shades of the same color to make them look more alive.
2. Once the mascots are dry, use your size 02 or 10mm brush to paint their individual backgrounds with the colors shown here, using two different shades to provide some depth to the backgrounds.
3. Once the backgrounds are dry, paint the frame of the crest and the banner with light yellow, leaving a fair number of white gaps to make it appear shiny.
4. Use shades of yellow ochre to apply shading to the crest and banner to create contrast.
5. Once it is dry, apply the lamp black to the crest folds and the folds in the banner, as well as the *H* in the center.
6. Lastly, use your gel pen to add small details, such as the lettering. Avoid outlining every facet; use it mostly on darker areas to underline the shadows and to provide small details.

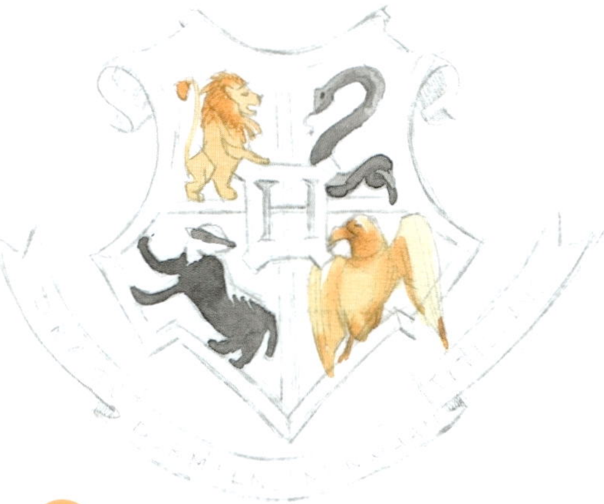

1

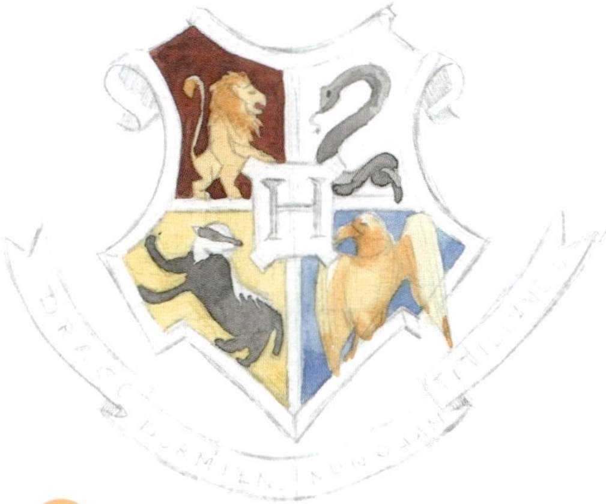

2

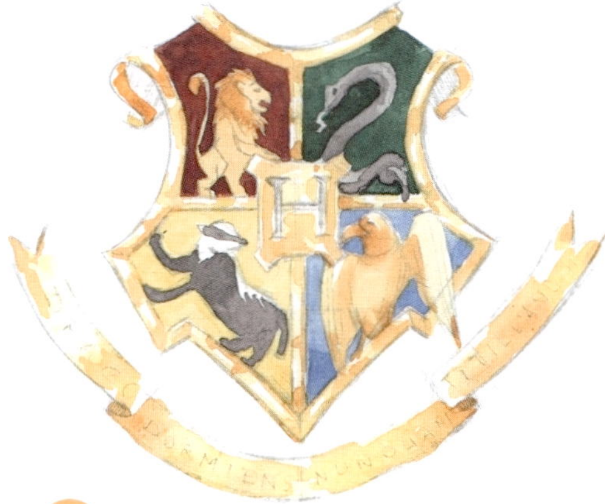

3

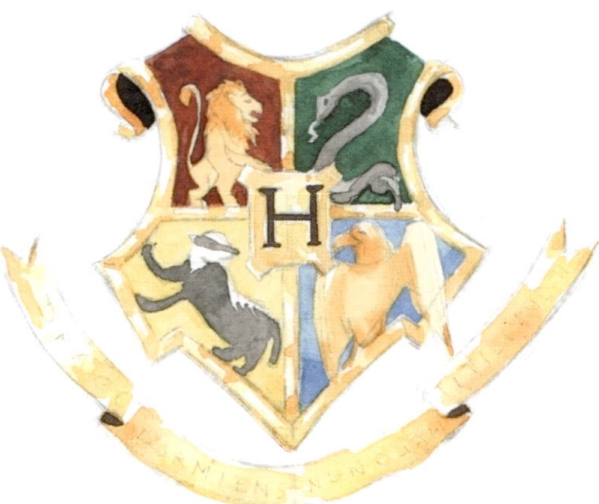

4 5

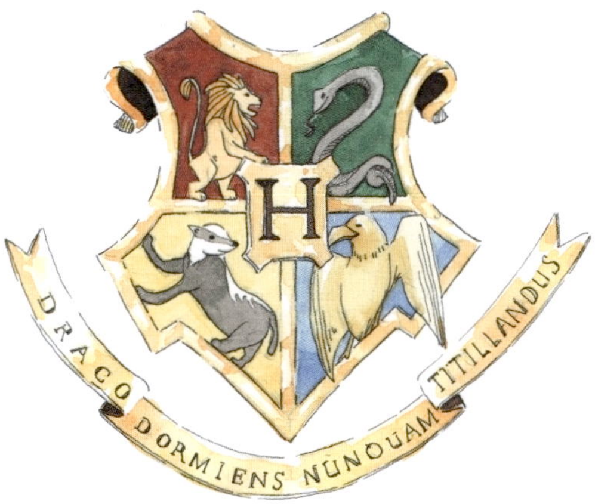

6

DIFFICULTY:

Gryffindor Crest

Bearing Gryffindor's scarlet and gold colors and featuring the Gryffindor lion, this crest evokes the qualities of those sorted into this house: courage, bravery, and determination.

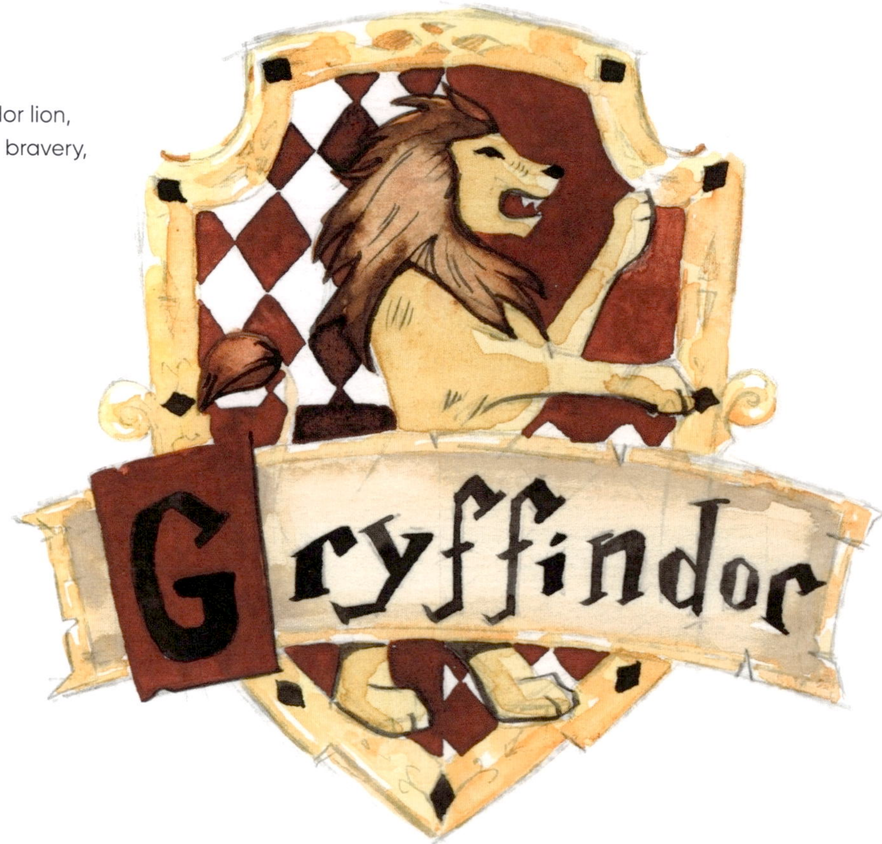

COLORS

LIGHT CADMIUM YELLOW
YELLOW OCHRE
BURNT UMBER
BEIGE
BURNT SIENNA
LAMP BLACK

RECOMMENDED SUPPLIES

Size 06 brush
Size 000 brush
Size 01 brush
Black gel pen

1. Begin by using your size 06 brush to apply light cadmium yellow to the entire lion.
2. Then, use yellow ochre to create the darker shades on the lion's face and body, as well as the base color for the mane.
3. After it is fully dry, use burnt umber to create the lion's mane, leaving areas for the yellow ochre to show through.
4. Now, apply light cadmium yellow to the entire frame of the crest, leaving a few white spots to simulate the reflection of light.
5. While that layer is still wet, use shades of light yellow ochre to create shading on the frame, mostly on the right side, to provide a better sense of dimension.
6. Apply a light shade of beige to the banner, adding darker shades while the base is still wet to provide some texture.
7. Once everything is dry, use your size 01 brush to begin filling in the background. The Gryffindor crest contains many different shades of red and brown, so be careful when mixing your colors so that they aren't too similar to each other, muddying the details. Use the very tip of your brush to paint the edges of the background first, with only a small amount of paint on your brush to create clean borders before filling inside them with shades of burnt sienna. This is especially key for the checkerboard pattern.
8. Once the background is dry, use your size 000 brush to add text to the banner. Painting text can be challenging, so it's often helpful to practice first. Focus on the angle of your brush and use your wrist to lead your brush up and down. If you prefer, you can also use your gel pen for the lettering.
9. Use your gel pen to add fine details, particularly to the lion and the details on the crest's frame.

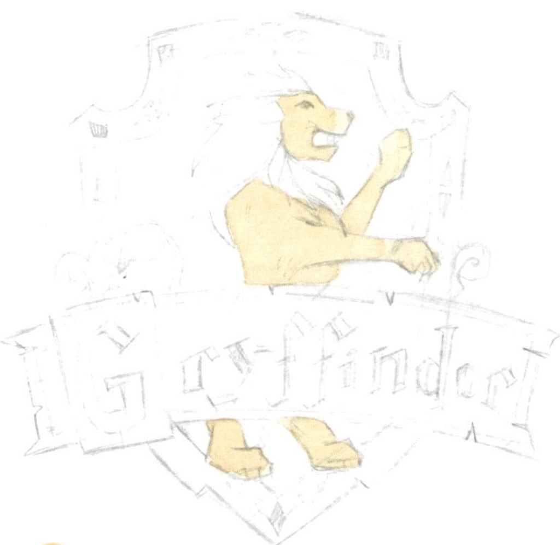

1

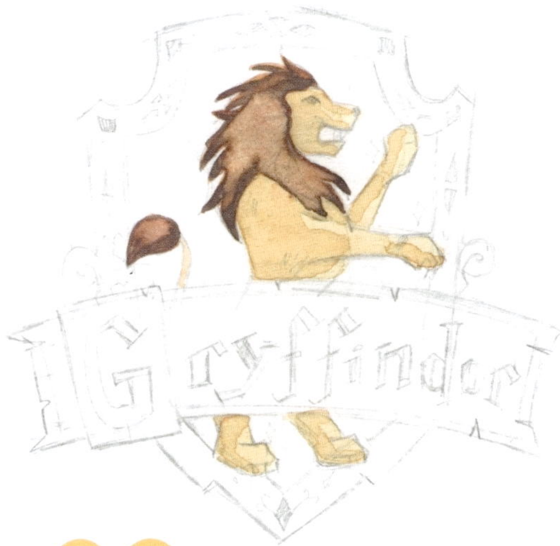

2 3

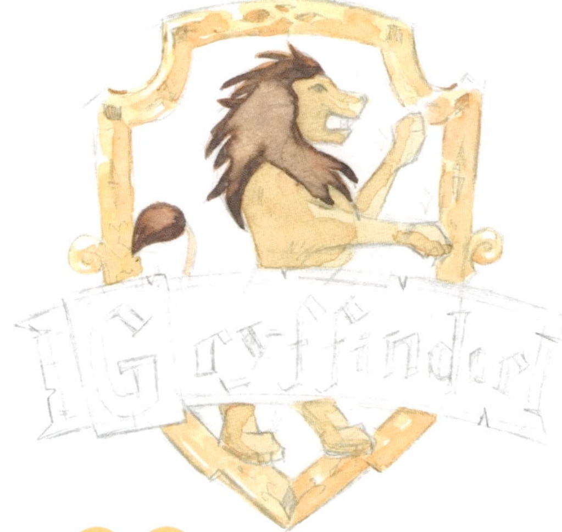

4 5

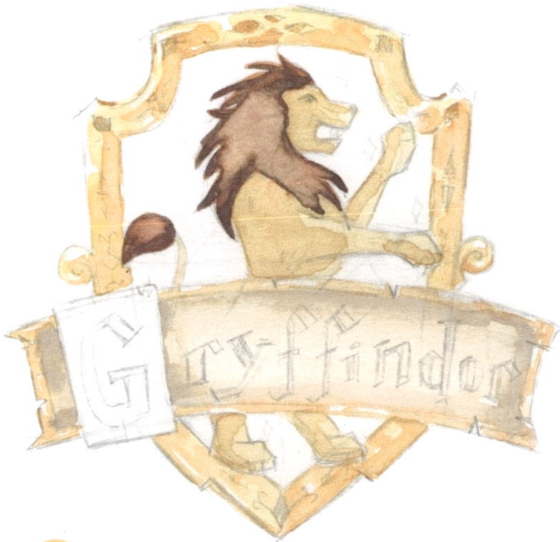

6

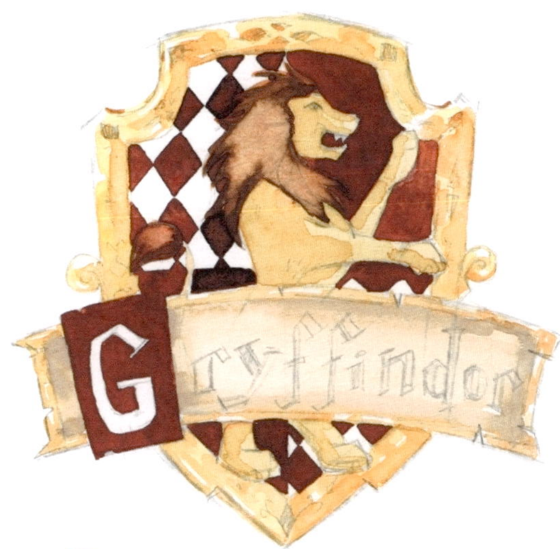

7

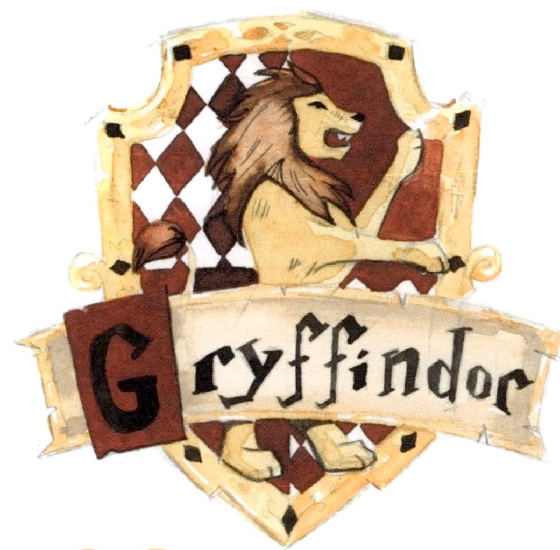

8 9

DIFFICULTY: ⚡⚡

Slytherin Crest

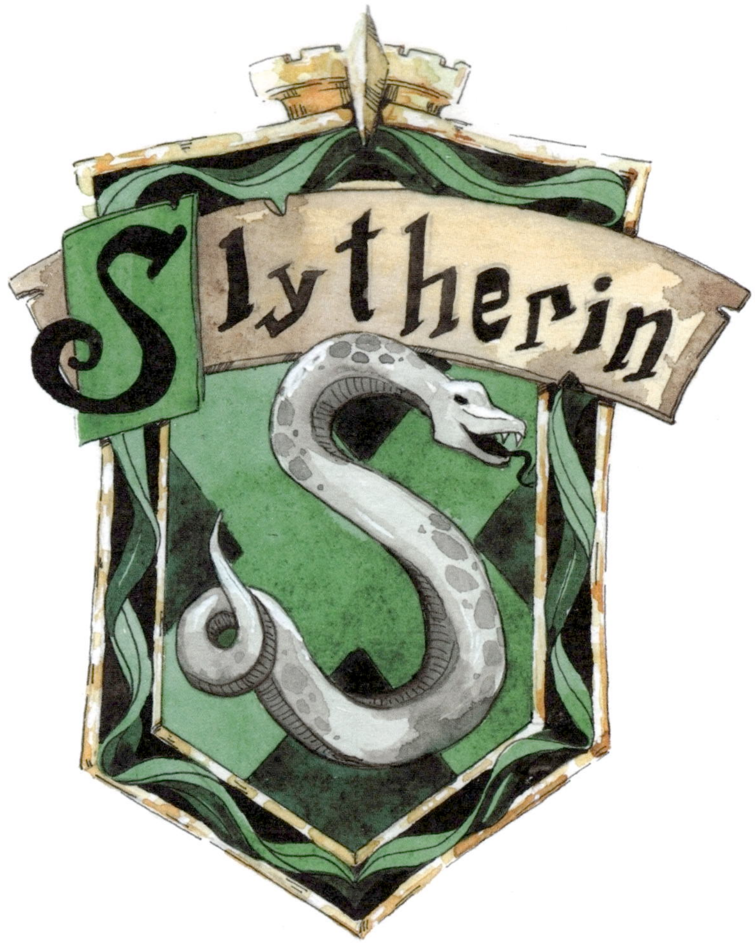

The silver serpent of the Slytherin crest represents the fact that the house's founder, Salazar Slytherin, was one of the first Parselmouths. Its members are known for their pride, ambition, and cunning.

COLORS

BEIGE

LIGHT GRAY

GRAY

SAP GREEN

VIRIDIAN HUE

LEMON YELLOW

YELLOW OCHRE

VANDYKE BROWN

LAMP BLACK

RECOMMENDED SUPPLIES

Size 01 brush

Size 06 brush

Size 000 brush

Size 6mm brush

Black gel pen

1. Begin by applying the light gray to the entire snake with your size 06 brush.
2. When that layer is dry, use the gray to shade the underside of the snake, along with the reptile's spots.
3. Once the snake is fully dry, tilt your size 01 brush with only a small amount of sap green to paint the edges with sharp, clean lines. Once you have painted the edges, fill the inside.
4. When the first layer of green is dry, apply shades of viridian hue to create the darker areas of the background. Pay close attention to creating straight, clean borderlines between those colors.
5. Using your size 000 brush, apply the lemon yellow to the frame pieces, leaving a few areas white to illustrate the reflective nature of the frame. While the first layer is still wet, follow that up with shades of yellow ochre to create nice transitions between the different shades on the frame.
6. Once these layers are all dry, it's time to create the base for the banner. To create the paper-like texture, begin by applying a light layer of beige over the banner with your size 06 brush.
7. While the first layer is still wet, put a little bit of diluted Vandyke brown on your brush and place it in a few places on the paper. Do not rub the brush around, but rather let the paint create the texture, using the darker shades closer to the edges for a better sense of dimension.
8. When it is dry, use your size 000 brush to create the text. It's often helpful to practice painting letters. Focus on the angle of your brush, and use your wrist to lead your brush up and down. If you prefer, you can also use your gel pen for the lettering.
9. Use your gel pen to add fine details, such as on the snake and on the background ribbons of the crest to finalize your piece.

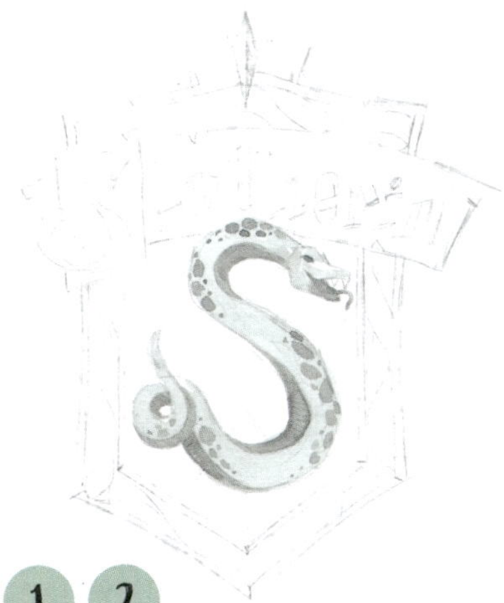

1 2

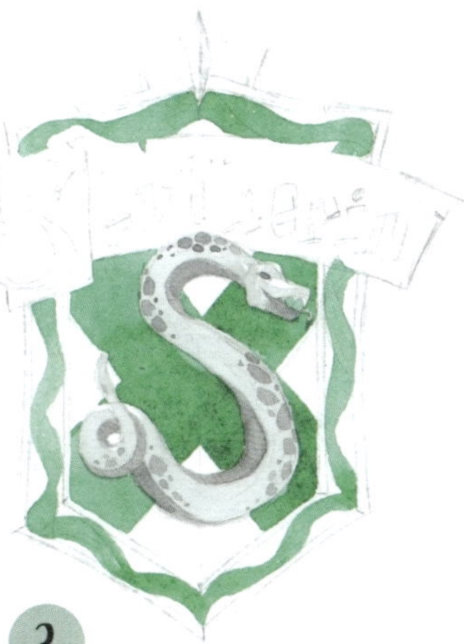

3

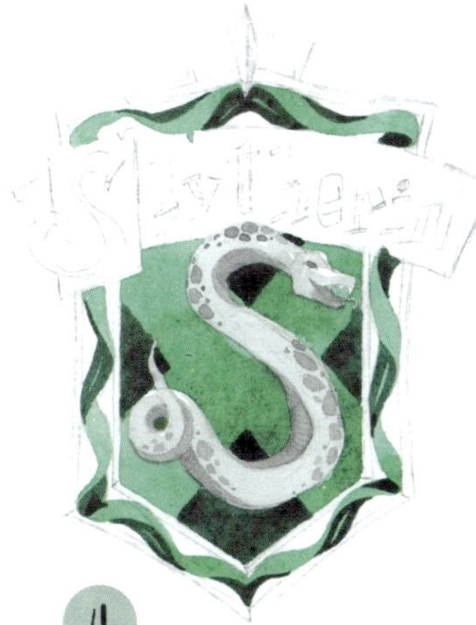

4

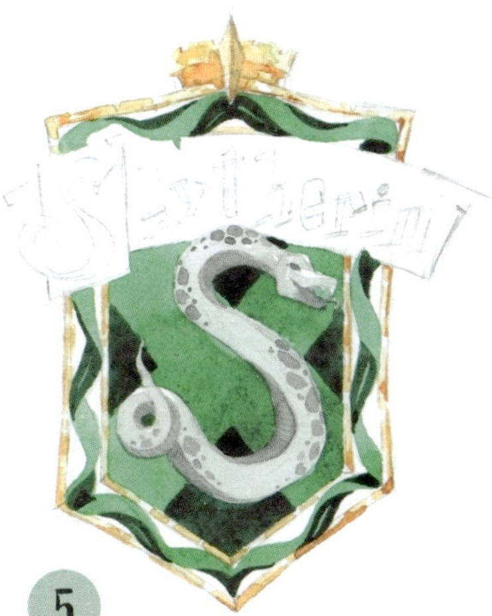

5

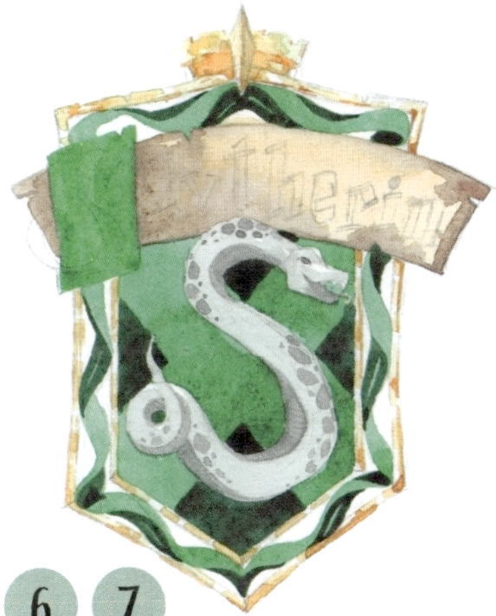

6 7

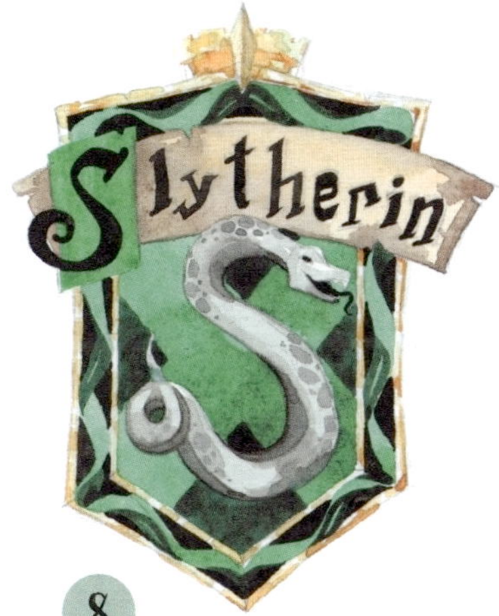

8

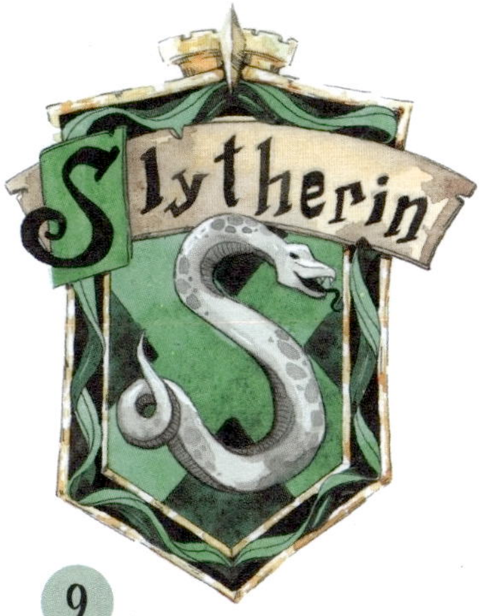

9

DIFFICULTY: ϟϟ

Ravenclaw Crest

Sporting the blue and bronze of the house, along with its emblematic raven, Ravenclaw's crest represents the wit, learning, and wisdom for which its members are known.

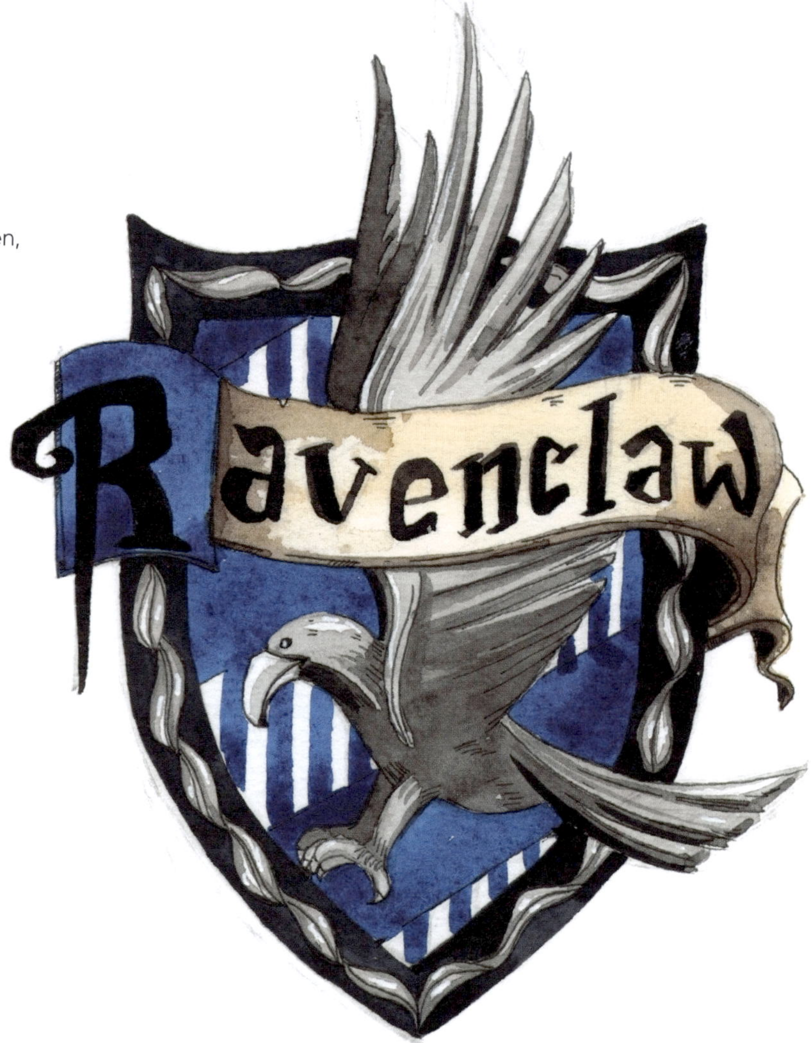

COLORS

- LIGHT GRAY
- GRAY
- COBALT BLUE
- INDIGO
- BEIGE
- VANDYKE BROWN
- LAMP BLACK

RECOMMENDED SUPPLIES

- Size 06 brush
- Size 02 brush
- Size 000 brush
- Size 6mm brush
- Black gel pen

1. Start by using your size 02 brush to paint the raven light gray.
2. Once the first layer is dry, apply a darker shade of gray, keeping the direction of the light coming from the upper right in mind as you apply the darker shade. Tilt your 02 brush and start painting from the root of the feathers, reducing the pressure and increasing the angle as you reach the tip of the feathers. This allows you to create clean lines that get thinner as you reach the end of each feather.
3. Once the raven is completely dry, use your size 6mm brush to apply the cobalt blue to the background, leaving clean lines to create the white stripes. Make sure your brush isn't too wet, and keep your brush tilted to achieve the best result.
4. Use your size 02 brush to apply the indigo to the outer part of the frame. Keep only a small amount of paint on your brush at once to reduce the risk of mistakes here.
5. Once it is dry, apply a light layer of beige over the banner with your size 06 brush to create a paperlike texture.
6. While the first layer is still wet, put a little bit of diluted Vandyke brown on your brush, and place it in a few places on the paper. Do not rub the brush around, but rather let the paint create the texture, using the darker shades closer to the edges for a better sense of dimension.
7. Once it is fully dry, use your size 000 brush to create the text. It's often helpful to practice painting letters first. Focus on the angle of your brush, and use your wrist to lead your brush up and down. You can also use your gel pen for the lettering if you'd like.
8. Use your gel pen to provide additional details, particularly on the raven's feathers and on the borderlines.

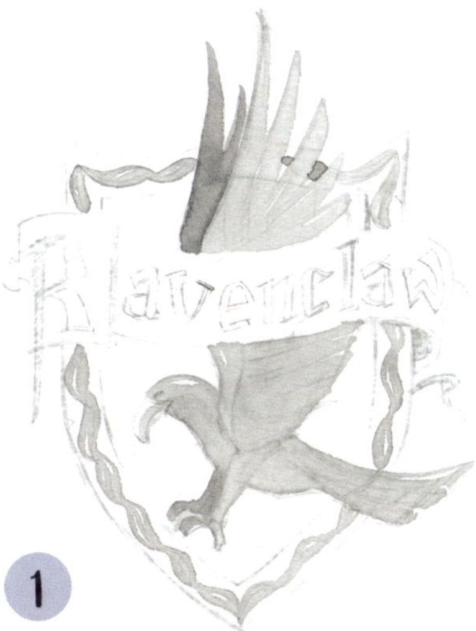

1

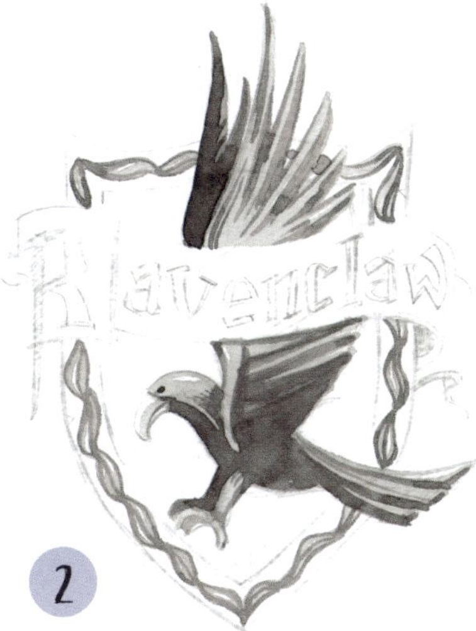

2

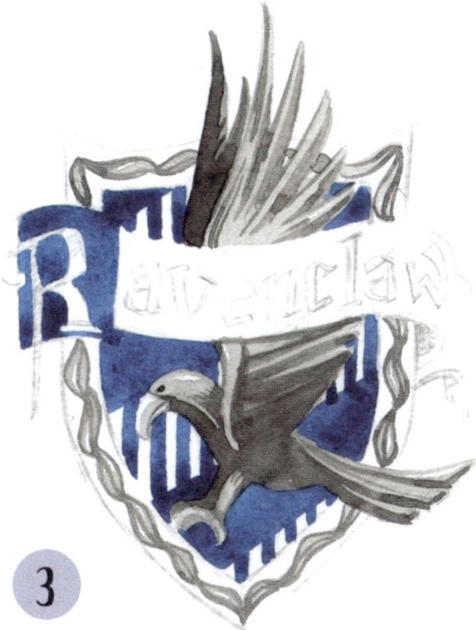

3

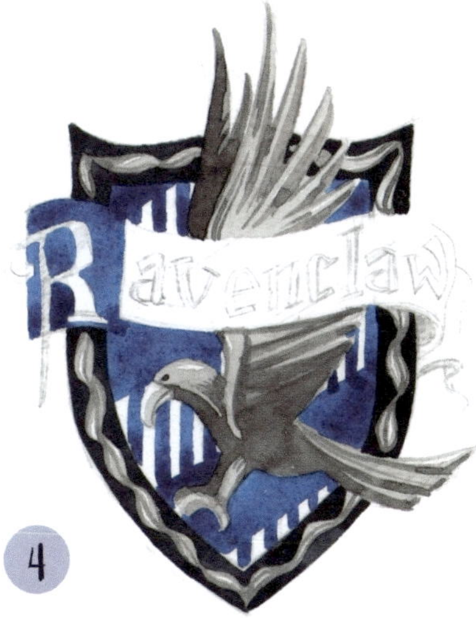

4

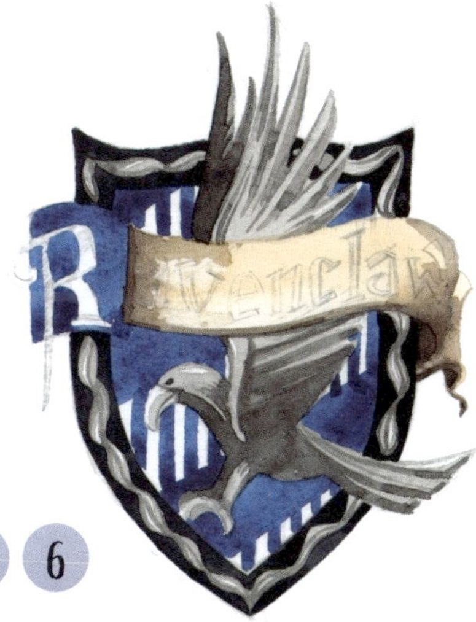

5 6

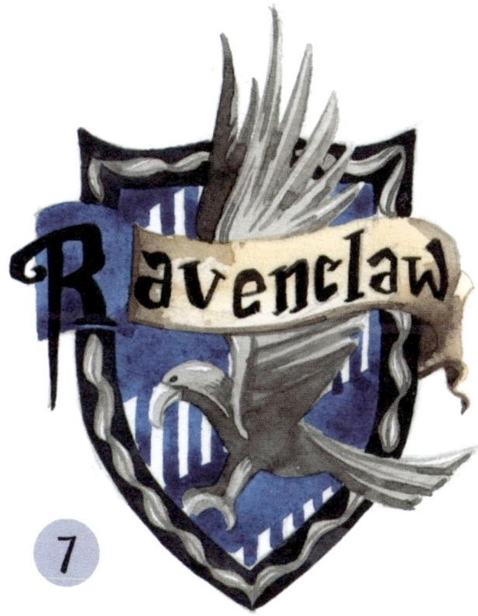

7

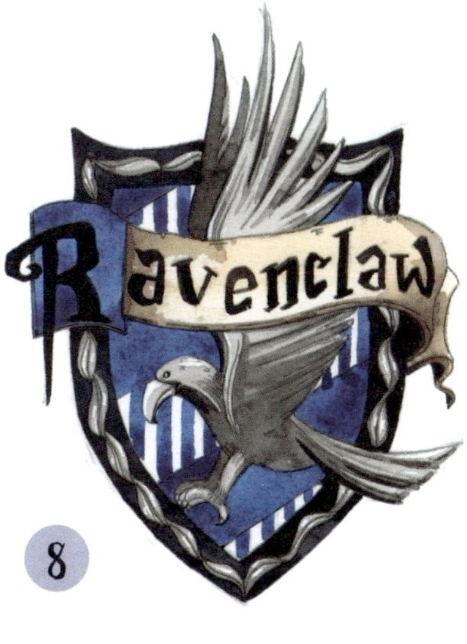

8

DIFFICULTY: ϟϟ

Hufflepuff Crest

Hufflepuffs are known for their dedication, patience, and loyalty. But much like the unassuming badger that graces the yellow and black Hufflepuff crest, they can be fierce when provoked, or when protecting something they care about.

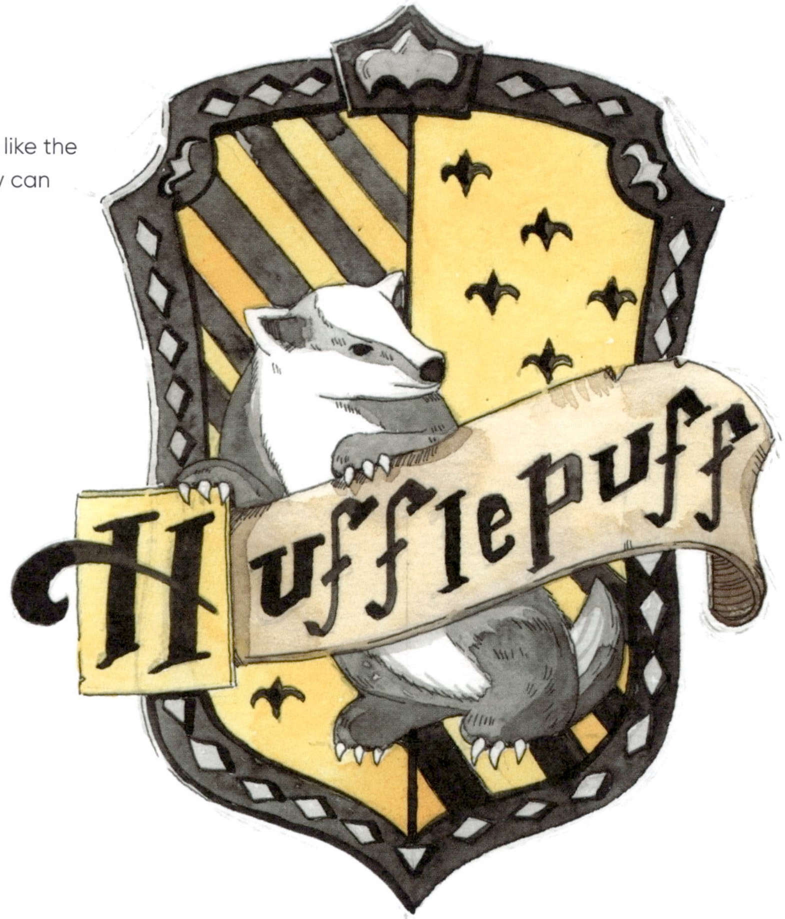

COLORS

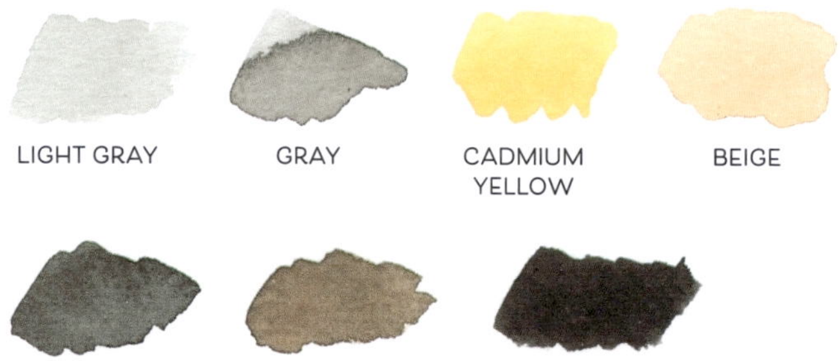

- LIGHT GRAY
- GRAY
- CADMIUM YELLOW
- BEIGE
- DARK GRAY
- VANDYKE BROWN
- LAMP BLACK

RECOMMENDED SUPPLIES

- Size 04 brush
- Size 02 brush
- Size 000 brush
- Size 6mm brush
- Black gel pen

1. Begin by using your size 02 brush to apply gray to the badger, leaving the appropriate body parts white, such as the head, belly, and claws.
2. Once the badger is dry, tilt your size 6mm brush to apply shades of cadmium yellow to the background, creating sharp edges where needed for the design. It is helpful to only use a small amount of paint on your brush at a time to ensure crisp edges.
3. For the frame, use your size 02 brush to place light gray over the entire frame.
4. When it's dry, carefully apply the dark gray around the frame with your size 000 brush to create the decorative elements, as well as the stripe element in the background. Start by painting the edges of the diamonds, then the border of the crest, and finally fill in between.
5. Once it is dry, apply a light layer of beige over the banner with your to size 04 brush to create a paperlike texture.
6. While the first layer is still wet, put a little bit of diluted Vandyke brown on your brush, and place it in a few places on the paper. Do not rub the brush around, but rather let the paint create the texture, using the darker shades closer to the edges for a better sense of dimension.
7. Once it is fully dry, use your size 000 brush to create the text. Text can be a challenge, and it's often helpful to practice painting letters first. Focus on the angle of your brush, and use your wrist to lead your brush up and down. You can also use your gel pen for the lettering if you'd like.
8. Continue using your size 000 brush to add shading to the frame, keeping in mind that the light is coming from the left, so the right side of the frame should be darker.
9. With your gel pen, add some fine details, particularly to the badger and banner to finalize this piece.

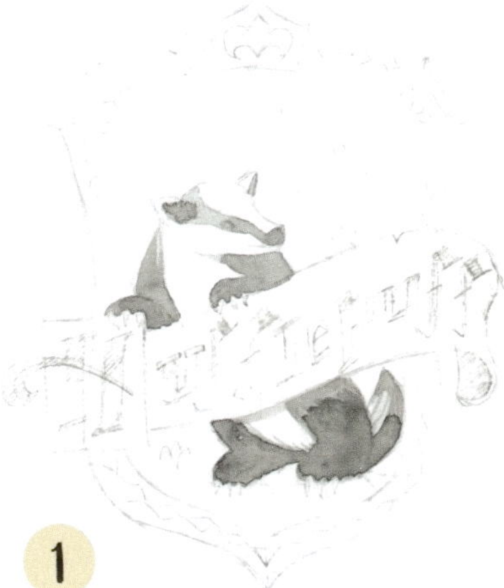

1

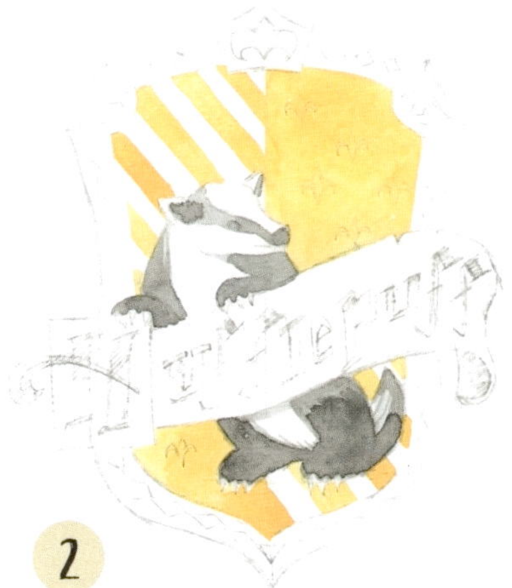

2

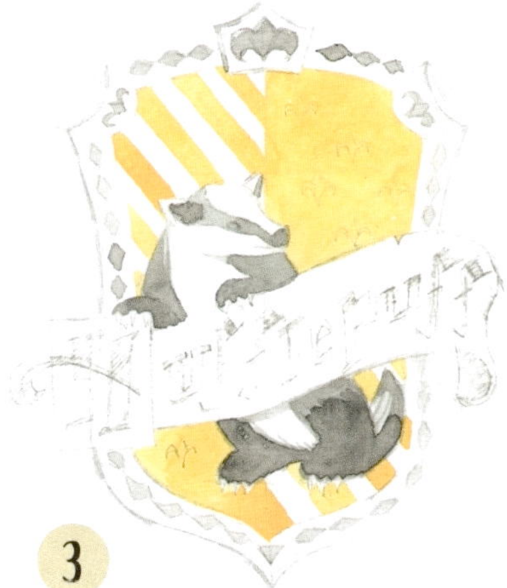

3

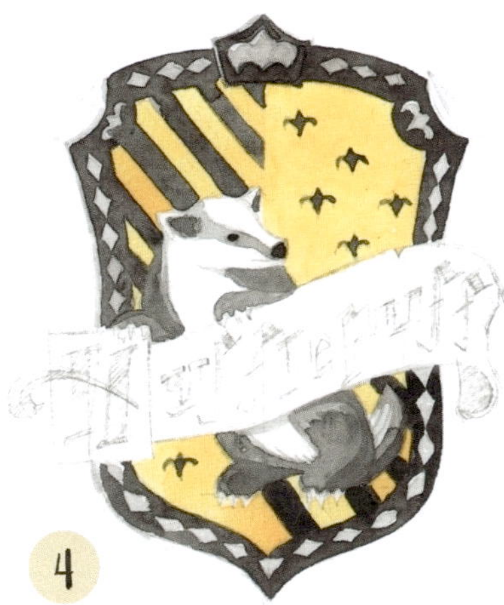

4

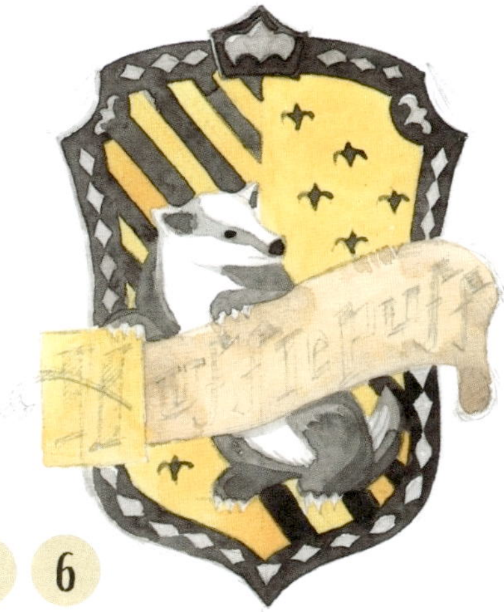

5 6

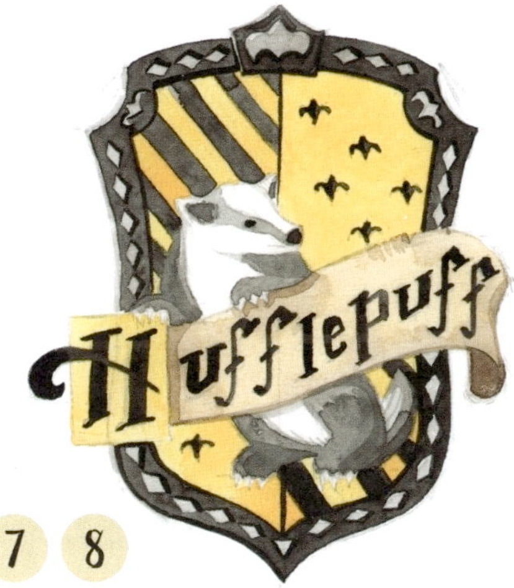

7 8

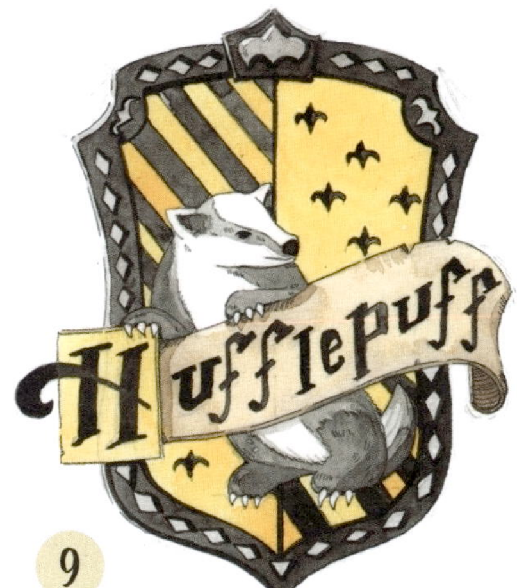

9

DIFFICULTY: ϟϟ

Nimbus 2000

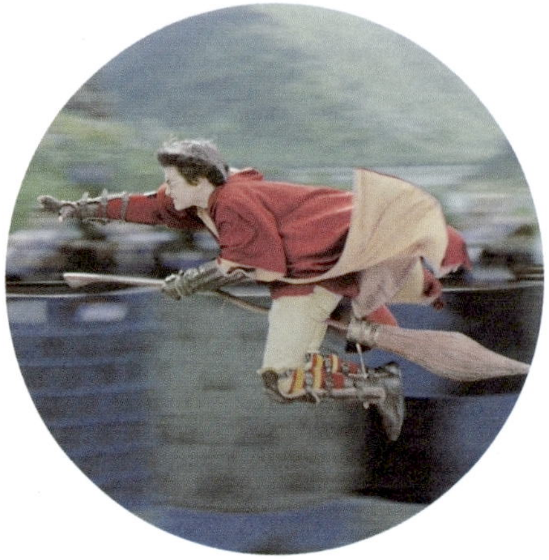

Harry receives this essential piece of Quidditch gear from Professor McGonagall when he joins the Gryffindor Quidditch team as the new Seeker in his first year.

"That's not just a broomstick, Harry. It's a Nimbus 2000!"
—Ron Weasley, *Harry Potter and the Sorcerer's Stone*

COLORS

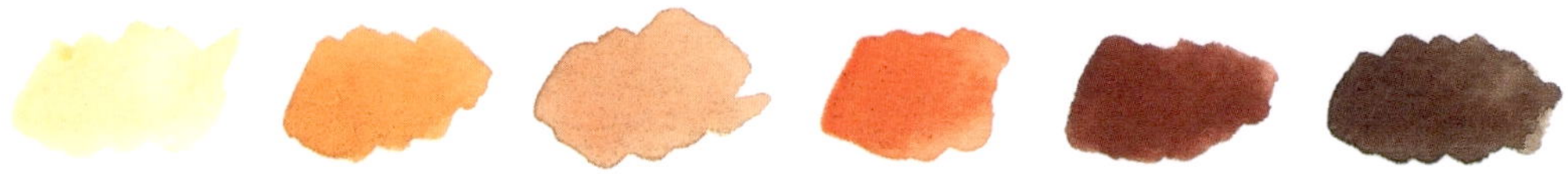

LIGHT LEMON YELLOW | RAW SIENNA | LIGHT SALMON | CADMIUM ORANGE | BURNT SIENNA | VANDYKE BROWN

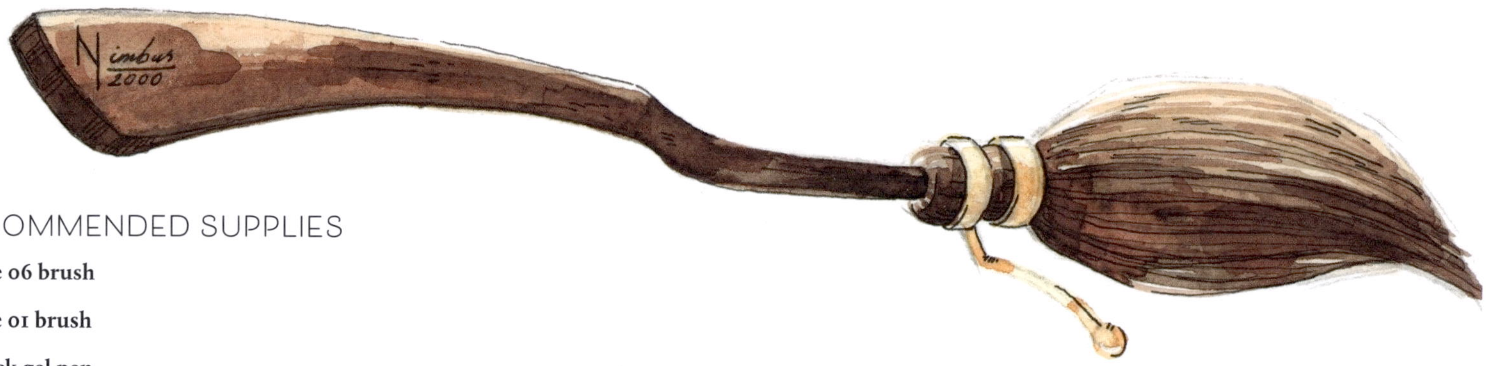

RECOMMENDED SUPPLIES

Size 06 brush

Size 01 brush

Black gel pen

1. Using your size 06 brush, apply a layer of light salmon to the entire handle of the Nimbus 2000.
2. Before the light salmon dries, add some cadmium orange to the handle as well, followed by Vandyke brown, blending to create the wooden texture. Use the tip of your brush with long lines from left to right to emphasize the texture. Allow the lighter shades to show through near the top where the light would hit it.
3. When the handle is fully dry, use your size 06 brush to apply a layer of light salmon to the broom tail.
4. While that layer is wet, add burnt sienna and some diluted Vandyke brown, blending them all over the tail, while keeping the lighter shade visible on the top and a few other spots.
5. When everything is dry, take your size 01 brush and use the tip of it to apply thin lines of Vandyke brown to the broom tail, creating a realistic texture.
6. Do the same on the broom handle, providing details to the wood texture.
7. Once everything is dry again, apply the light lemon yellow to the metal rings on the tail and the kickstand. Then, while that is still wet, apply a small amount of raw sienna to these same elements, to create a more realistic look.
8. While it is still wet, apply highlights of cadmium orange, blending to create smooth transitions.
9. When it is fully dry, use your gel pen to write "Nimbus 2000" on the handle and to add any additional small details you'd like.

DIFFICULTY: ⚡⚡

The Golden Snitch

"What do I do with it?"

"You catch it. Before the other team's Seeker. You catch this, the game is over. You catch this, Potter, and we win."
—Harry Potter and Oliver Wood, *Harry Potter and the Sorcerer's Stone*

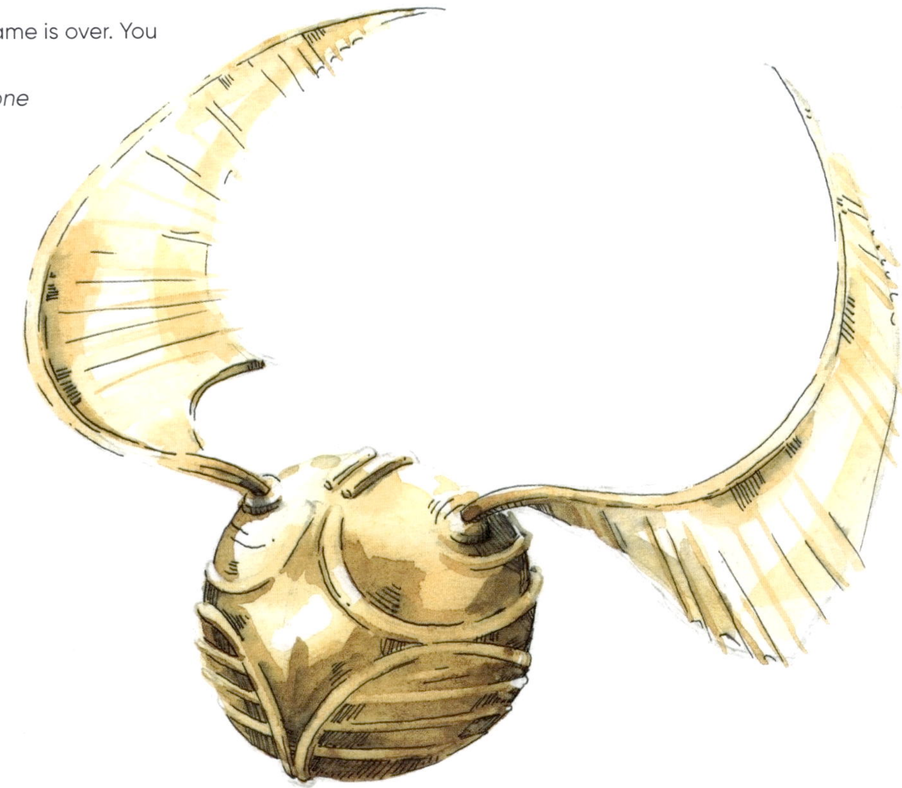

COLORS

LIGHT LEMON YELLOW

LEMON YELLOW

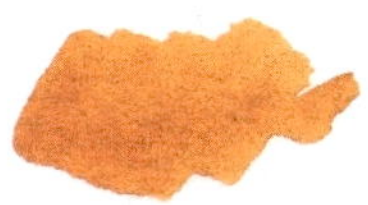

CADMIUM ORANGE

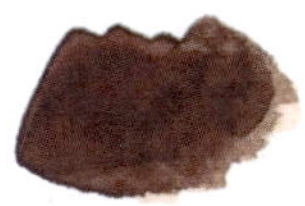

BURNT UMBER

RECOMMENDED SUPPLIES

Size 06 brush

Size 000 brush

Black gel pen

1. Using a size 06 brush, start by applying light lemon yellow all over, leaving a few white gaps here and there to simulate points where the light hits the snitch. It can be helpful to take a look at how light hits other gold objects to get a sense of how light reflects on gold textures.
2. Apply the lemon yellow over the upper- and midportions of the ball and the raised detail lines, leaving parts of the light lemon yellow exposed.
3. Use cadmium orange to color in the bottom portion of the ball, leaving spaces where the light would hit it to show the lemon yellow and light lemon yellow.
4. Lightly brush cadmium orange in spots along the wing spines and where the lemon yellow will meet burnt umber.
5. Use the burnt umber to color the bottom portion of the Golden Snitch, blending at the edges of the cadmium orange, but leaving the raised detailed lines alone so that the lighter shade shows.
6. Take your size 000 brush to add details once the other layers dry. Apply darker shades just beside the lighter ones to create a sharp contrast, which helps identify the material of the Snitch. Consider how the light hits your Golden Snitch and use burnt umber to apply dark lines on the underside of the details, and anywhere else that would be in shadow. Use the tip of your brush while applying fine details, and always hold your brush tilted with only a small amount of paint on it.
7. Once all of the paint is dry, use your gel pen to add some small final lines and to sharpen up any areas as needed.

DIFFICULTY: ⚡⚡⚡

Hagrid's Hut

"There's no Hogwarts without you, Hagrid."
—Harry Potter, *Harry Potter and the Chamber of Secrets*

COLORS

- LIGHT GRAY
- LIGHT VIRIDIAN HUE
- GRAY
- LIGHT INDIGO
- LIGHT CADMIUM ORANGE
- CADMIUM ORANGE
- BURNT SIENNA
- PAYNE'S GRAY

RECOMMENDED SUPPLIES

Size 02 brush
Size 10mm brush
Black gel pen
White gel pen

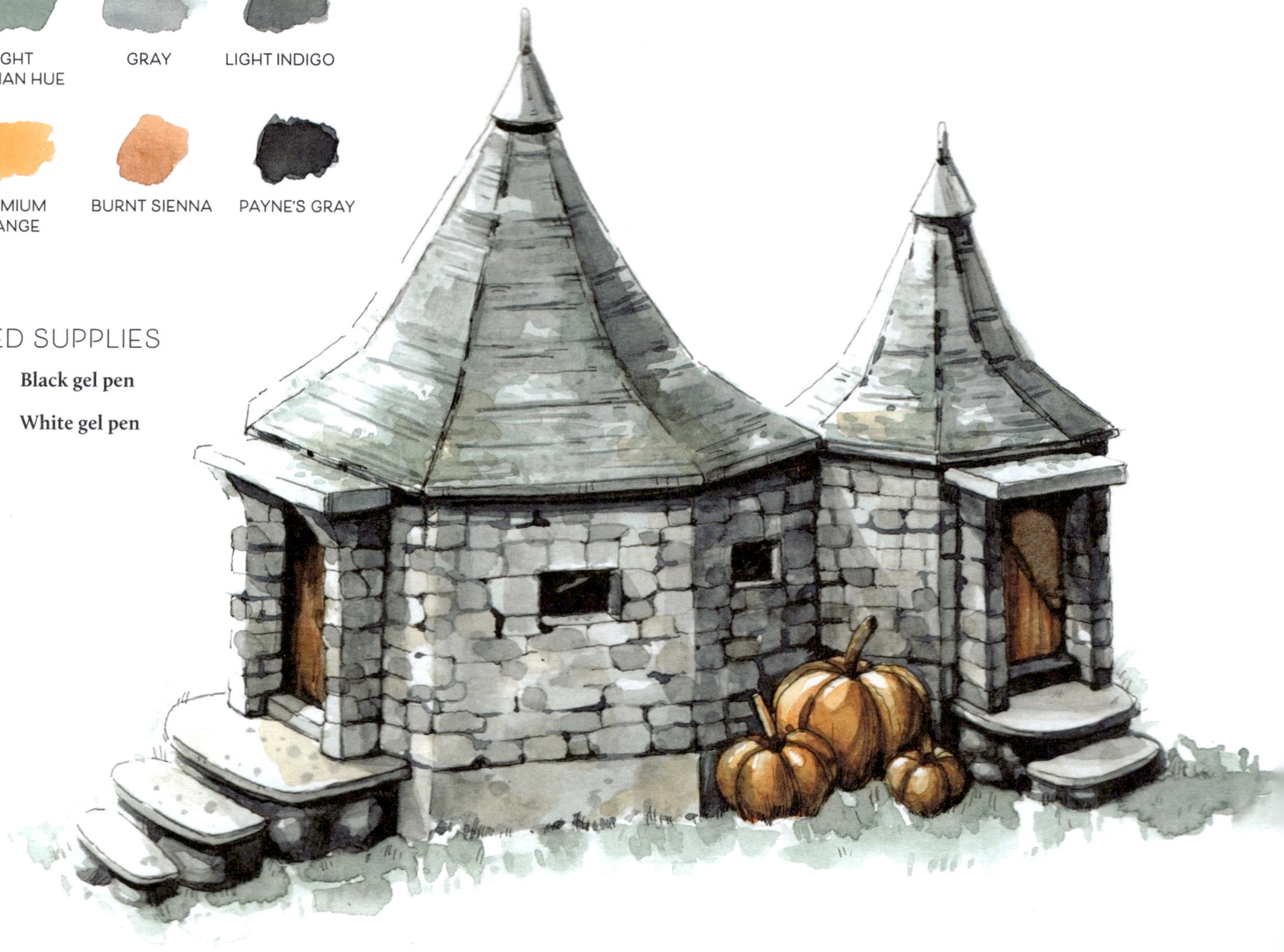

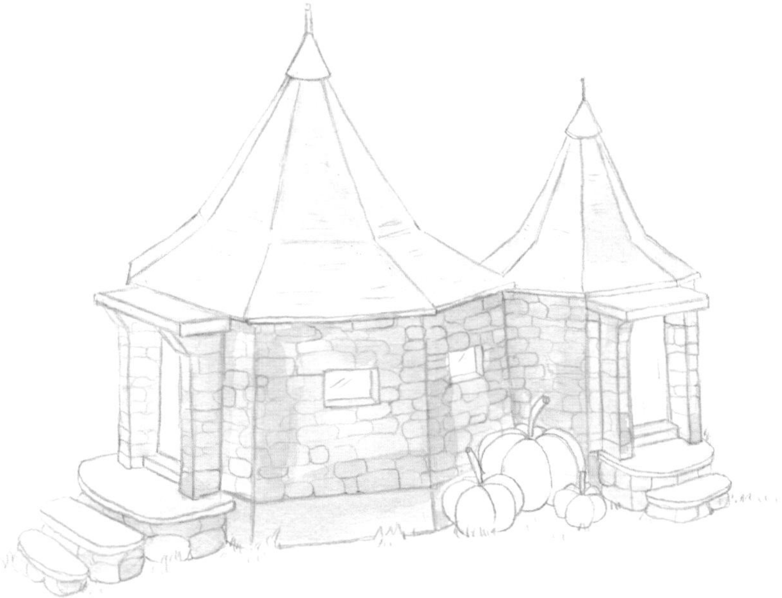

1 Paint almost the entire hut with light gray. Leave the pumpkins, windows, and door unpainted.

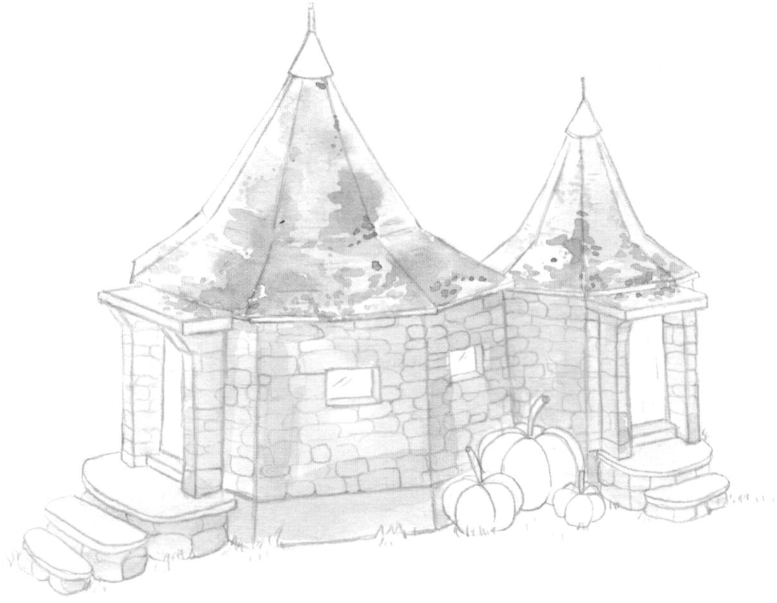

2 Before it dries, apply light viridian hue on the roof to create the moss effect underneath.

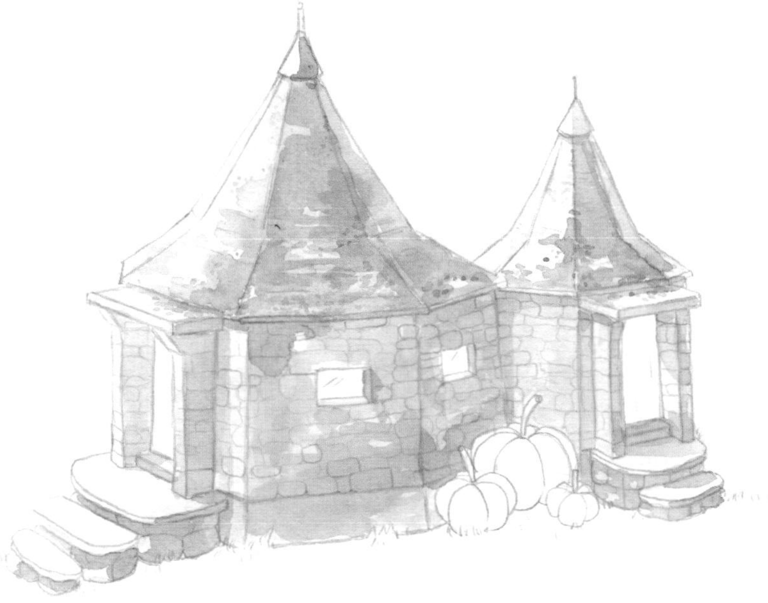

3 Use your size 02 brush and add gray on the hut, keeping the light source in mind. Make sure to leave the left and top sides of the hut lighter.

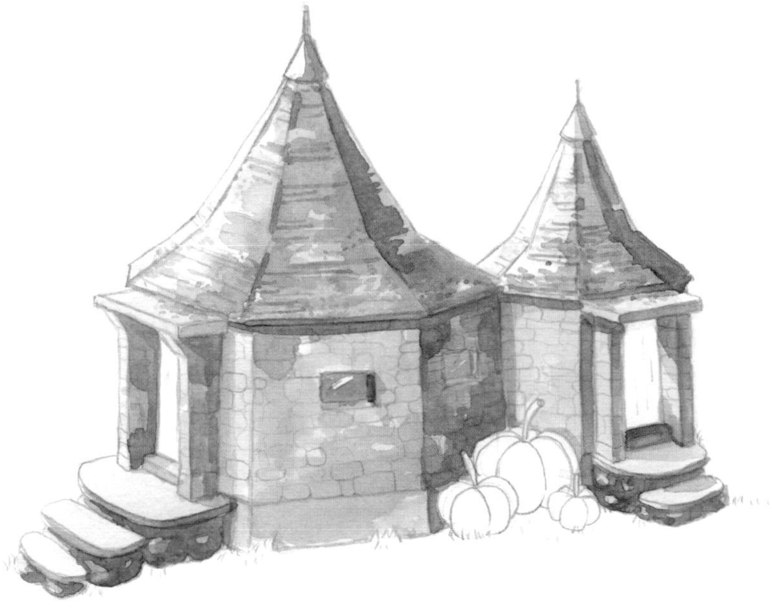

4 Once it's dry, add light indigo on the hut with your size 02 brush. Use this darker shade mostly where the shadows are the strongest, such as the right side of the hut, under the roof, and under the stairs.

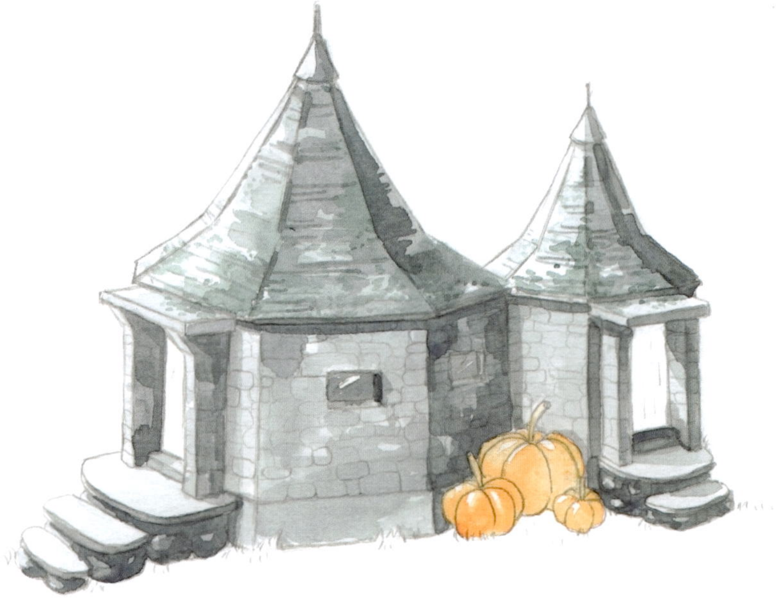

5 While painting the roof, make sure to use horizontal lines to create the roof texture.

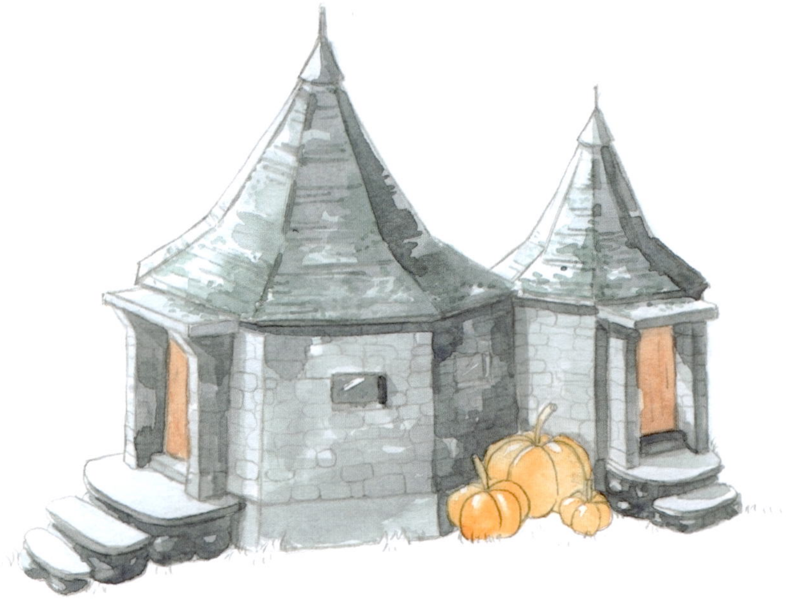

6 Paint the pumpkins with light cadmium orange and try to leave some lighter areas on the left top of them to emphasize their round shape.

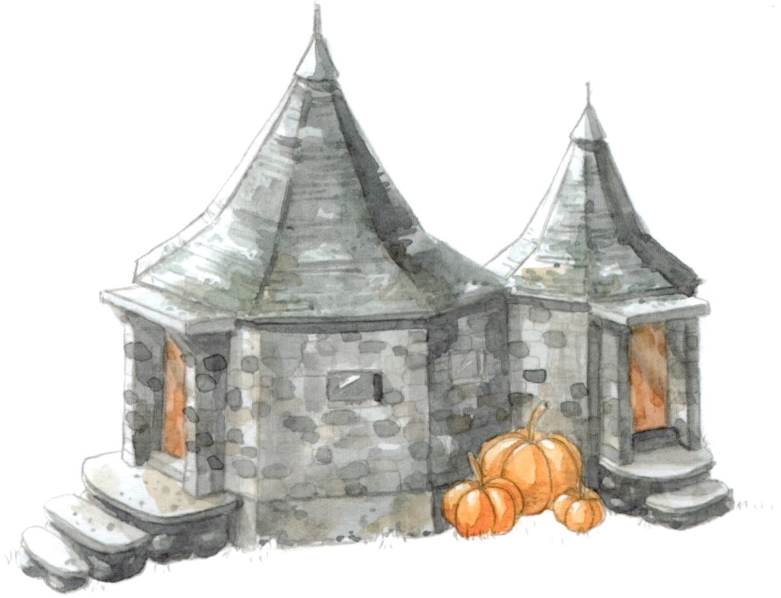

9 Once it's dry, add some light cadmium orange to the hut to make it look more organic.

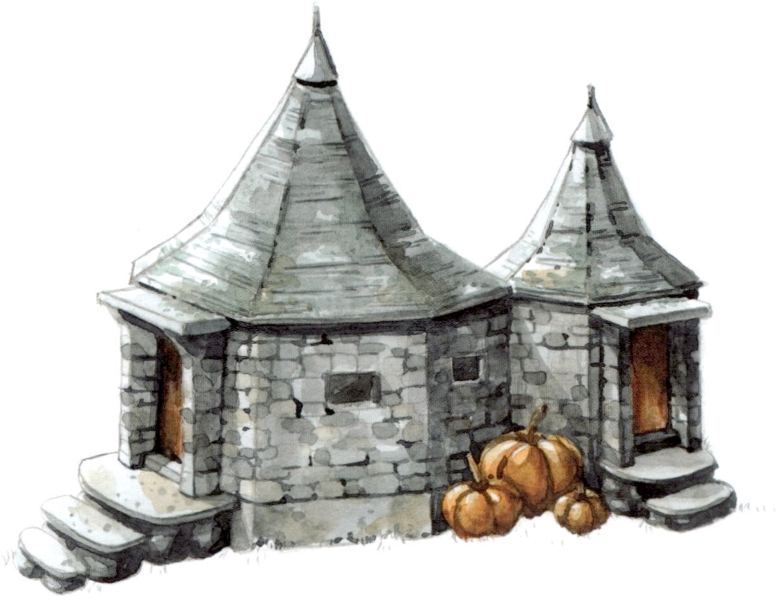

10 Use your size 02 brush to apply Payne's gray where the shadows are the deepest.

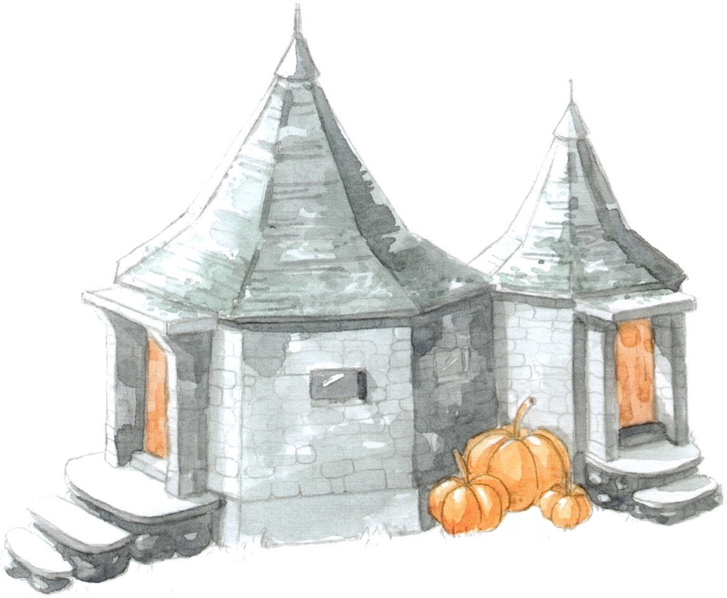

7 Paint the doors with shades of burnt sienna and add a sharper shade of cadmium orange on the pumpkins to support their unique shape.

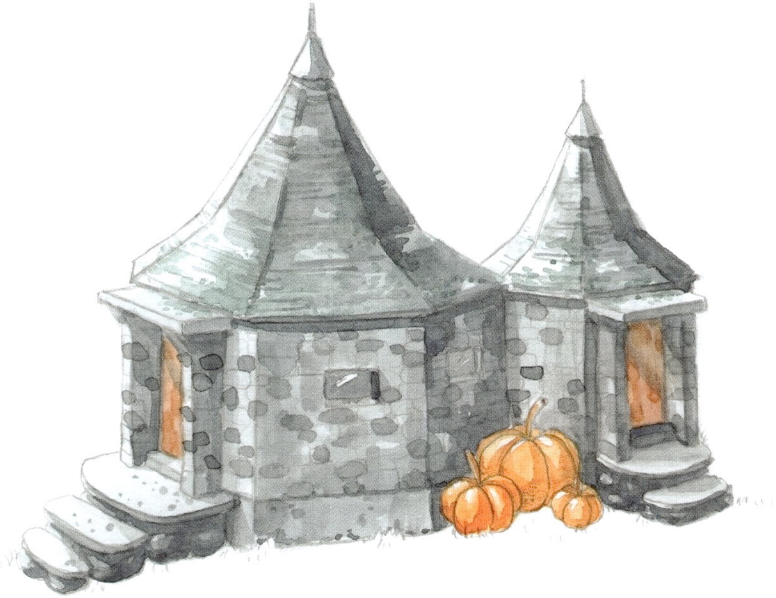

8 Use your size 10mm flat cut brush to add a brick effect on the hut with light indigo. Avoid covering the entire hut with this texture.

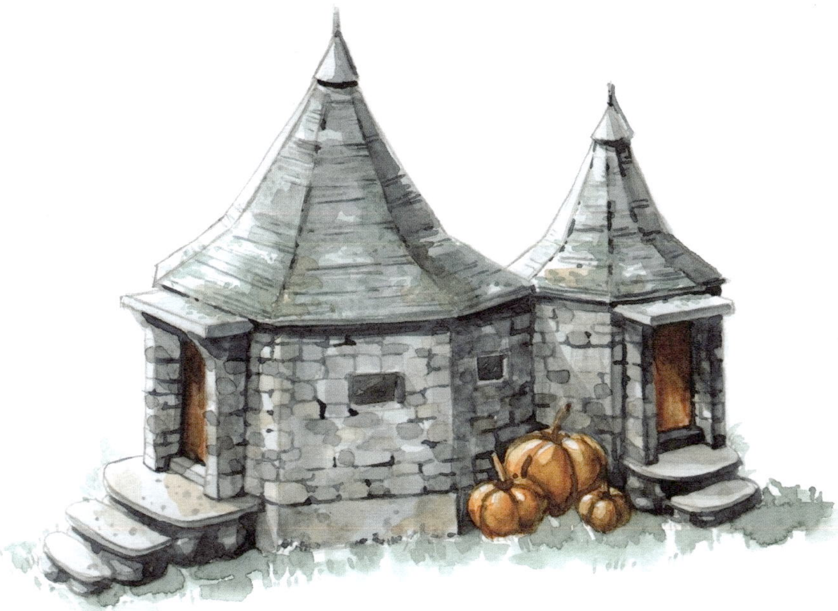

11 Use your size 10mm brush and paint the grasses with light viridian hue. Move your brush up and down in the direction of grasses to achieve a better result.

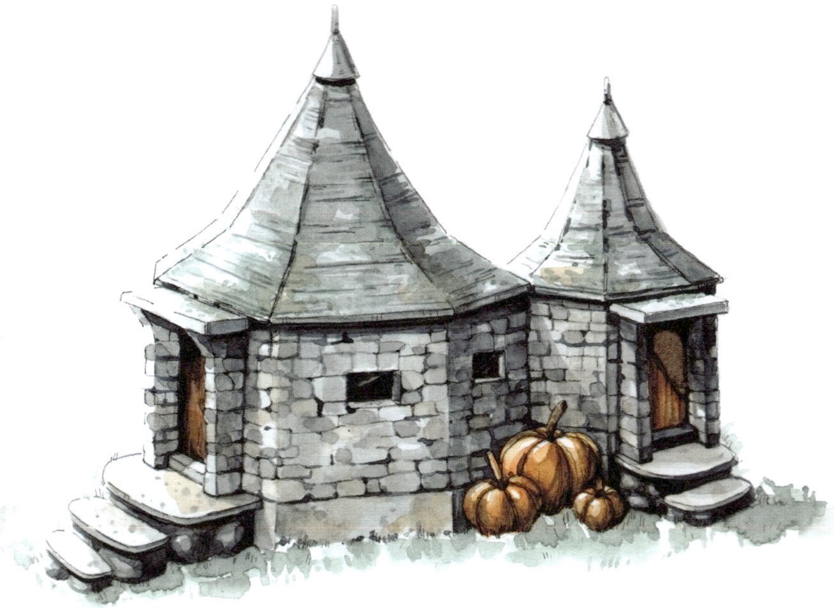

12 Use your gel pens to refine any last details and thin shadows, especially between bricks.

DIFFICULTY: ⚡⚡

Golden Egg

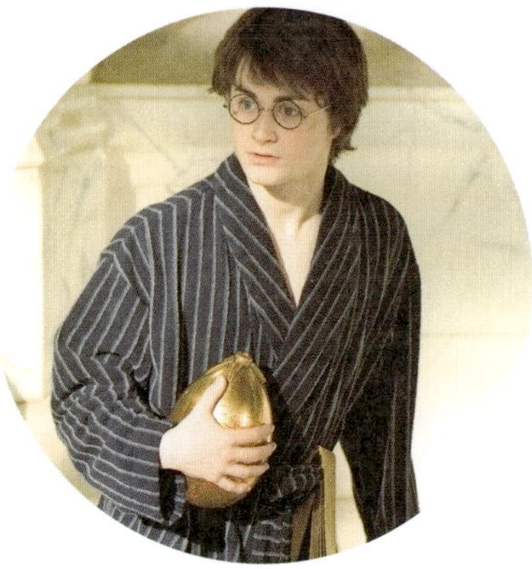

"Come seek us where our voices sound,

We cannot sing above the ground,

An hour long you'll have to look,

To recover what we took."

—The Golden Egg, *Harry Potter and the Goblet of Fire*

COLORS

LIGHT LEMON YELLOW

LEMON YELLOW

CADMIUM ORANGE

BURNT UMBER

LAMP BLACK

RECOMMENDED SUPPLIES

Size 04 brush

Size 06 brush

Black gel pen

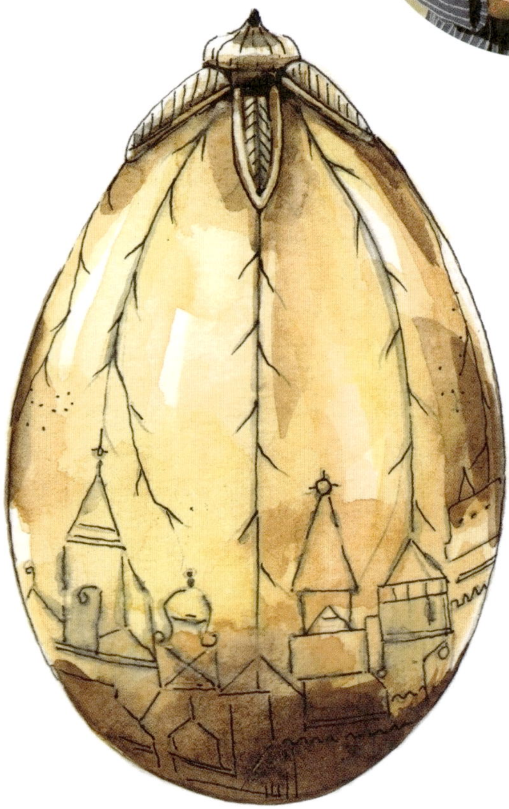

1. Use your size 06 brush and apply light lemon yellow to almost the entire egg. Make sure to leave some white gaps to create a nice metal reflection effect.
2. While the first layer is still wet, apply lemon yellow on some areas to have various shades of yellow on the surface.
3. Next, apply cadmium orange with your size 04 brush. Use this color mostly on the side and bottom of the egg to add dimension. Light colors must remain where the light is hitting the most—in this case the top and middle areas.
4. Let it dry and apply burnt umber on the edges and under the egg. Tilt your brush to create some sharp straight lines between colors so it will support the metal look of the egg.
5. Once everything is dry, apply lamp black with a size 04 brush sparingly, careful to avoid losing the gold color of the egg.
6. Now take your gel pen and add fine details on the carvings and textures.

DIFFICULTY: ϟϟϟ

Dobby

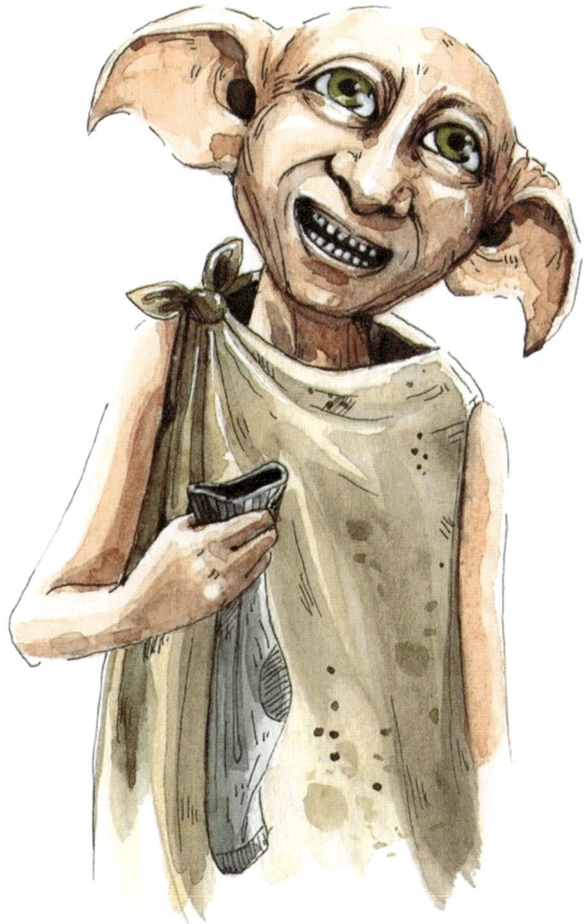

Dobby is a loyal and brave house-elf and stout friend. Though he once served the Malfoys, through Harry's help he was freed, becoming a free house-elf, beholden to no one. His bravery and self-sacrifice make him a truly unique house-elf and ally.

"Master has given Dobby a sock! Master has presented Dobby with clothes. Dobby is free!"
—Dobby, *Harry Potter and the Chamber of Secrets*

COLORS

LIGHT PINK

BURNT SIENNA

LIGHT SAP GREEN

PALE GREEN

RAW UMBER

LIGHT GRAY

DARK GRAY

RECOMMENDED SUPPLIES

Size 06 brush

Size 01 brush

Black gel pen

1. Add water to your size 06 brush, and apply a diluted shade of light pink to all of Dobby's skin, leaving white at the tip of his nose.
2. While that layer is still wet, use a darker shade of light pink on the skin, primarily on the right side, leaving the lighter layer to show through in many areas.
3. When that is fully dry, use your size 01 brush to add some burnt sienna to the darkest areas of the skin, particularly on the inner ears, lower ear tips, and neck. Smooth out any transitions with a wet brush to avoid having sharp contrast on the skin.
4. Once the skin is fully dry, use your 01 brush to add some final details on the skin, such as the wrinkles under his eyes, shadows on his eyelids, and on his cheekbones.
5. When the previous layer is dry, apply the light sap green to the eyes and to Dobby's shirt.
6. Once the light sap green is dry, add pale green to Dobby's eyes and to his shirt. Use a clean, wet brush to smooth the transition between shades on his shirt to create a better textile-like texture.
7. Next, apply a light shade of raw umber to make the shirt appear old and dirty.
8. For the sock, use your size 06 brush to apply a layer of light gray across the entire sock.
9. While it is still wet, apply dark gray, blending into the light gray layer, but leaving the dark gray most concentrated in the toe and heel of the sock.
10. Your gel pen is very useful in this piece. Use it to color the pupils and to add darker shades under the eyelids, inside the mouth, and between Dobby's teeth.

DIFFICULTY: ⚡⚡

The Marauder's Map

Created by James Potter, Remus Lupin, Sirius Black, and Peter Pettigrew during their time as students at Hogwarts, the Marauder's Map shows the movements of everyone in the castle or on the school grounds. It proves very useful to the group until it is eventually confiscated by the caretaker, Argus Filch. After liberating it from Filch, Fred and George Weasley use it to pull their infamous pranks. The twins eventually gift the map to Harry, seeing that his need for it is greater than theirs.

"I solemnly swear that I am up to no good."
—George Weasley, *Harry Potter and the Prisoner of Azkaban*

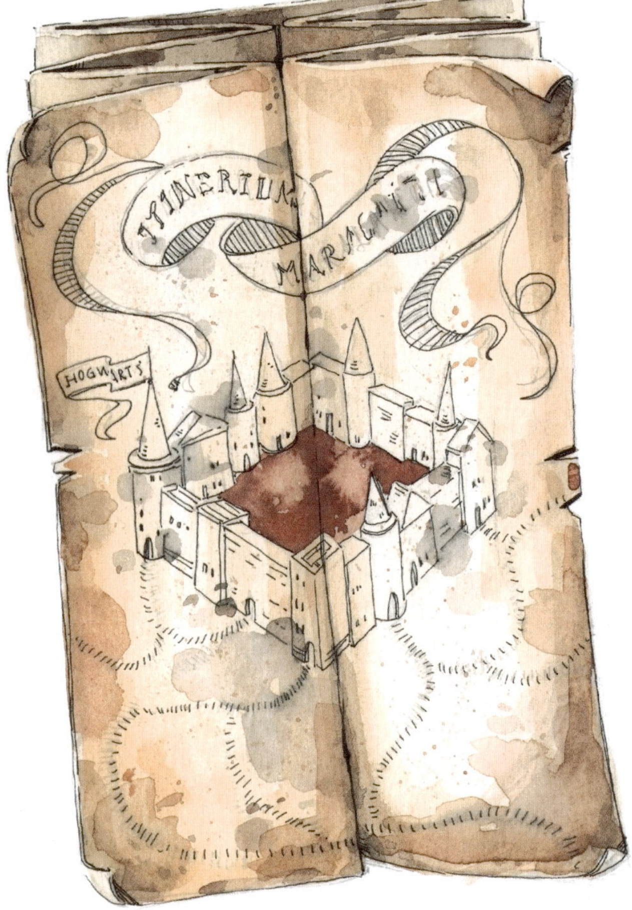

COLORS

LIGHT SALMON

SALMON

BURNT UMBER

SEPIA

BURNT SIENNA

RECOMMENDED SUPPLIES

Size 10 brush

Size 02 brush

Size 06 brush

Black gel pen

1. With your size 10 brush, take a good amount of plain water and apply it all over the map.
2. Using light salmon, touch the paper gently with your brush, just enough to leave behind paint here and there. The water will carry it around to create a nice texture.
3. Repeat this with the salmon, burnt umber, and sepia one by one before the paper gets too dry. Be sure to use the darker shades more near the edges.
4. Once it is fully dry, tilt your size 02 brush to place sepia between the folded pages in fine lines, adding dimension.
5. Apply a small amount of burnt sienna to the center of the castle with your size 02 brush to control the color. Use a clean, wet brush to touch the paint once or twice to create waves of color.
6. Use your size 06 brush to splash a small bit of sepia over the page as well, helping to create the aged look.
7. Add fine details with your gel pen to finish your piece.

DIFFICULTY: ⚡⚡

Love Potion

Weasleys' Wizard Wheezes carries a stock of pleasantly packaged love potions, but as Ron found out when he eats some dosed candies from Romilda Vane meant for Harry, the real thing is nothing to mess with.

"It's no joke! I'm in love with her."

"All right, fine, you're in love with her. Have you ever actually met her?"

"No . . . can you introduce me?"
—Ron Weasley and Harry Potter, *Harry Potter and the Half-Blood Prince*

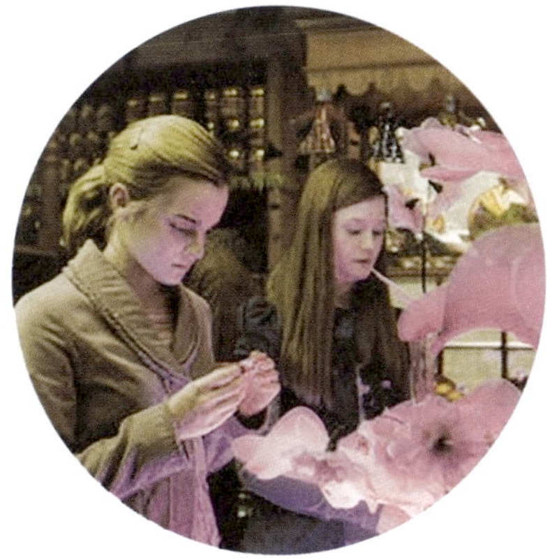

COLORS

LIGHT ROSE | CADMIUM RED | PURPLE LAKE | LIGHT SALMON

VANDYKE BROWN | CADMIUM YELLOW | YELLOW OCHRE | BURNT UMBER

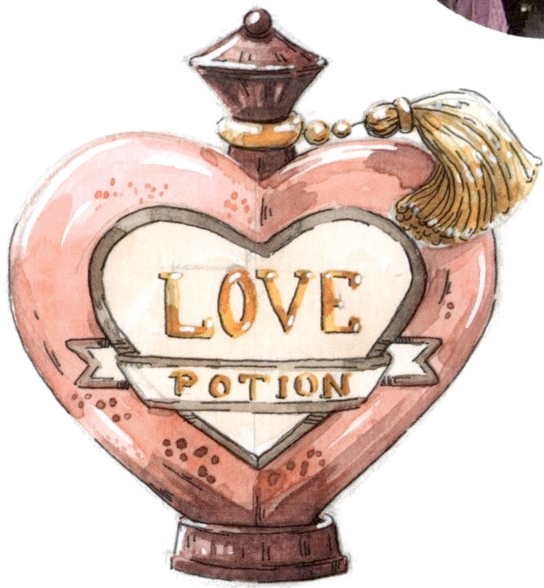

RECOMMENDED SUPPLIES

Size 04 brush

Size 01 brush

Size 000 brush

White gel pen

1. With your size 04 brush, add some water to a bit of the light rose on your palette, and apply to the outer part of the bottle, leaving the label white for now. Move in the direction of the bottle shape, leaving a few white spaces to create reflections on the glass.
2. While this layer is still wet, add a darker shade of light rose to the bottom of the bottle, leaving the top the lighter shade and blending to create smooth transitions.
3. When this layer is dry, use your size 01 brush to apply small dots of purple lake to the bottle.
4. When the bottle is fully dry, paint the bottle label with light salmon. Add small touches of Vandyke brown while the light salmon is still wet to create a paperlike texture.
5. Once the label is dry, add Vandyke brown to the label frame.
6. Use your size 000 brush to add the text in cadmium red.
7. Apply cadmium yellow to the ring and tassel. While still wet, apply yellow ochre to the tassel as well, leaving areas for the lighter shade to show through, providing contrast.
8. When everything is dry, add some water to a portion of the purple lake on your palette. Apply this shade to both the bottle stopper and the base.
9. While that layer is still wet, apply darker shades of purple lake to both pieces, leaving some lighter spaces where the light hits it.
10. Use your white gel pen to add highlights to the label, stopper, and base.

DIFFICULTY: ⚡⚡

Weasleys' Wizard Wheezes Logo

Located in Diagon Alley, this successful joke shop was founded by George and Fred Weasley. They have a booming business selling practical jokes and other items, such as love potions, a likeness of Dolores Umbridge riding a unicycle, Sticky Trainers, and Peruvian Instant Darkness Powder.

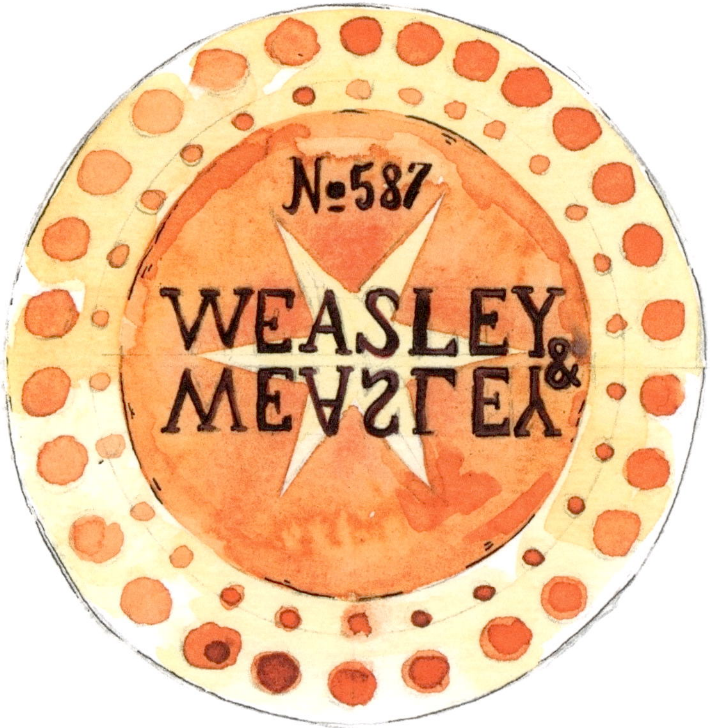

COLORS

- LIGHT LEMON YELLOW
- CADMIUM YELLOW
- CADMIUM ORANGE
- CADMIUM RED
- PURPLE LAKE

RECOMMENDED SUPPLIES

- Size 06 brush
- Size 01 brush
- Black gel pen

1. Use your size 06 brush to apply the light lemon yellow to the outer edge and the middle star. Tilt your brush to have as much control as possible.
2. While that layer is still wet, apply the cadmium yellow to portions of the same areas, blending to create smooth transitions.
3. Once the yellow dries, paint the center circle cadmium orange, being careful to stay outside of the star by painting around its edges first.
4. Add some shading with cadmium red, particularly on the outer edge of the inner circle.
5. Use your size 01 brush to add dots of cadmium orange and cadmium red.
6. Once dry, pick up concentrated purple lake with your size 01 brush, being sure the brush is relatively dry. Hold it straight and use the tip to carefully add the lettering.
7. If you wish, you can use your gel pen to sharpen the edges on the lettering as well.

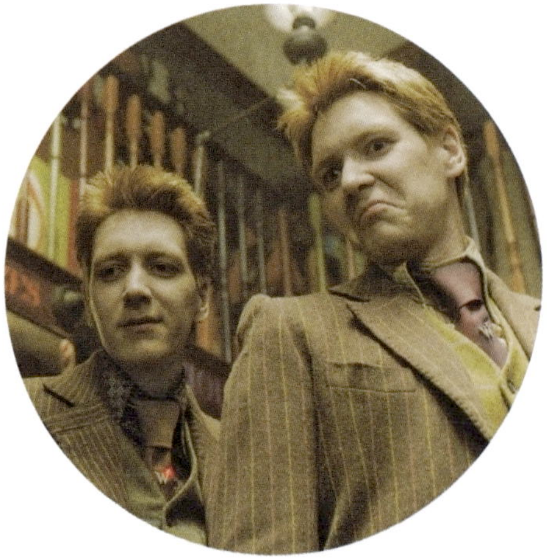

DIFFICULTY: ⚡⚡

Stag Patronus

"A powerful memory, the happiest you can remember. Allow it to fill you up. . . . A full-bodied Patronus is the most difficult to produce, but shield forms can also be equally useful against a variety of opponents. . . . Just remember, your Patronus can only protect you for as long as you stay focused."
—Harry Potter, *Harry Potter and the Order of the Phoenix*

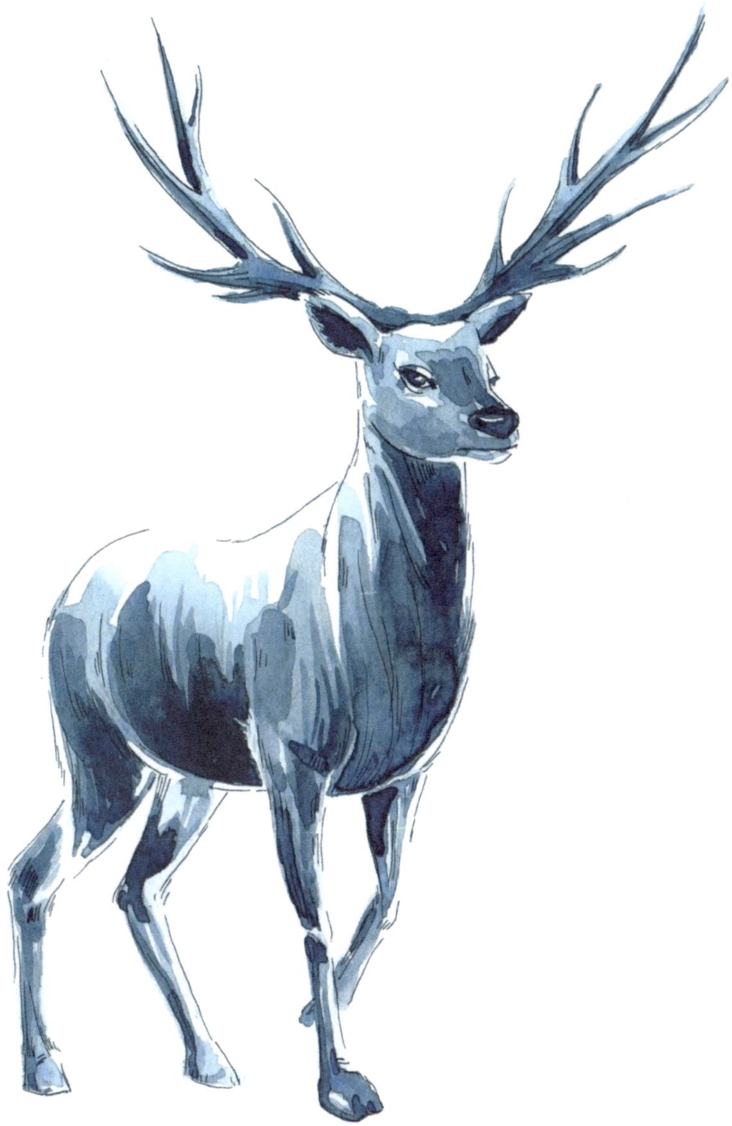

COLORS

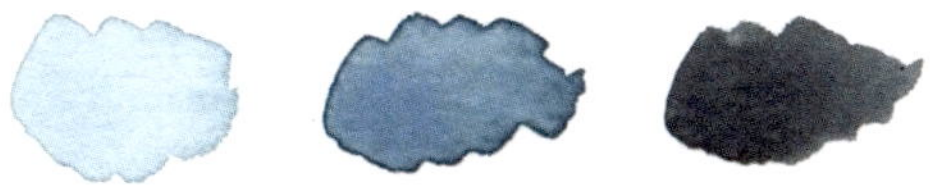

LIGHT INDIGO INDIGO IVORY BLACK

RECOMMENDED SUPPLIES

Size 06 brush

Size 02 brush

Black gel pen

1. Using your size 02 brush, put a tiny bit of light indigo on the tip, using it to start painting from the tip of the antlers, tilting your brush as you move farther down the antlers to create thicker lines.
2. While this first layer is still wet, apply a layer of indigo, blending with the light indigo on the antlers.
3. Using a size 06 brush, cover the rest of the stag with the light indigo as well, leaving large white gaps on the top of the body to reflect the light effect.
4. Before the light indigo dries, apply a layer of indigo, blending to achieve a smoky watercolor effect on the stag. Leave some lighter areas around the face, neck, the tops of the ears, behind the legs, and the top of its back. Be very careful while applying this layer to the face, as misplaced lines can be very noticeable here. Because our light source is on the left, be sure to use darker shades mostly on the lower-right bottom, such as under the stag's belly.
5. When the previous layers are completely dry, grab the ivory black and apply it to the inner ears, on the nose, under the neck, on the bottom of the antlers, and under the belly.
6. To smooth out transitions between colors, dip a clean brush into water. Remove the extra water and rub gently between the colors to smooth the edges.
7. To finish, use your gel pen or a very small brush to create the eyes.

DIFFICULTY: ⚡⚡

Death Eater Mask

While certainly intimidating, the main purpose of Death Eater masks is to hide the Death Eaters' identities. By concealing their allegiance, the Death Eaters were able to hide in plain sight throughout wizard society.

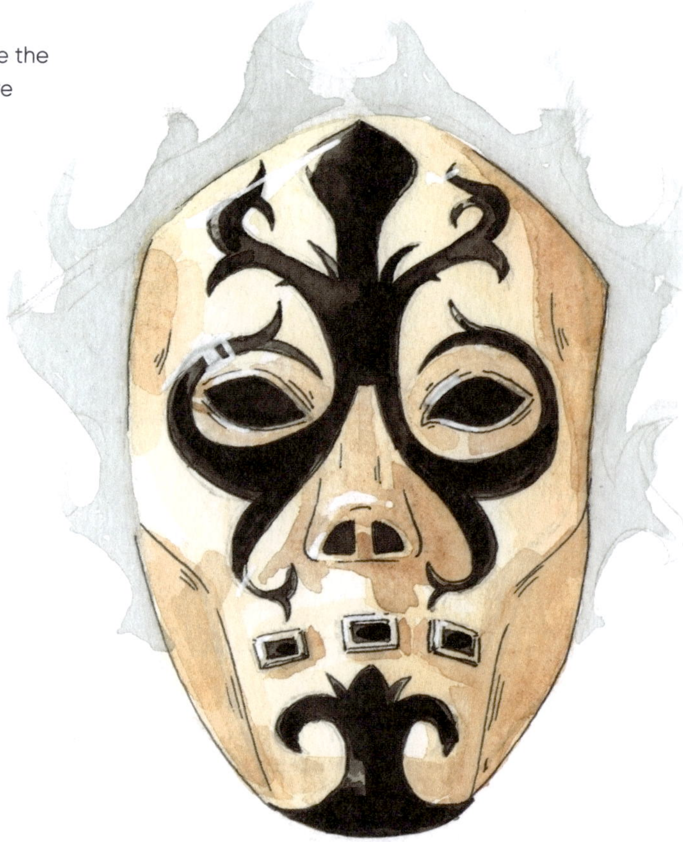

COLORS

LIGHT CADMIUM YELLOW

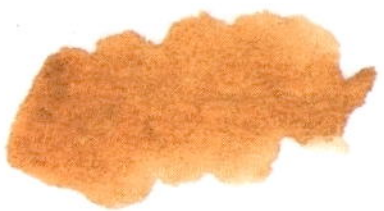

RAW SIENNA

LAMP BLACK

GRAY

RECOMMENDED SUPPLIES

Size 10 brush

Size 02 brush

Black gel pen

White gel pen

1. Using a size 10 brush, apply light cadmium yellow over most of the mask. Leave a few areas white, particularly the tip of the nose, left side of the forehead, and the left cheekbone, to create the metallic shine.
2. When the first layer is dry, apply the raw sienna on the darker areas of the mask, such as the contours on the temples, cheeks, and around the nose. Keep in mind how the light would hit the mask. Use your own face as an example to gain a better understanding of shadow and light reflections on this mask.
3. When it is all dry, use your 02 brush to add the lamp black. After filling in the black design, tilt your brush and keep it in contact with the paper to draw the straight, fine lines found on the raised facets of the mask.
4. Use your gel pen to add any details too fine for your brush, such as around the eyes and nose.
5. Once everything else is dry, use your size 02 brush to apply the flames in gray. Tilt your brush to create sharp, thin edges on the flames.
6. You can use a white gel pen to add additional bright spots as needed to complete the mask.

DIFFICULTY: ϟϟ

Tom Riddle's Diary and Basilisk Fang

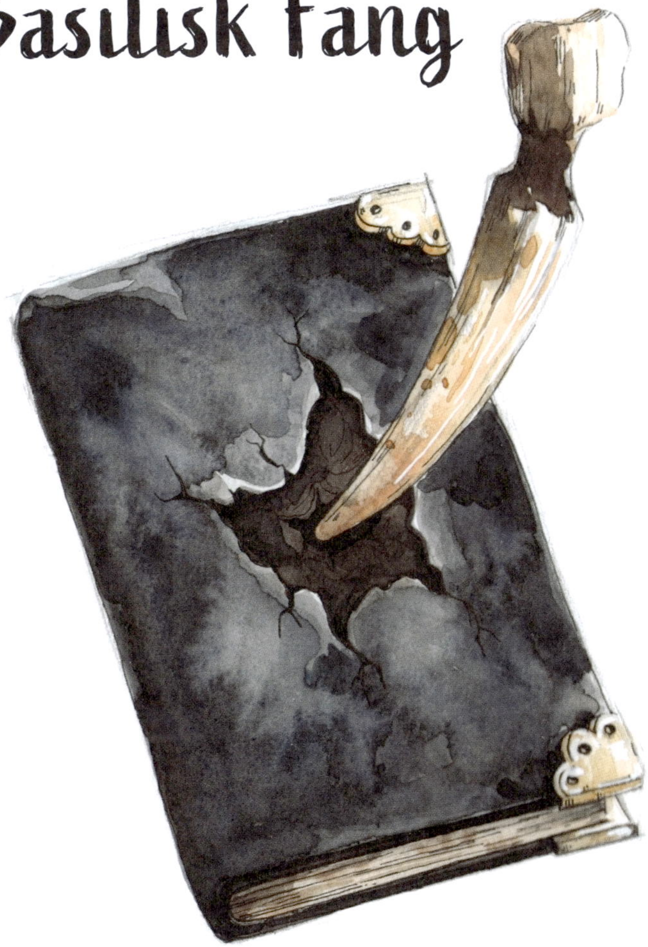

"Funny, the damage a silly little book can do,
especially in the hands of a silly little girl."
—Tom Riddle, *Harry Potter and the Chamber of Secrets*

COLORS

LIGHT GRAY

INDIGO

IVORY BLACK

LIGHT SALMON

LIGHT LEMON YELLOW

YELLOW OCHRE

RAW UMBER

RECOMMENDED SUPPLIES

Size 10 brush

Size 06 brush

Size 02 brush

Size 000 brush

Black gel pen

1. With your size 10 brush, take a good amount of plain water, and apply it all over the diary's cover.
2. With gentle touches of your brush, add light gray, indigo, and ivory black one by one to the cover. Just touch the wet areas enough to leave the paint behind, letting the water carry the paint to create an amazing texture. Continue doing this until the cover reaches the desired color and texture.
3. Once it is completely dry, add some more controlled shading to the book with those same colors, being sure to highlight the torn edges with lighter shades.
4. Use your size 06 brush to apply light lemon yellow over the entire Basilisk fang, as well as the pages and book corners.
5. Before that layer dries, add some shades of yellow ochre and raw umber, blending to create smooth transitions and shadows.
6. With your 02 brush, add light salmon to the fang as well.
7. When it is dry, use your size 000 brush to add lines to the fang with the raw umber, as well as to the paper, creating distinct pages along the bottom.
8. Use your gel pen to add finishing fine details.

DIFFICULTY: ⚡⚡

Bertie Bott's Every-Flavour Beans

"Bertie Bott's Every-Flavour Beans?"

"They mean every flavor. There's chocolate and peppermint and there's also spinach, liver, and tripe. George swears he got a bogey-flavored one once."
—Harry Potter and Ron Weasley, *Harry Potter and the Sorcerer's Stone*

COLORS

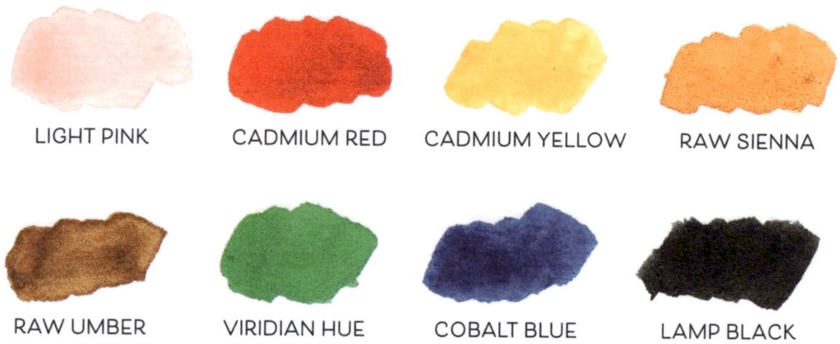

RECOMMENDED SUPPLIES

Size 10 brush

Size 02 brush

Black gel pen

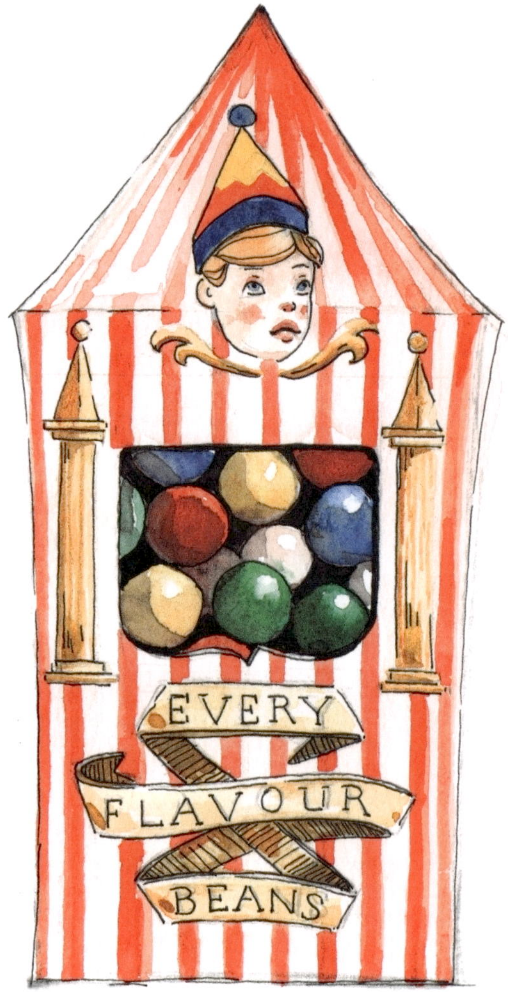

1. With your size 10 brush, apply light pink all over the box.
2. With your size 02 brush, use cadmium red to fill the stripes on the tent. Keep your brush tilted to keep level pressure and achieve fine, straight lines.
3. When the tent is dry, use the tip of your size 02 brush to add details to the face and paint the hat. Don't use too much water here as you want your colors to stay brightly pigmented and easily controlled in this small area.
4. Apply a light shade of cadmium yellow to the ribbon and pillars, adding raw sienna while the yellow is still wet to create smooth transitions.
5. With your size 02 brush, paint the candies various colors, leaving a small white gap on the upper part where the light hits them to make them look round and shiny.
6. Once everything is dry, add lamp black between the candies to achieve a more realistic look.
7. Finish by using your gel pen to add small details to the face and text.

DIFFICULTY: ⚡⚡

The Monster Book of Monsters

Assigned reading for any students enrolled in Hagrid's Care of Magical Creatures class, The Monster Book of Monsters requires careful handling.

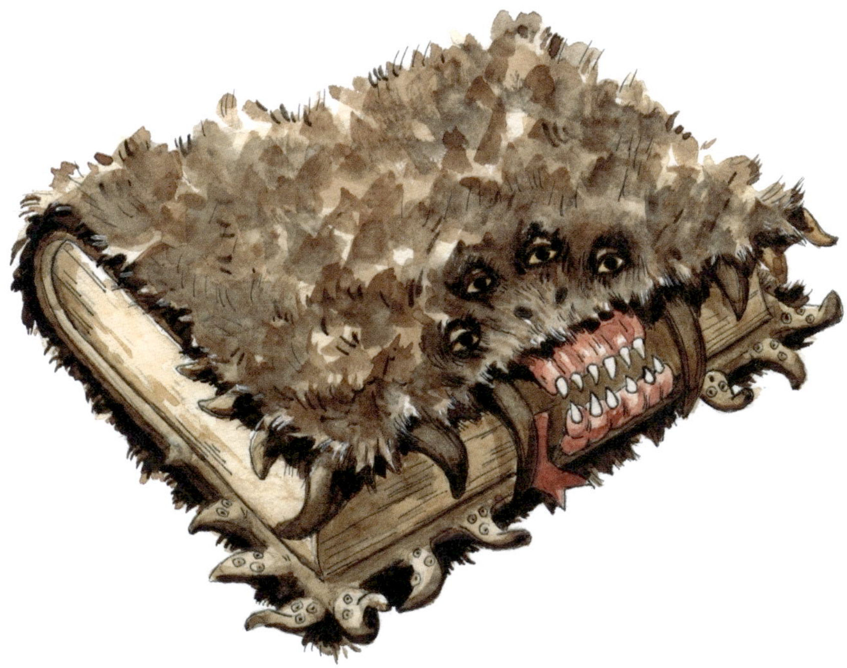

COLORS

LIGHT LEMON YELLOW

LIGHT BURNT UMBER

BURNT UMBER

RAW UMBER

LIGHT CADMIUM RED

VANDYKE BROWN

RECOMMENDED SUPPLIES

Size 02 brush

Size 10mm brush

Black gel pen

White gel pen

1. Using your size 02 brush, apply light lemon yellow over the entire book, except for the mouth, teeth, and tongue.
2. Once it is dry, apply some light burnt umber with your size 02 brush on the pages to create shading and differentiate the pages. Use the tip of your brush to create thin lines.
3. When that layer is fully dry, apply some light burnt umber on the tentacles with your size 02 brush. Leave some areas with light lemon yellow to create some dimension.
4. Take some burnt umber and add it mostly under the tentacles to emphasize their shapes.
5. Once everything is dry, paint the gums and the tongue with light red. Dilute the color with water to create two different shades of it and apply the paint by following the anatomy of the teeth.
6. Take your size 10mm flat cut brush and some burnt umber and start to color the fur by swinging your wrist left and right like you are dusting. That will help you create a messy fur effect.
7. Do the same with raw umber once the first layer is dry.
8. Take your size 02 brush and grab some Vandyke brown to add the darkest tones to the fur.
9. Use your white gel pen to add some lighter hairs on the cover if needed and use the black gel pen to finalize any remaining small details on your painting.

DIFFICULTY: ϟϟϟ

Chocolate Frog

"These aren't real frogs, are they?"

"It's just a spell. Besides, it's the cards you want. Each pack's got a famous witch or wizard. I've got about five hundred meself."
—Harry Potter and Ron Weasley, *Harry Potter and the Sorcerer's Stone*

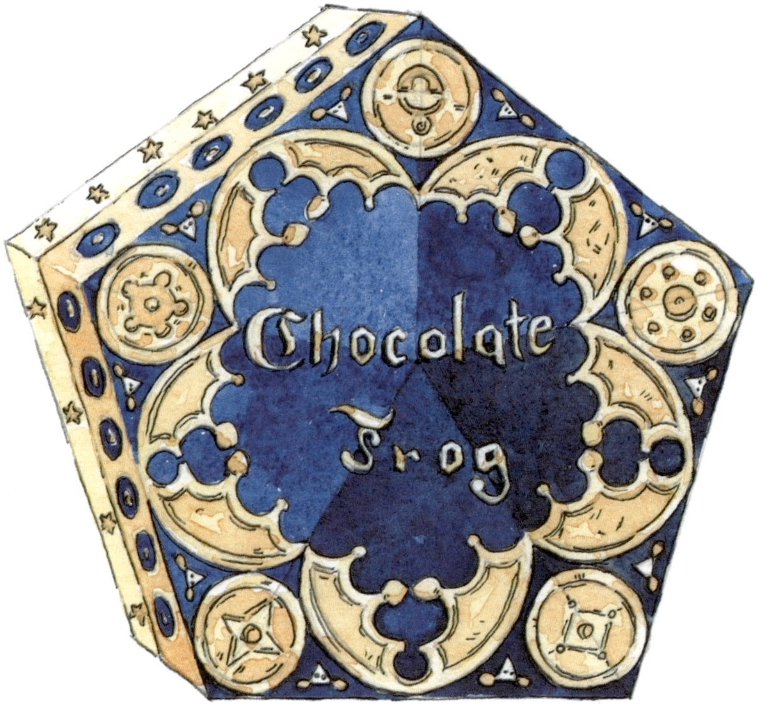

COLORS

LIGHT LEMON YELLOW

YELLOW OCHRE

LIGHT COBALT BLUE

COBALT BLUE

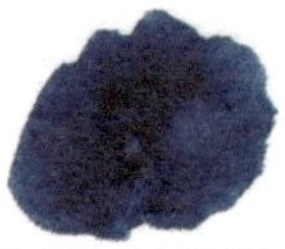
DARK COBALT BLUE

RECOMMENDED SUPPLIES

Size 04 brush

Size 02 brush

Size 000 brush

Black gel pen

1. Begin by using your size 000 brush to apply the light lemon yellow on the patterns and text. Don't worry if you make any mistakes, as they will be covered by the blue later.
2. When that layer is dry, use the same brush to apply yellow ochre to add dimension and details to the patterns.
3. To paint the box, be sure to use a slightly different shade of blue on each of the five facets to provide a sense of dimension. Start by using your size 000 brush to take a small amount of paint to paint around the patterns and text. Take your time here and use the tip of your brush to fill the right areas without painting over the text and textures.
4. After you have completed those detailed areas, use your size 02 or 04 brush to fill the rest of the surface with the varying shades of blue. Let it dry and then follow the same process on the next surface with slightly darker shades.
5. To finalize your box, use your gel pen to add additional details, especially around the text and patterns.

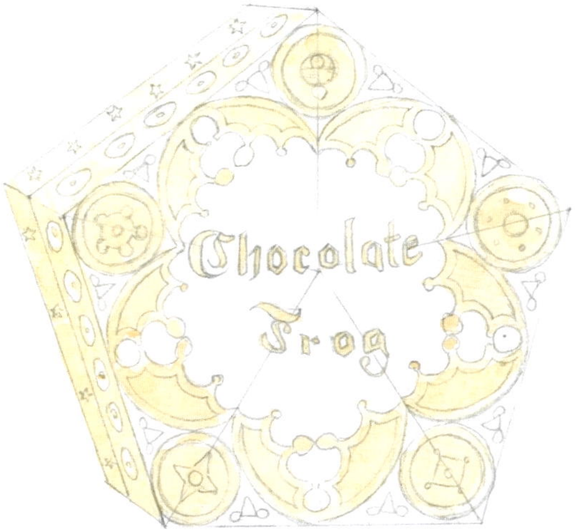
Chocolate
Frog

1

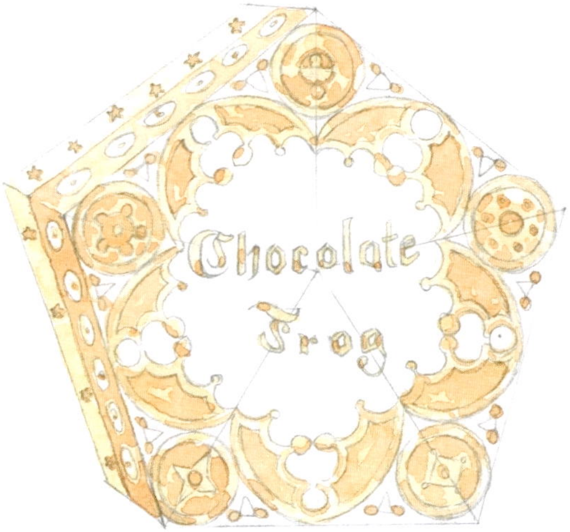
Chocolate
Frog

2

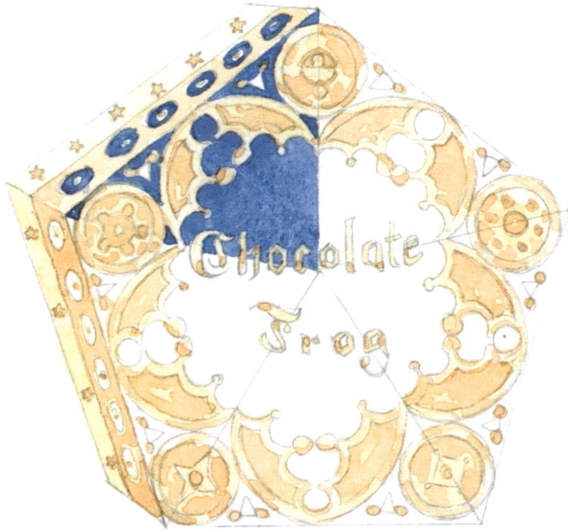
Chocolate
Frog

3

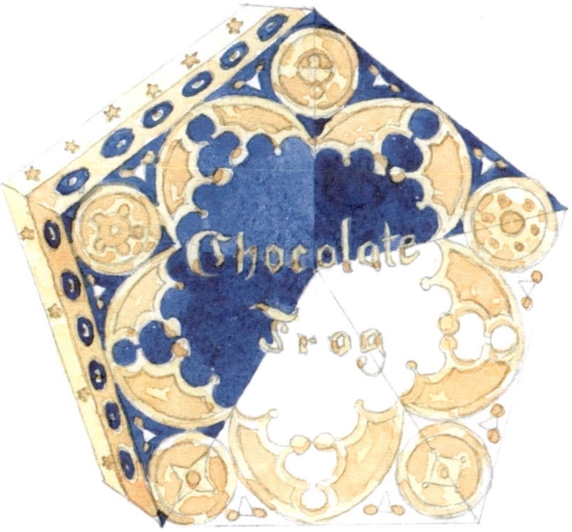
Chocolate
Frog

4

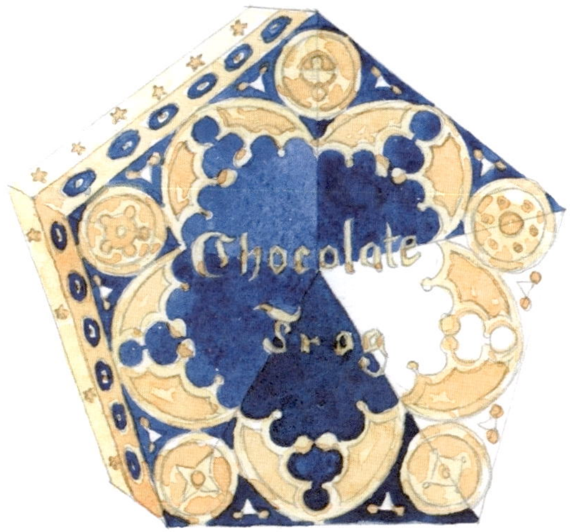
Chocolate
Frog

4

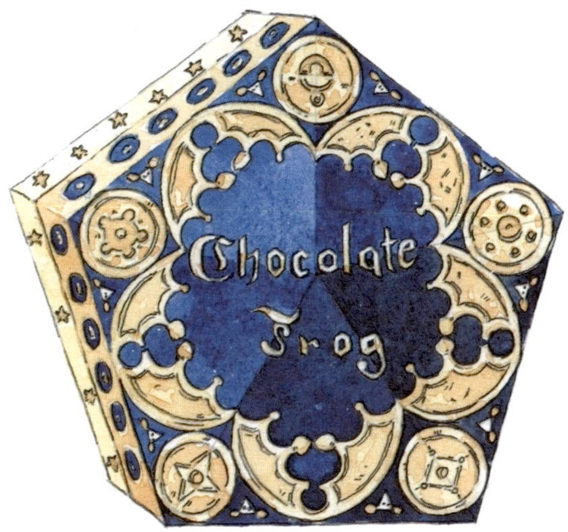
Chocolate
Frog

5

DIFFICULTY: ϟϟϟ

Hogwarts Castle

Serving as the main building for Hogwarts School of Witchcraft and Wizardry, Hogwarts castle is an impressive sight, towering over the Great Lake. The castle's seven stories are supported by magic, and it holds an impressive 142 staircases from its deepest dungeons to its tallest turrets.

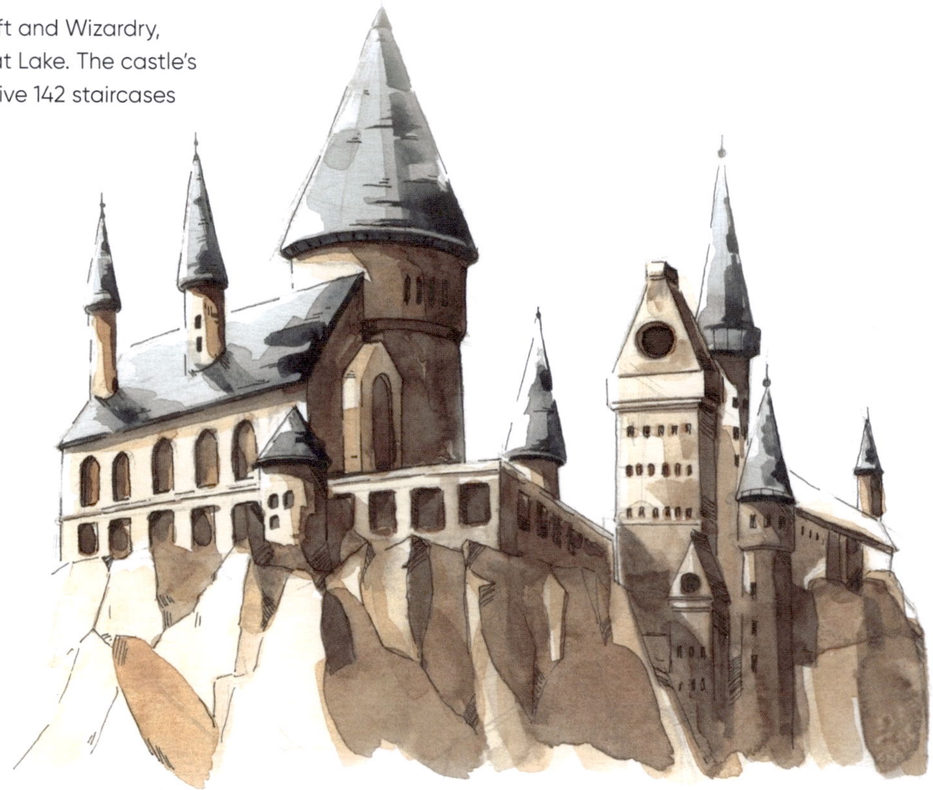

COLORS

BEIGE

YELLOW OCHRE

LIGHT RAW UMBER

RAW UMBER

LIGHT INDIGO

INDIGO

RECOMMENDED SUPPLIES

Size 06 brush

Size 10mm brush

Size 10 brush

Black gel pen

1. Begin by using your size 10 brush to apply the lightest shade of beige over the entire castle and the underpinning cliff face, leaving the gray roofs alone for now.
2. While this first layer is still wet, add some darker touches with the yellow ochre and light raw umber to avoid having a plain base color.
3. Assuming a light source on the left, build up the shading on the right side of the castle using darker shades of light raw umber and raw umber. No need to be perfect! Just be sure that the shadows are on the right side. This will help the castle look three-dimensional.
4. While the castle is drying, apply the light indigo to the roofs. While this layer is still wet, add some darker touches of diluted indigo, remembering to place the darker touches on the right.
5. While the roofs dry, return to the castle. Use your size 06 brush to apply a second shade of light raw umber and raw umber to the castle, keeping in mind that the darker areas should be on the right. Tilt your brush down to create straight lines on the edges of the castle.
6. Once this is dry, use your size 10mm brush to place windows and additional shadows with the darker shades in your palette.
7. Let this fully dry, then apply an even darker shade to deepen the shadows until you feel like you've achieved the desired effect.
8. Use your 10mm brush to apply indigo to details on the roofs in horizontal lines, as well as under the roofs, windows, and towers to enhance their dimensions. This helps create the nice brick effect.
9. Grab your gel pen and add line details on the cliff and building edges and fine details on the windows. There is no need to define every detail; just enhance the general shape.

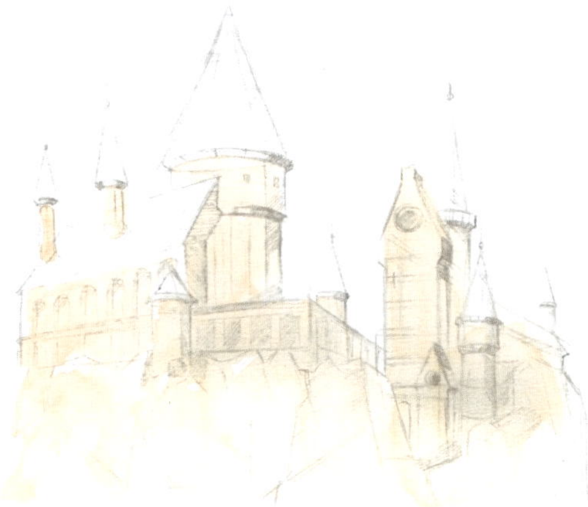

1 2 3

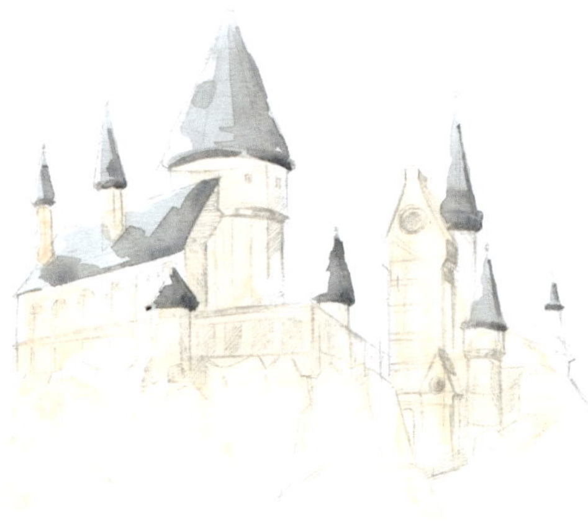

4

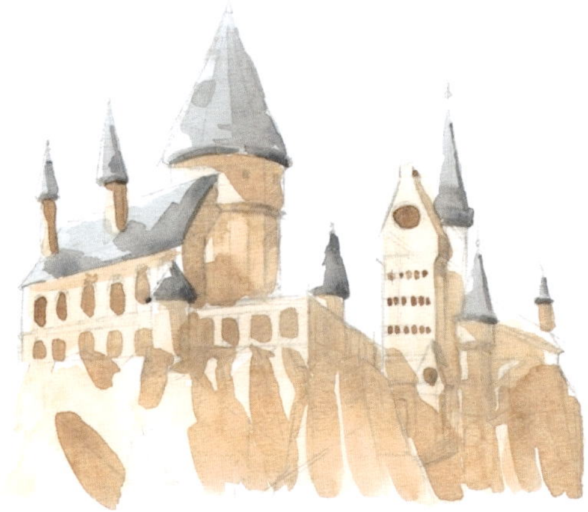

5 6

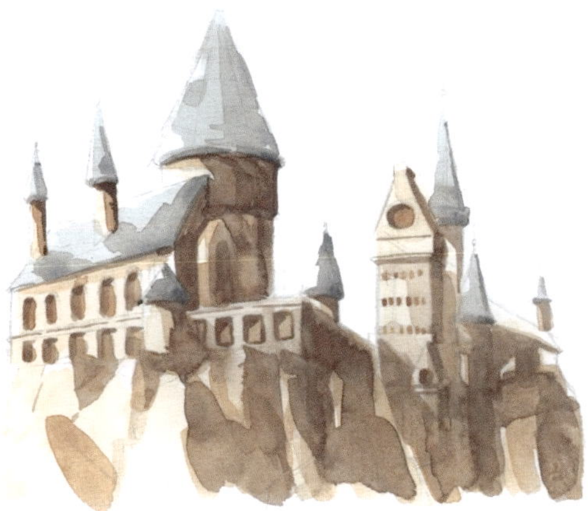

7

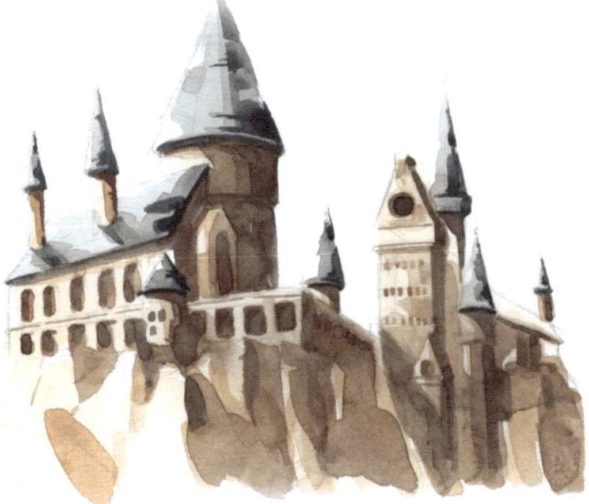

8

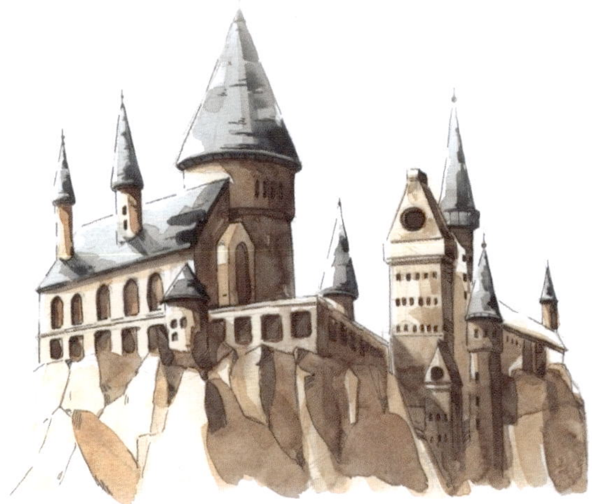

9

DIFFICULTY: ϟϟϟ

Howler

"Look everyone! Weasley's got himself a Howler."
—Seamus Finnigan, *Harry Potter and the Chamber of Secrets*

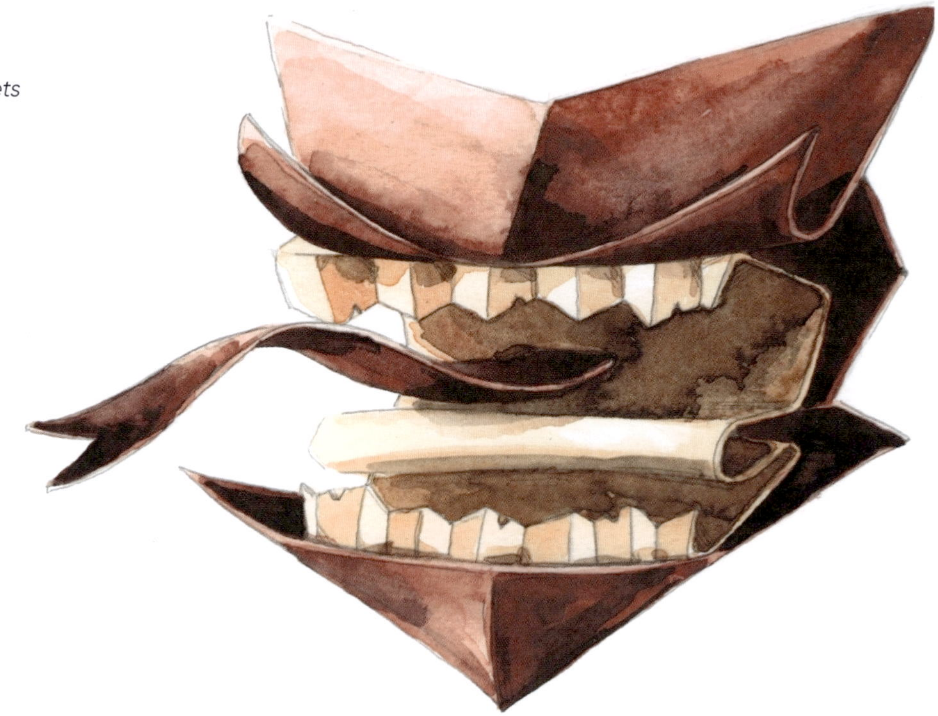

COLORS

LIGHT SALMON

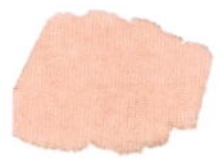
LIGHT BURNT SIENNA

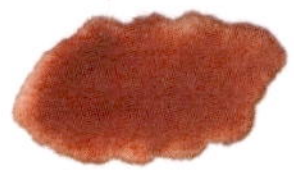
BURNT SIENNA

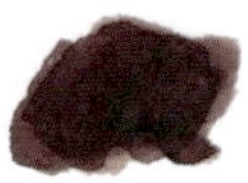
LAMP BLACK

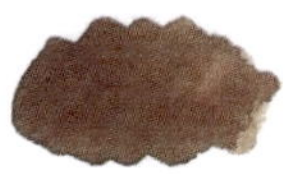
VANDYKE BROWN

RECOMMENDED SUPPLIES

Size 06 brush

Size 02 brush

Black gel pen

White gel pen

1. Using a size 06 brush, apply light salmon all around the letter, including the teeth. Use the tip of your brush to create clean sharp edges by starting to paint from the left top portion and moving down.
2. When the first layer is dry, use your size 02 brush to add shading to the letter with the light burnt sienna in clean, straight lines.
3. Once this is dry, apply the Vandyke brown in the darkest shadows inside the mouth and behind the teeth and tongue to sharpen the shades on the letter.
4. Once the letter is fully dry, add a large amount of water to your burnt sienna to create a light version of the color. Begin painting with this lightest shade over the entire envelope and tongue.
5. While this layer is still wet, apply a darker, but still not the darkest, shade of burnt sienna, blending to create smooth transitions, leaving the upper part of the envelope and the top part of the tongue for the lightest shade to show through.
6. When that layer is dry, add the darkest burnt sienna to the heavily shadowed portions of the envelope, toward the back and the bottom.
7. Darken your Vandyke brown with a little bit of lamp black to add one final layer of shadow to the letter. Be sure to only apply this color where the shadows are the deepest.
8. Use your gel pens to add some thickness to the paper and envelope edges.

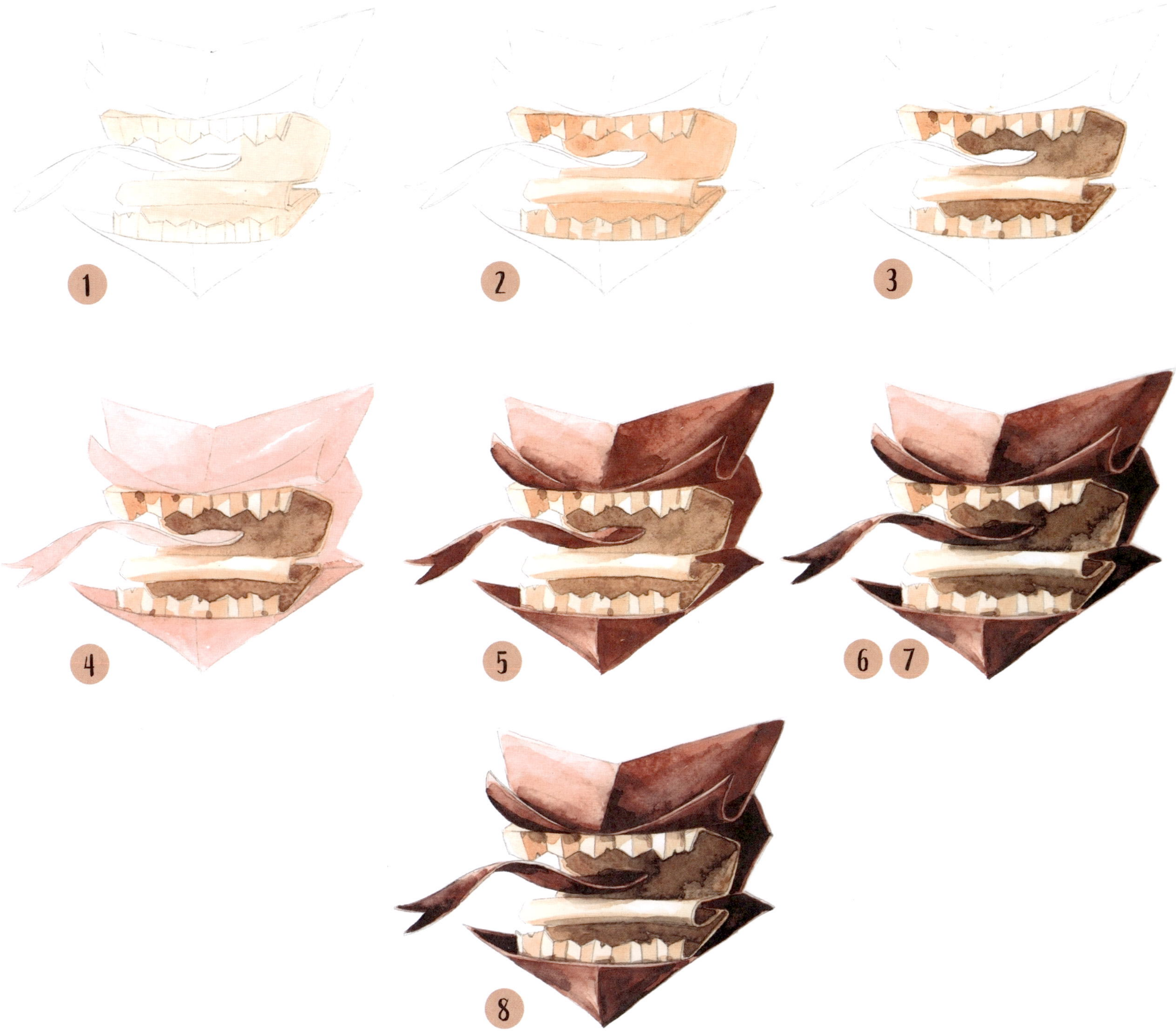
1
2
3
4
5
6
7
8

DIFFICULTY: ⚡⚡⚡

Time-Turner

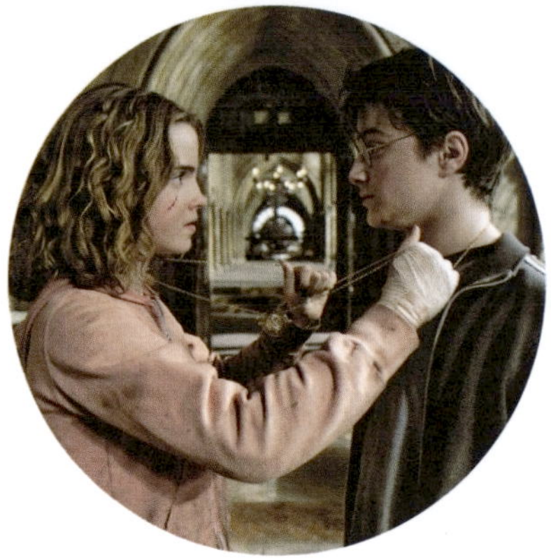

"Mysterious thing, time. Powerful and, when meddled with, dangerous. Sirius Black is in the topmost cell of the Dark Tower. You know the laws, Miss Granger. You must not be seen. And you would do well, I feel, to return before this last chime. If not, the consequences are too ghastly to discuss. If you succeed tonight, more than one innocent life may be spared. . . . Oh, by the way, when in doubt, I find retracing my steps to be a wise place to begin. Good luck."
—Professor Dumbledore, *Harry Potter and the Prisoner of Azkaban*

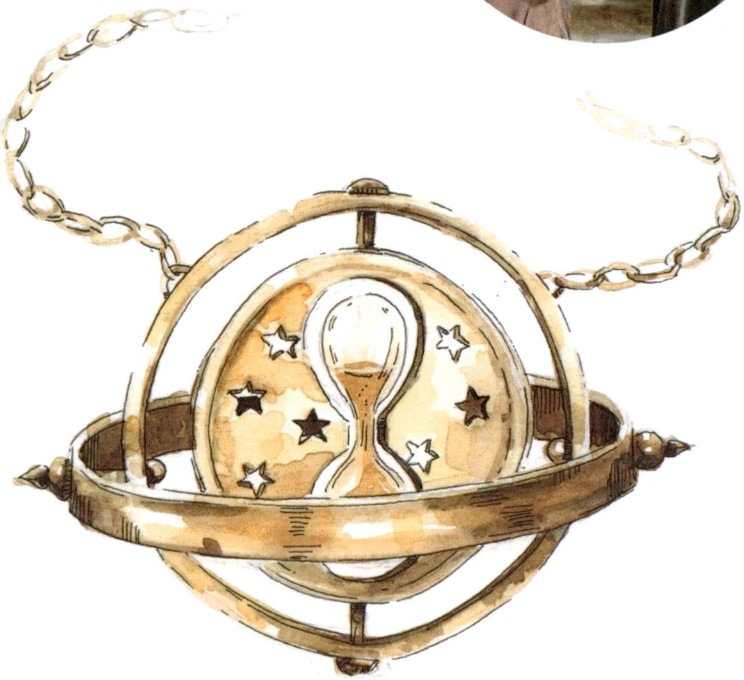

COLORS

LIGHT CADMIUM YELLOW

CADMIUM YELLOW

RAW SIENNA

BURNT UMBER

VANDYKE BROWN

RECOMMENDED SUPPLIES

Size 02 brush

Black gel pen

1. Dip your size 02 brush into water, and fill the hourglass. Grab a tiny bit of light cadmium yellow, touch the middle of the hourglass, and let the color fade around.
2. Continue applying the light cadmium yellow throughout, leaving a few white gaps to simulate where the light reflects off of the gold.
3. Before that layer dries, apply the cadmium yellow and let it fade into the light cadmium yellow for a soft transition between the shades over the entire Time-Turner.
4. When it is almost dry, take a tiny amount of raw sienna, and add it to the Time-Turner to create shallow shadows. Tilt your brush so you can better control the placement.
5. Repeat this process with the burnt umber, creating deeper shadows. Use the lightest and darkest shades side by side to emphasize the contrast in between and better define the gold material.
6. Use the Vandyke brown to create the darkest shadows, like those along the inside edges of the horizontal bar of the Time-Turner.
7. Use your gel pen to separate the various sections of the Time-Turner from each other and to add the many fine details on this object.

DIFFICULTY: ⚡⚡⚡

The Dark Mark

An infamous symbol used by Voldemort and his most trusted followers, the Dark Mark inspires fear in all who see it, whether appearing on the forearms of Death Eaters or in the sky above the site of any heinous acts they might commit.

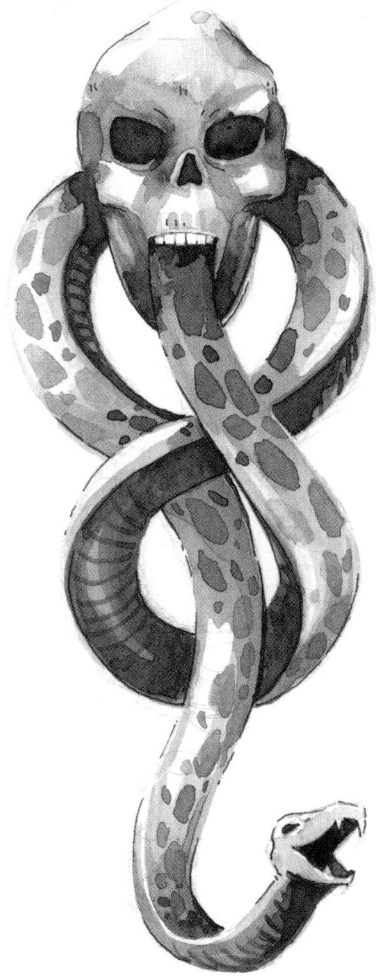

COLORS

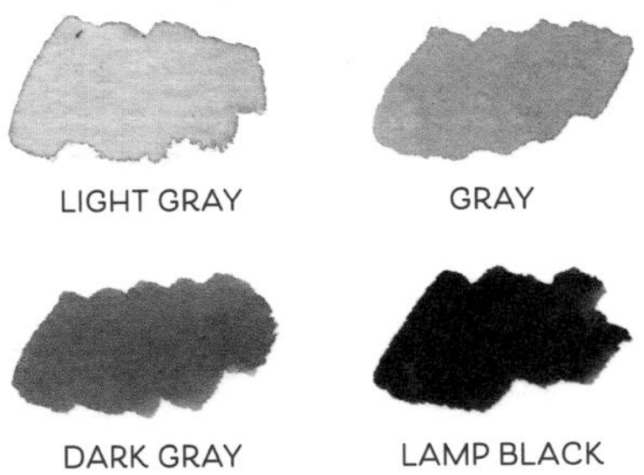

RECOMMENDED SUPPLIES

Size 06 brush
Size 01 brush
Size 10 brush
Black gel pen

1. Using your size 06 brush, apply the light gray to the skull, tilting your brush to more easily follow the contours. Leave some white areas to help simulate the light hitting it, particularly on the top of the skull, cheekbones, and upper lip.
2. While that first layer is still wet, apply a layer of gray, blending from the light gray into the deeper areas.
3. Once those layers are dry, add dark gray to the contours of the skull, particularly the eyes and on the bottom part of the chin.
4. Using your size 10 brush, apply light gray over the whole snake, leaving a few areas as white to simulate where the light hits it.
5. While the light gray is still wet, apply the gray to some of the spots on the snake, and blend it along the body, considering the play of light and shadow.
6. When the previous layers are dry, add the dark gray, especially under the body of the snake and behind the skull.
7. When this is dry, use your size 01 brush to apply gray to add some texture to the snake.
8. Once everything has dried, add the lamp black to the darkest areas of the image, such as inside the mouth and behind the skull.
9. Finish this off by using the gel pen to add fine lines on the underside of the snake.

DIFFICULTY: ϟϟϟ

The Whomping Willow

The students at Hogwarts are no strangers to dangerous plant life, but the Whomping Willow is in a class of its own for displays of aggression. Harry and Ron find this out when Ron accidently flies his father's treasured Ford Anglia into the willow's branches.

COLORS

LIGHT INDIGO

INDIGO

LIGHT GRAY

GRAY

DARK GRAY

PAYNE'S GRAY

LAMP BLACK

RECOMMENDED SUPPLIES

Size 02 brush	**Size 000 brush**
Size 04 brush	**Black gel pen**
Size 06 brush	**White gel pen**

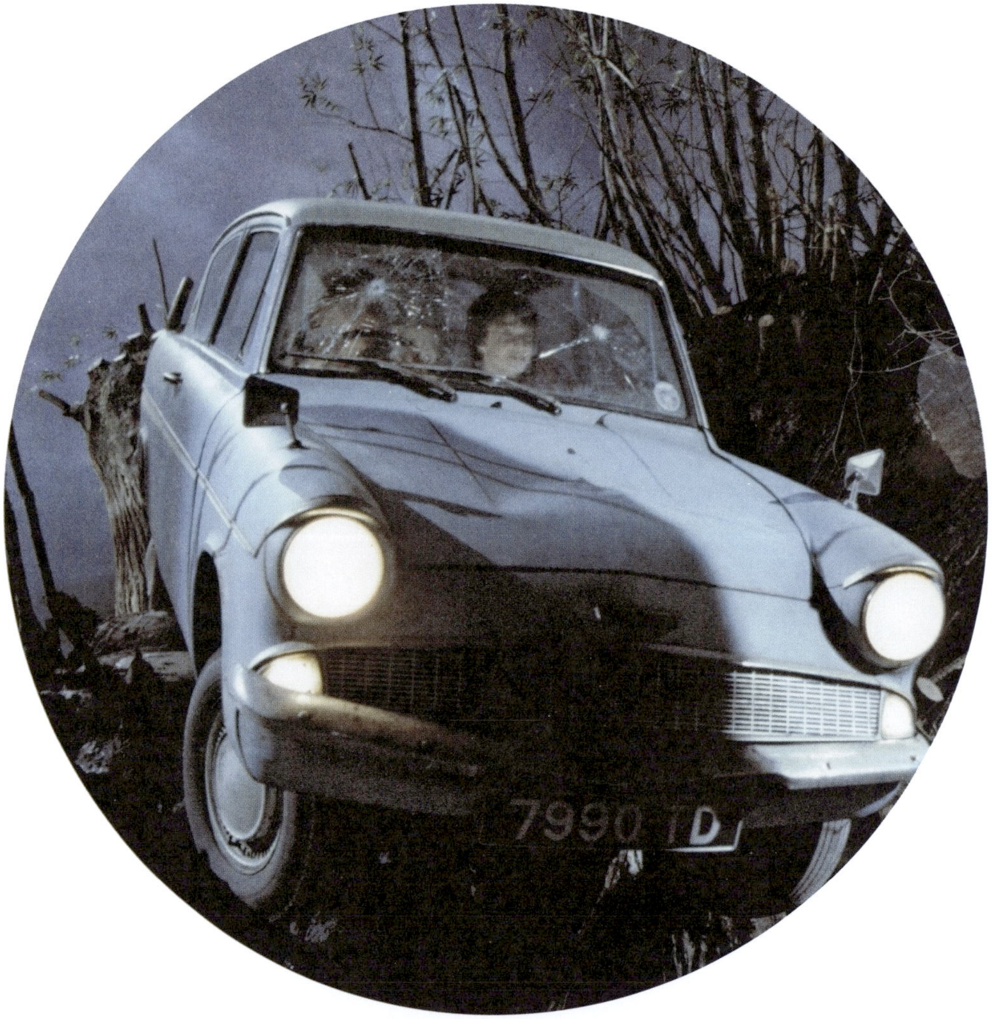

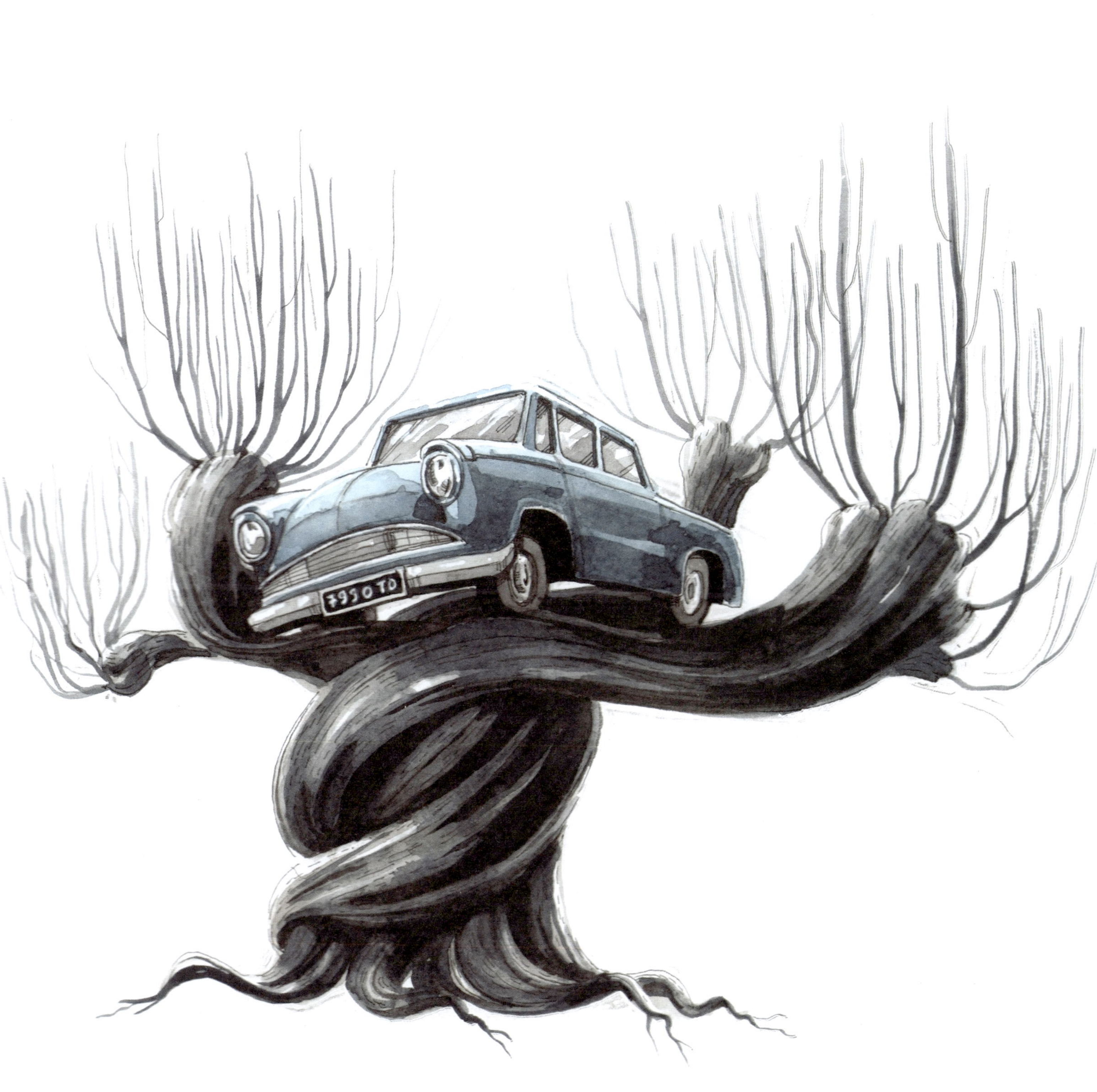
7950 TD

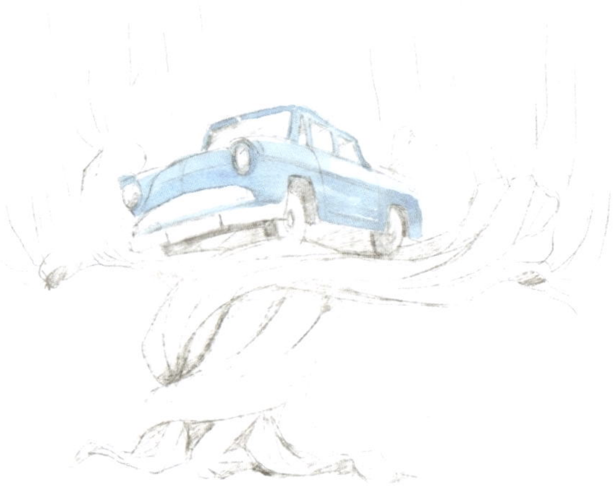

1 Using your size 02 brush, begin by applying light indigo to the car body, leaving a few white areas to create a nice reflection on the metal surface.

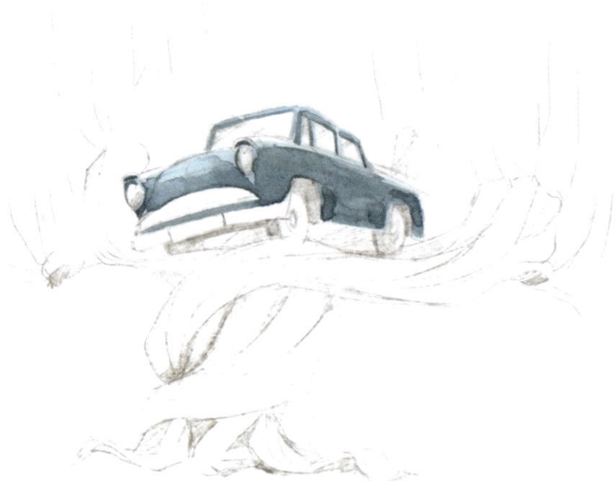

2 While the first layer is still wet, apply a second, slightly darker, shade of indigo so they blend into a nice texture. Keep in mind the way the light falls when adding the darker shade.

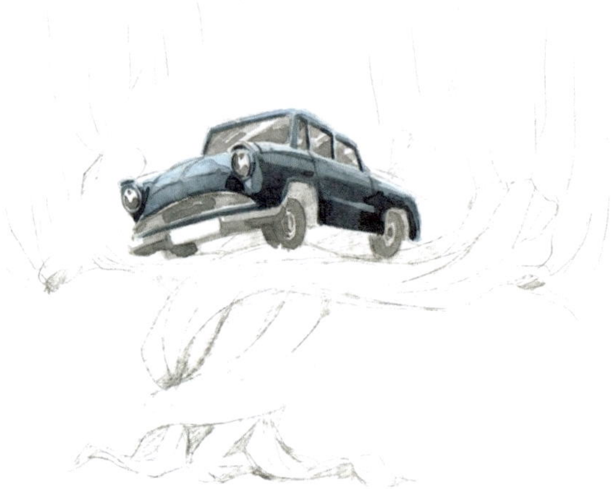

5 With your size 04 brush, apply the darkest shade of indigo to the car, avoiding a flat appearance by creating shadowed areas.

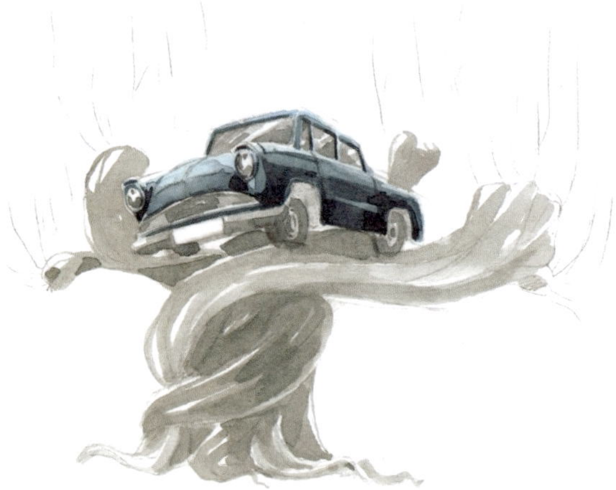

6 Now that the car is coming together, use your size 06 brush to apply the first layer of gray to the tree overall. Think of it as a group of very thick threads wrapped around each other when considering where you will apply shadows.

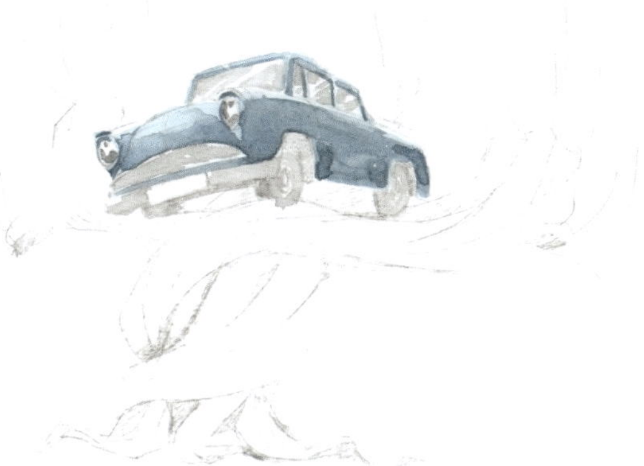

3 When that is dry, apply the light gray to the windows, headlights, hubcaps, and grille.

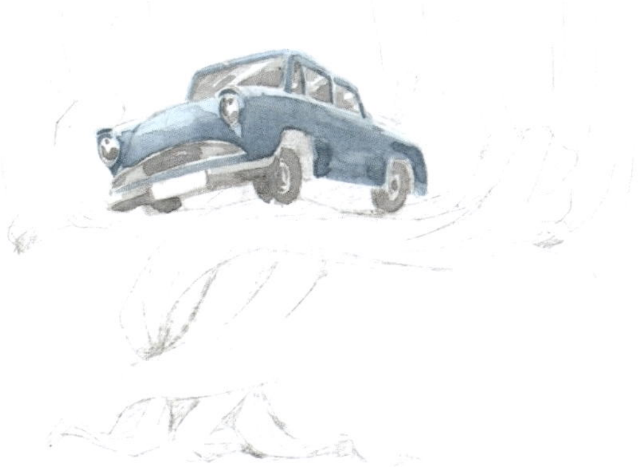

4 Once the light gray is dry, use your size 000 brush to apply dark gray, adding fine details to those same areas.

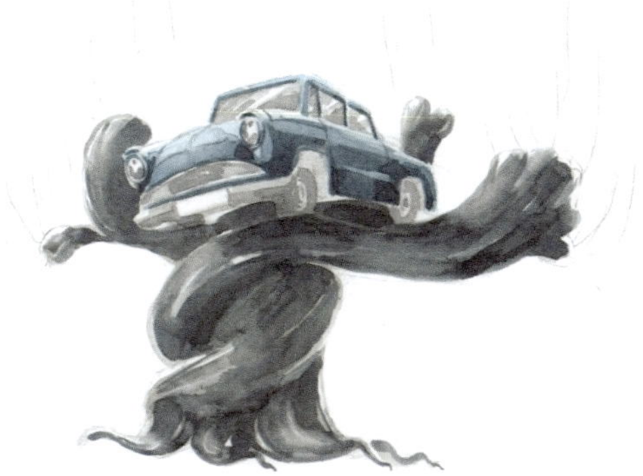

7 Mix indigo with Payne's gray, and apply it to the tree. Use a shade with more indigo and then one with more gray in it to give the tree dimension and depth. Always keep the light source in mind, and leave some light gray areas to better highlight its shape.

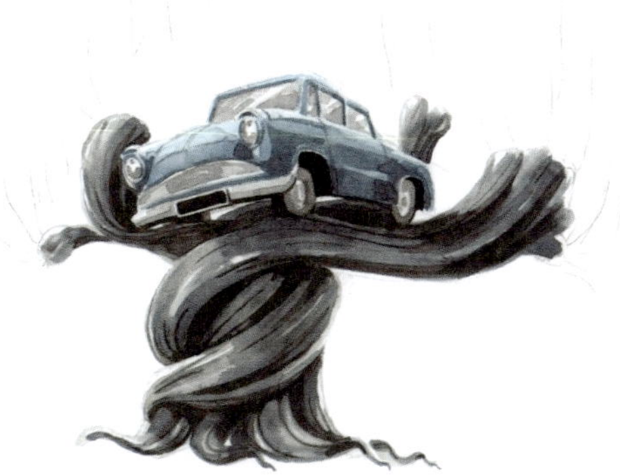

8 Wait for the previous layer to dry, then use your 000 brush to add darker details to the tree with Payne's gray and lamp black. Dip a clean brush in water, and use it to smooth any harsh transitions between shadows and light if needed.

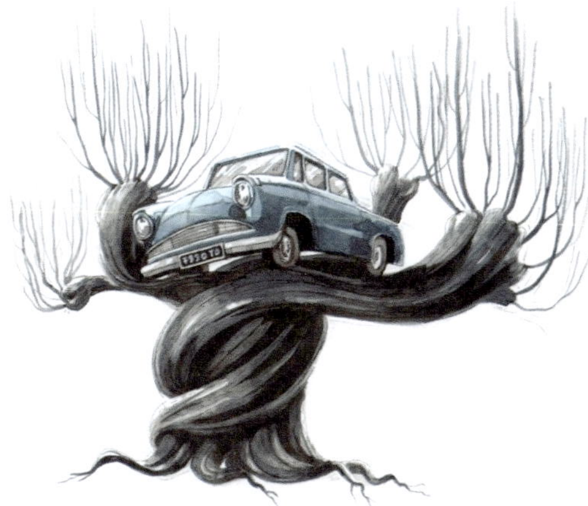

9 Use the same brush to add a few final details on the car as well. You can also use your gel pen to ensure you have clean lines. Your white gel pen is also helpful to emphasize some areas, like the headlights and windows.

DIFFICULTY: ϟϟϟ

The Knight Bus

"Welcome to the Knight Bus, emergency transport for the stranded witch or wizard. My name is Stan Shunpike and I will be your conductor for this evening."
—Stan Shunpike, *Harry Potter and the Prisoner of Azkaban*

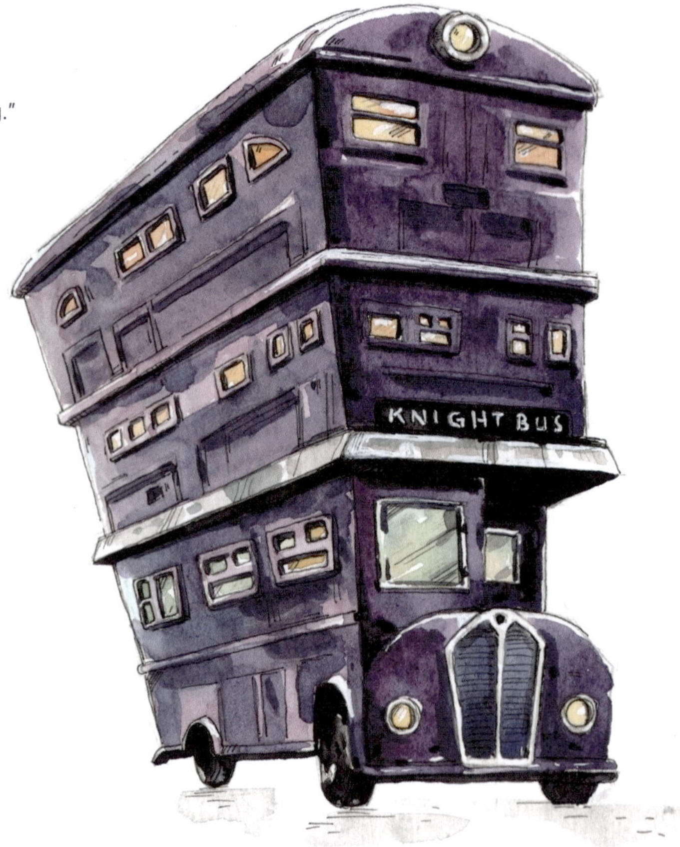

COLORS

LIGHT DIOXAZINE PURPLE
LIGHT INDIGO
DIOXAZINE PURPLE
INDIGO
LIGHT GRAY
LAMP BLACK
CADMIUM YELLOW
LIGHT TURQUOISE
LIGHT EMERALD

RECOMMENDED SUPPLIES

Size 06 brush
Size 01 brush
Size 000 brush
Black gel pen
White gel pen

1. With your size 01 brush, paint the top two tiers of windows with varying shades of cadmium yellow and light emerald. Use different shades on each window to create a more realistic look.
2. While the windows dry, apply light gray to the wheels and bottom deck roof. Do the same with the light turquoise and indigo for the windows on the lower level of the bus. Use different shades on each window to make it more realistic.
3. Once the windows are dry, use your 06 brush, and apply a layer of light purple over almost the entire bus, leaving a few white gaps where the light hits it most sharply.
4. While the lighter layer is still wet, apply the light indigo, followed by the dioxazine purple. Always start at the bottom and paint up to the light source.
5. Once it is fully dry, add sharper shadows with the dioxazine purple, making sure one side of the bus is darker than the other to emphasize the three-dimensional effect.
6. Use your 000 brush with lamp black to create the darkest shades, like the wheels and Knight Bus sign.
7. When everything is dry, use your black gel pen to add small, but necessary, details to the bus, particularly on the window frames and headlamps to give them some depth.
8. Use your white gel pen to write the name of the bus and to add a few bright touches to the windows and headlamps.

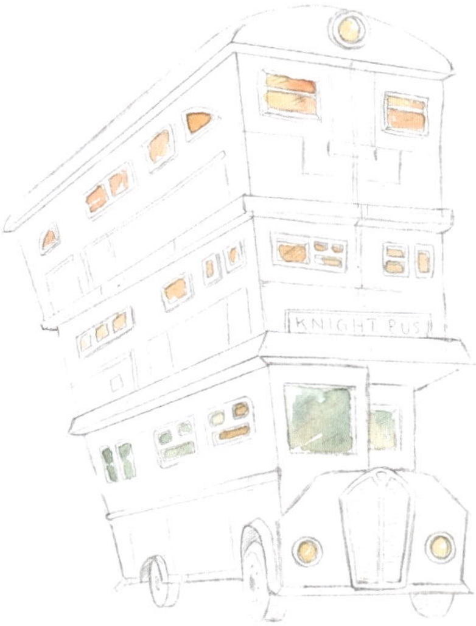

1

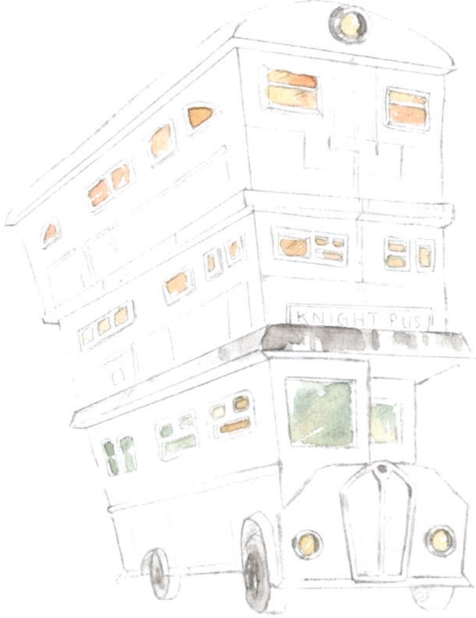

2

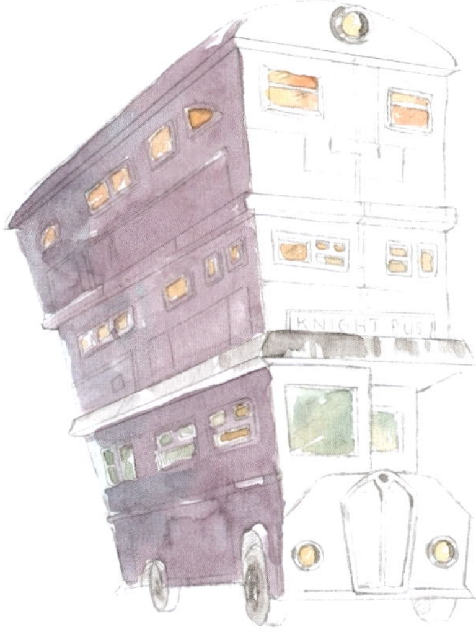

3

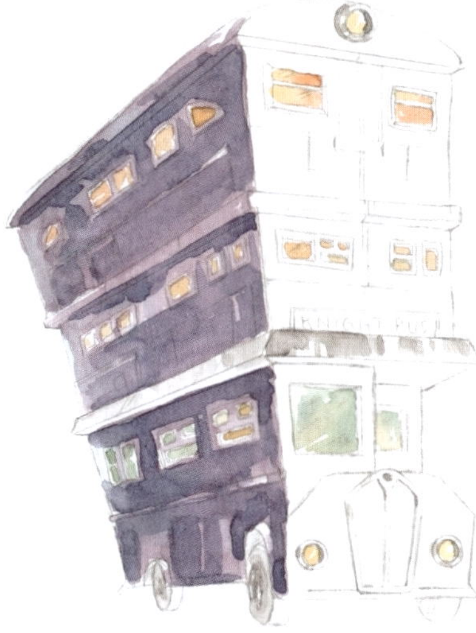

4

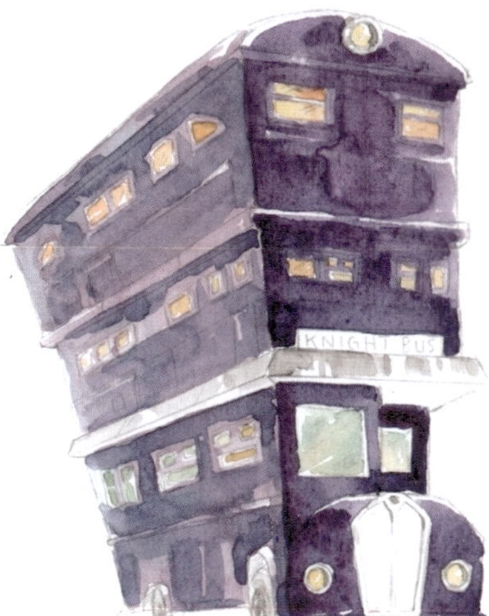

4

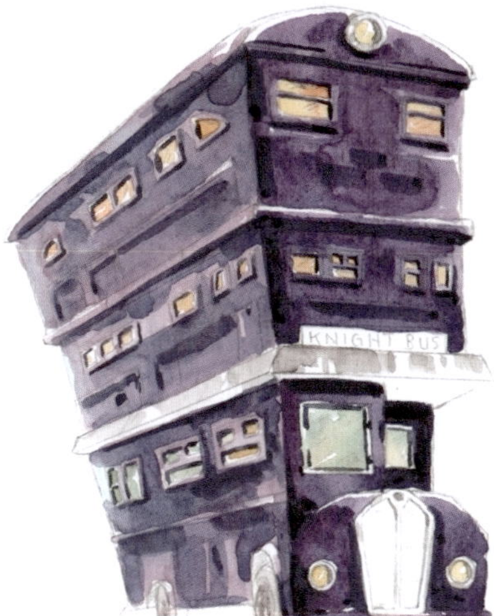

5

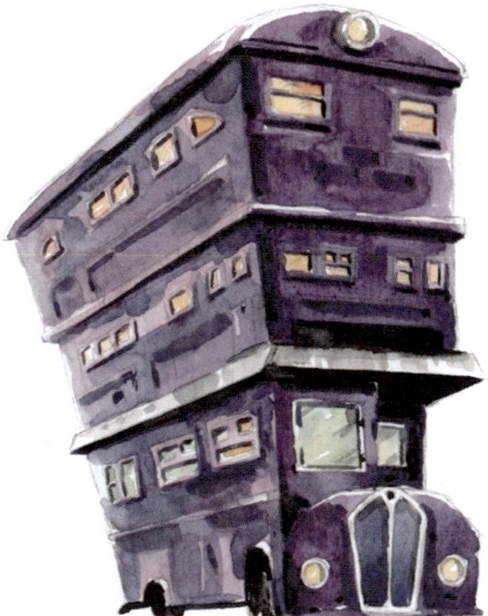

6

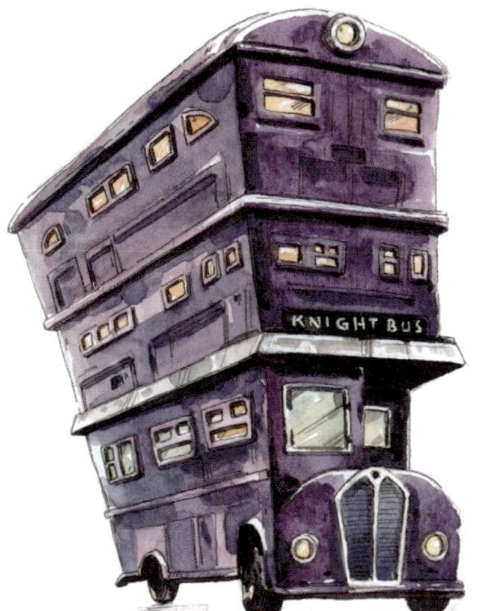

7 8

DIFFICULTY: ϟϟϟ

Hogwarts Express

Accessed only from the hidden Platform 9¾, the Hogwarts Express runs from London's busy King's Cross station (unbeknownst to the hurrying Muggles) to the Hogsmeade Station, ferrying students to and from Hogwarts. It runs at the beginning and end of every term, and also carries students home on holiday breaks.

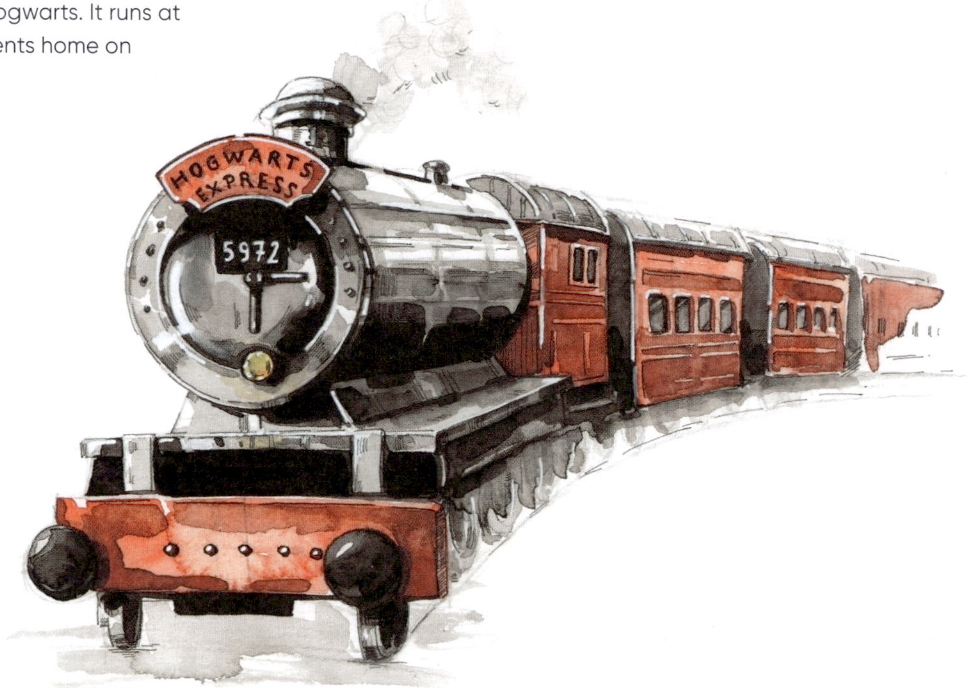

COLORS

- LIGHT GRAY
- DARK GRAY
- LIGHT CADMIUM RED
- CADMIUM RED
- BURNT SIENNA
- LAMP BLACK

RECOMMENDED SUPPLIES

Size 01 brush	**Black gel pen**
Size 04 brush	**White gel pen**

1. With your size 04 brush, begin by painting the engine and car roofs the lightest shade of gray. Leave some white areas on the left side and top to convey the metallic texture.
2. Once this layer is dry, use your size 01 or thinner brush to apply a second layer with darker gray. Because the light source is on the left, use darker shades mostly on the right side of the engine, leaving lighter areas on the left to simulate the light shining on them.
3. With your size 04 brush, apply light cadmium red to the cars. Use a varying amount of water on your brush with the light red to paint different areas, creating a nice watercolor effect, instead of a flat red color.
4. Once that layer dries, apply a darker shade of red with your size 01 brush, paying attention to your light and shadows.
5. Once the previous layer is dry, apply some thin lines, additional shading, and details for the doors and windows.
6. After everything is dry, carefully apply lamp black to the shaded areas on the engine and between the cars.
7. Use both your white and black gel pens to add a great deal of the detail on this piece, such as the lettering and numbers, as well as to sharpen the details and metal effect on the cars.

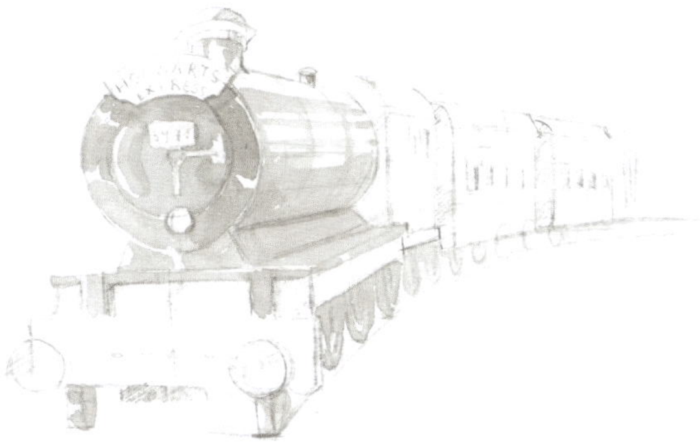

1

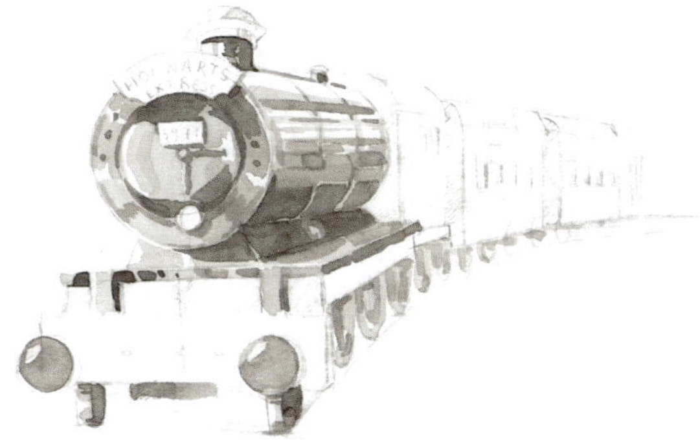

2

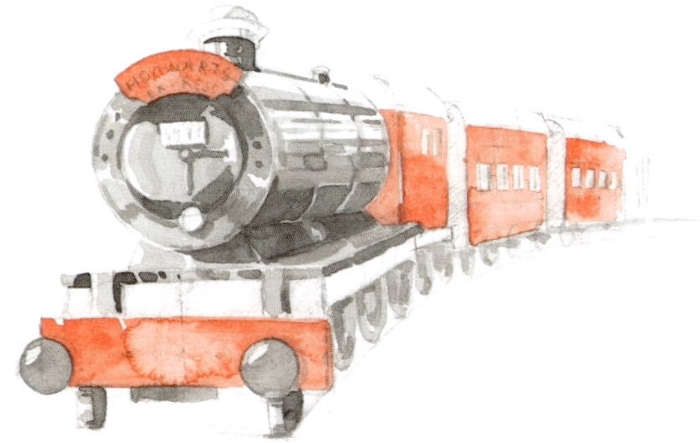

3

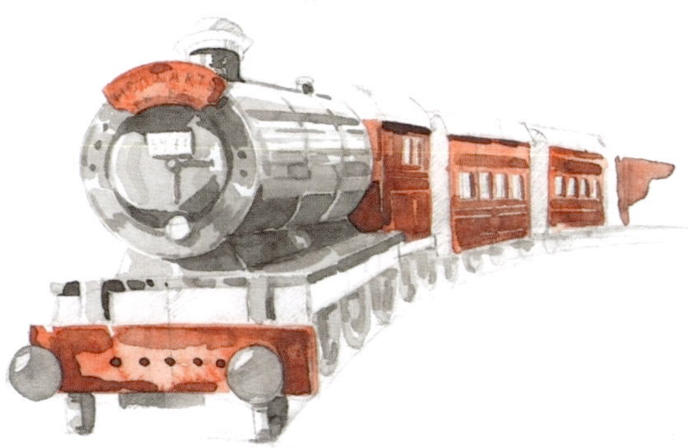

4

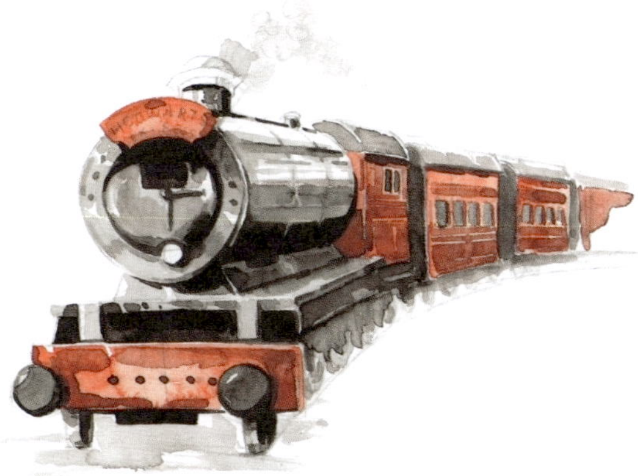

5 6

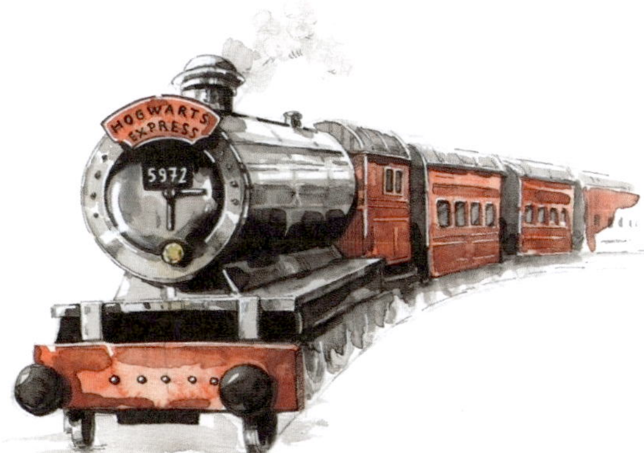

7

DIFFICULTY:

The Forbidden Forest

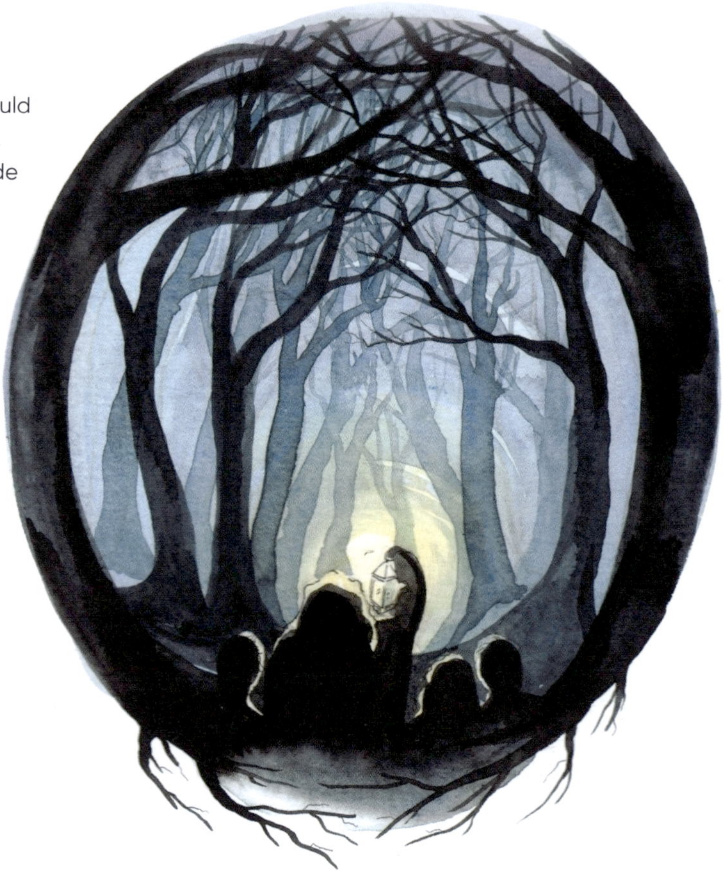

"A pity they let the old punishments die. There was a time when detention would find you hanging by your thumbs in the dungeons. God, I miss the screaming. You'll be serving detention with Hagrid tonight. He's got a little job to do. Inside the Dark Forest."
—Argus Filch, *Harry Potter and the Sorcerer's Stone*

COLORS

LEMON YELLOW

LIGHT TURQUOISE

TURQUOISE

INDIGO

LAMP BLACK

RECOMMENDED SUPPLIES

Size 08 brush

Size 000 brush

Size 06 brush

Black gel pen

1. Start by using your size 06 brush to apply lemon yellow in a rough oval, making the light from Hagrid's lamp.
2. While it is still wet, use your size 08 brush to apply turquoise. Start with a lighter shade near the yellow light source, blending the colors for a smooth transition. While it is still wet, apply darker shades of turquoise expanding outward, with the darkest shades closest to the edges, leading your brush in circles to create nice oval transitions between shades.
3. Once those layers are fully dry, mix a good amount of water with the indigo to create a very light shade of it. Use your 000 brush to paint the first, lightest group of trees near the center of the image. Tilt your brush and decrease the pressure while increasing the angle as you paint toward the edge of the branches to create thin, organic lines.
4. Use a slightly darker shade of indigo as you paint the second group of trees moving out from the center of the image.
5. When dry, start the third group of trees with the same brush with a slightly darker shade of indigo. Make some slight changes to each tree so they each have their own individual characteristics.
6. After this is dry, use the lamp black to paint the outermost trees and the characters' silhouettes, being sure to leave some lighter areas to illustrate the light's reflection on the characters' head and shoulders.
7. Use your gel pen to add a few fine details, such as those on Hagrid's lamp.

1

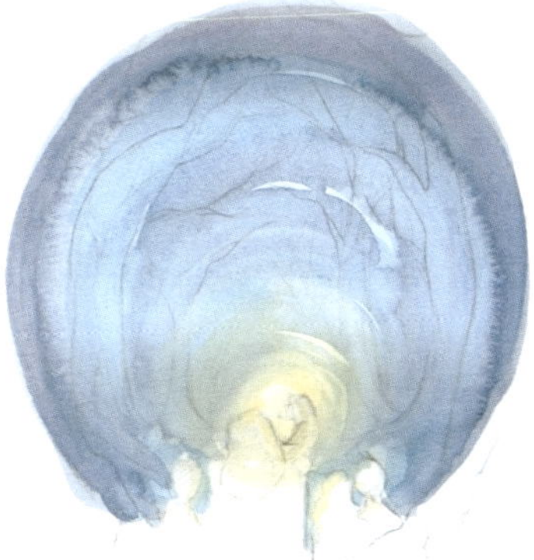

2

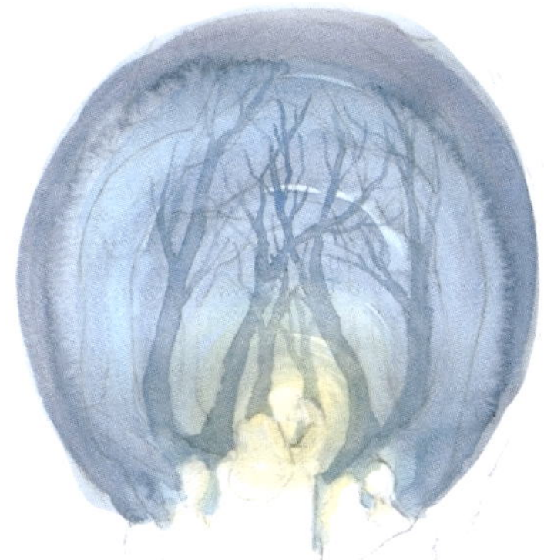

3

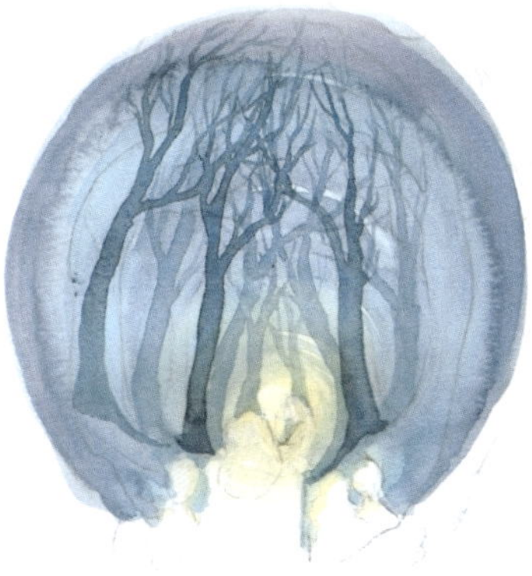

4

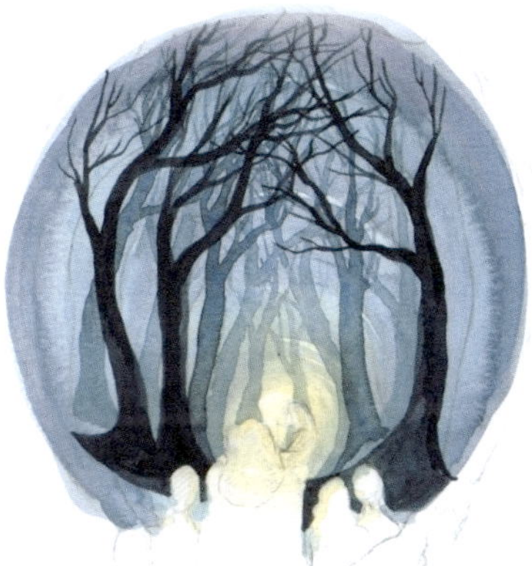

5

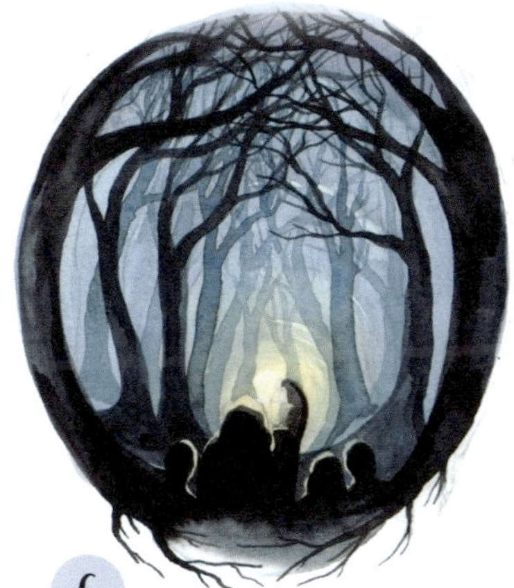

6

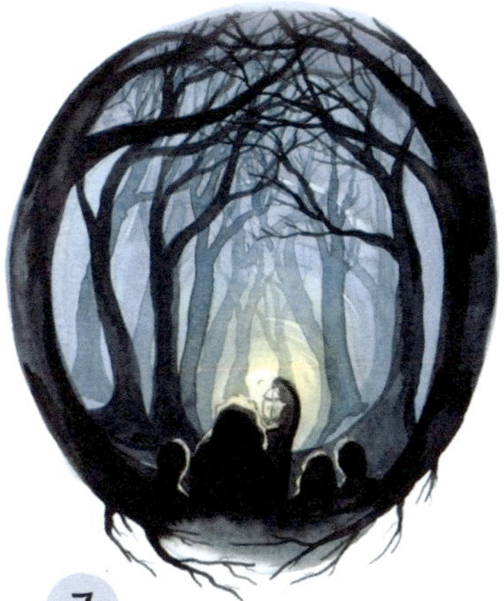

7

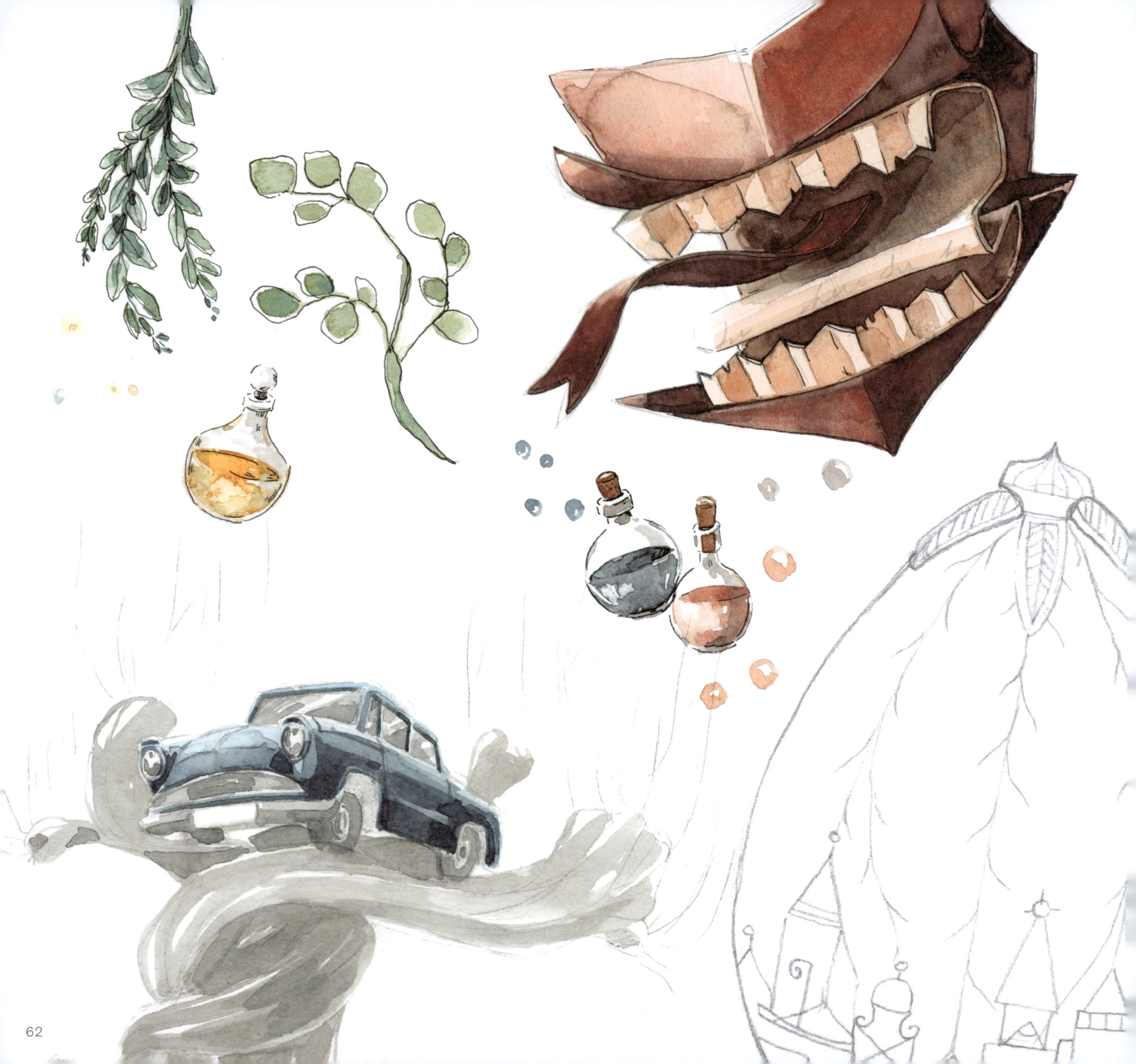

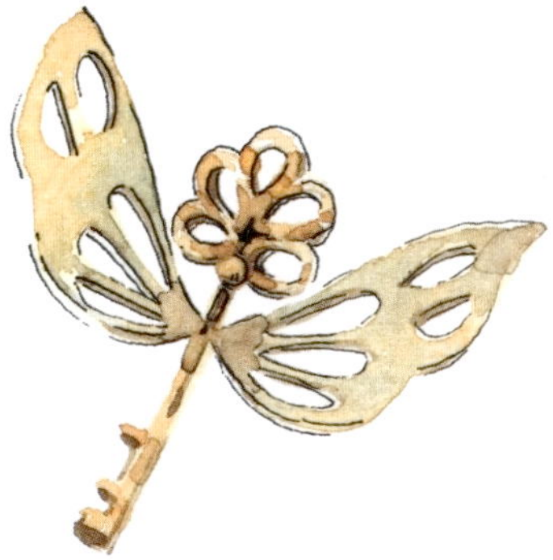

Watercolor Sketches

The following pages contain sketches corresponding to each illustration and set of instructions printed on premium watercolor paper. Just select the sketch you'd like to watercolor, gently tear it out, and you're ready to begin painting your very own magical creations!

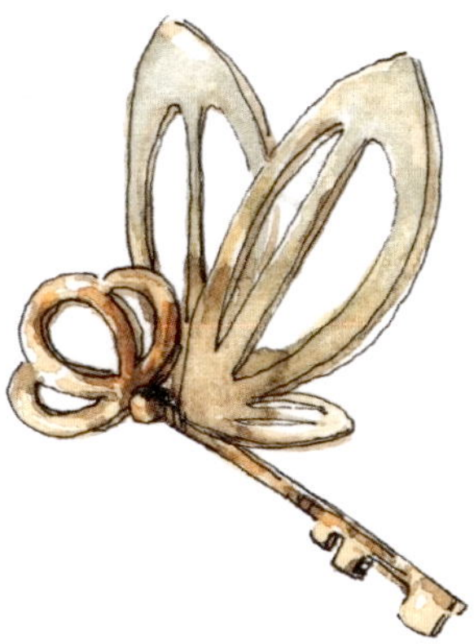

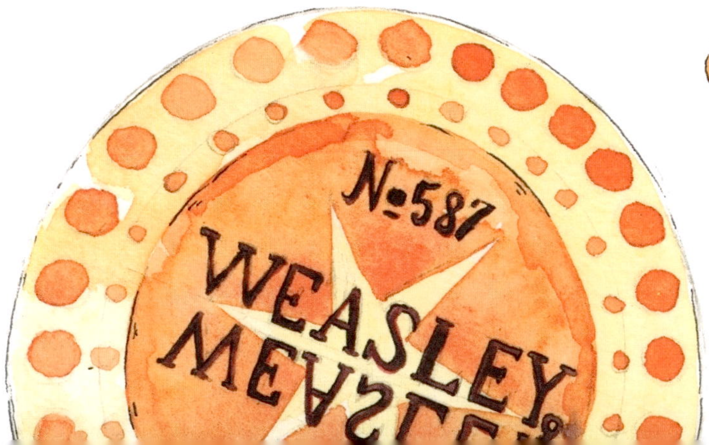

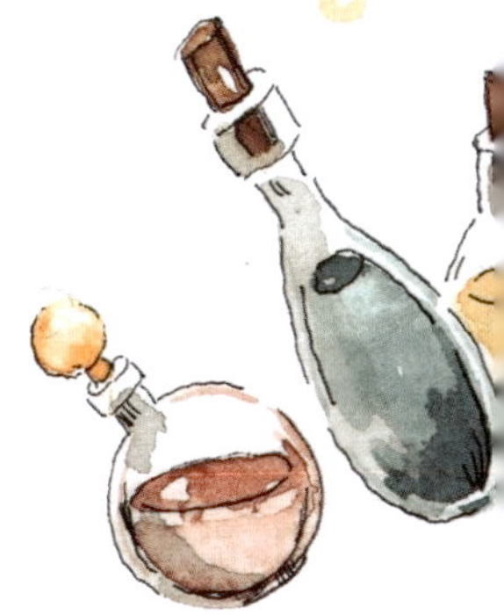

The Sorting Hat

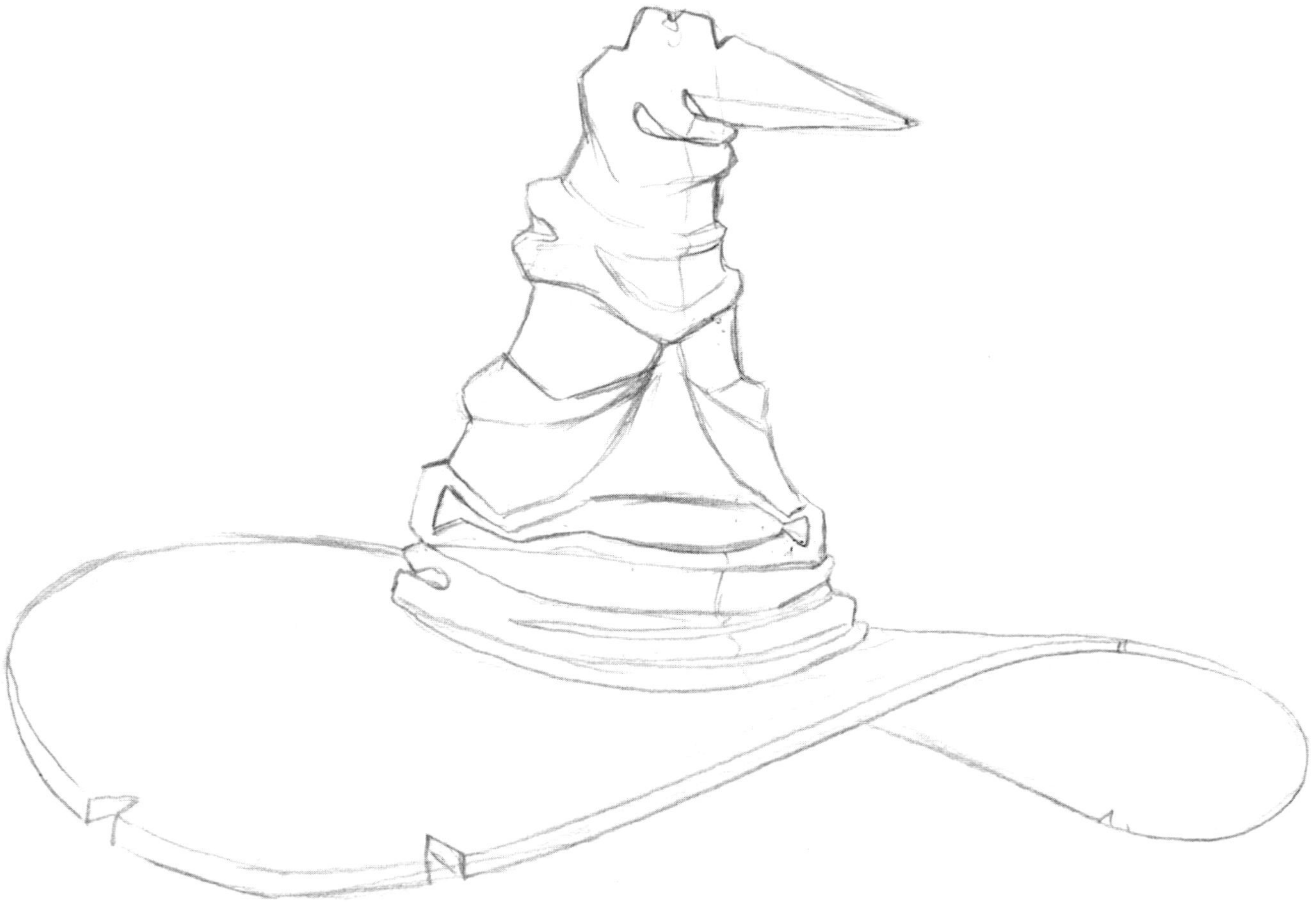

Happee Birthdae Cake

HAPPEE
BIRTHDAE
HARRY

Platform 9¾ Sign

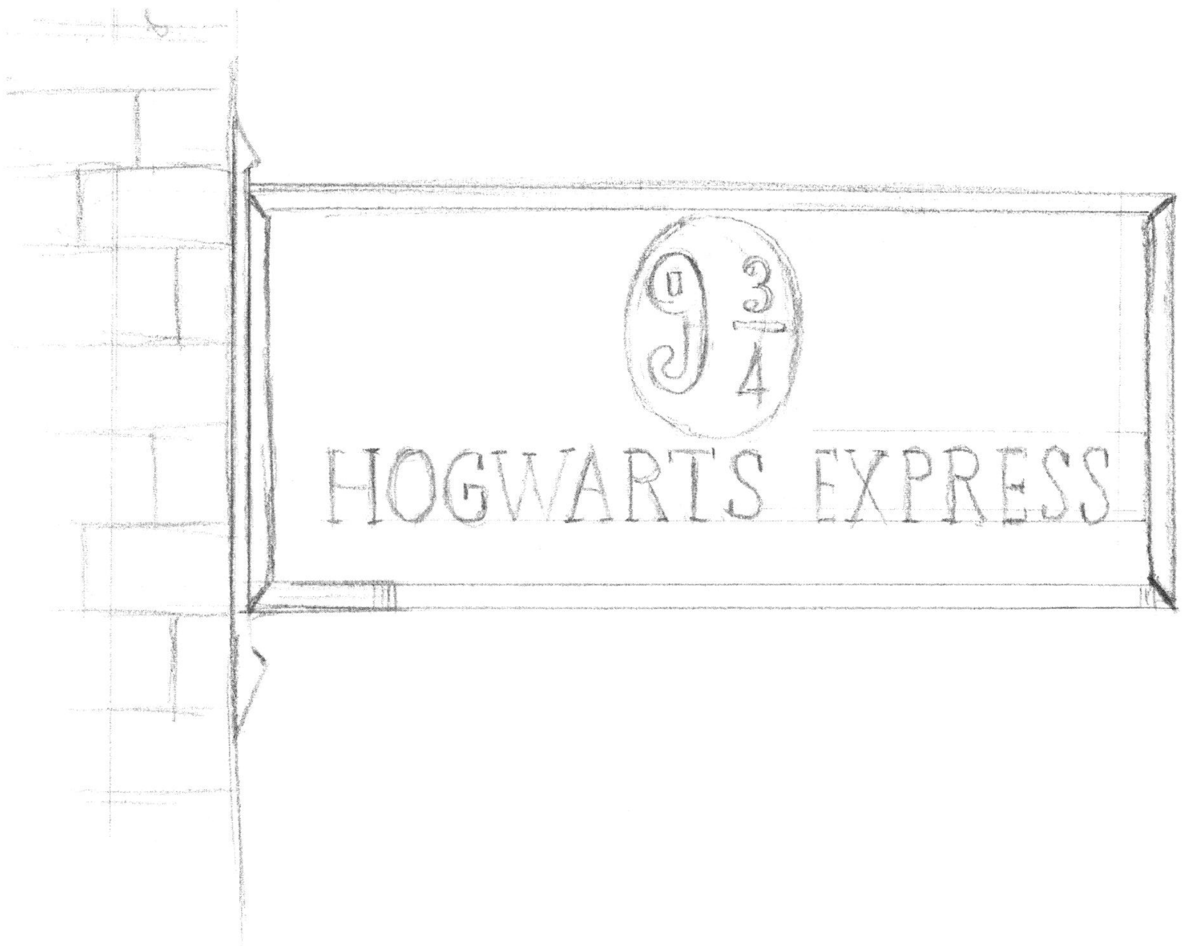
9 3/4
HOGWARTS EXPRESS

Cauldron

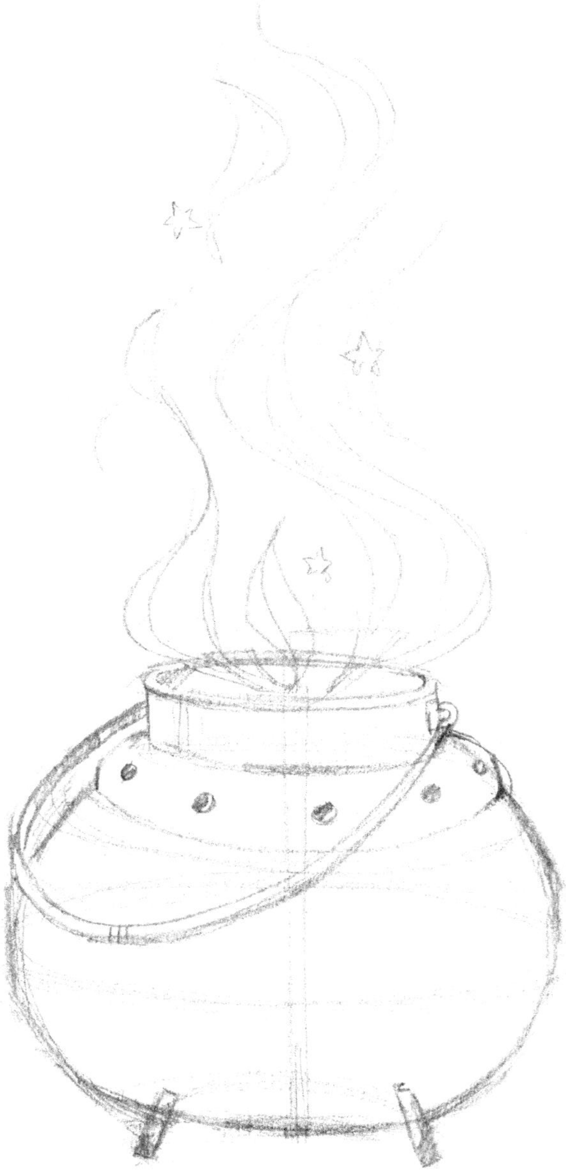

Hedwig Holding a Letter

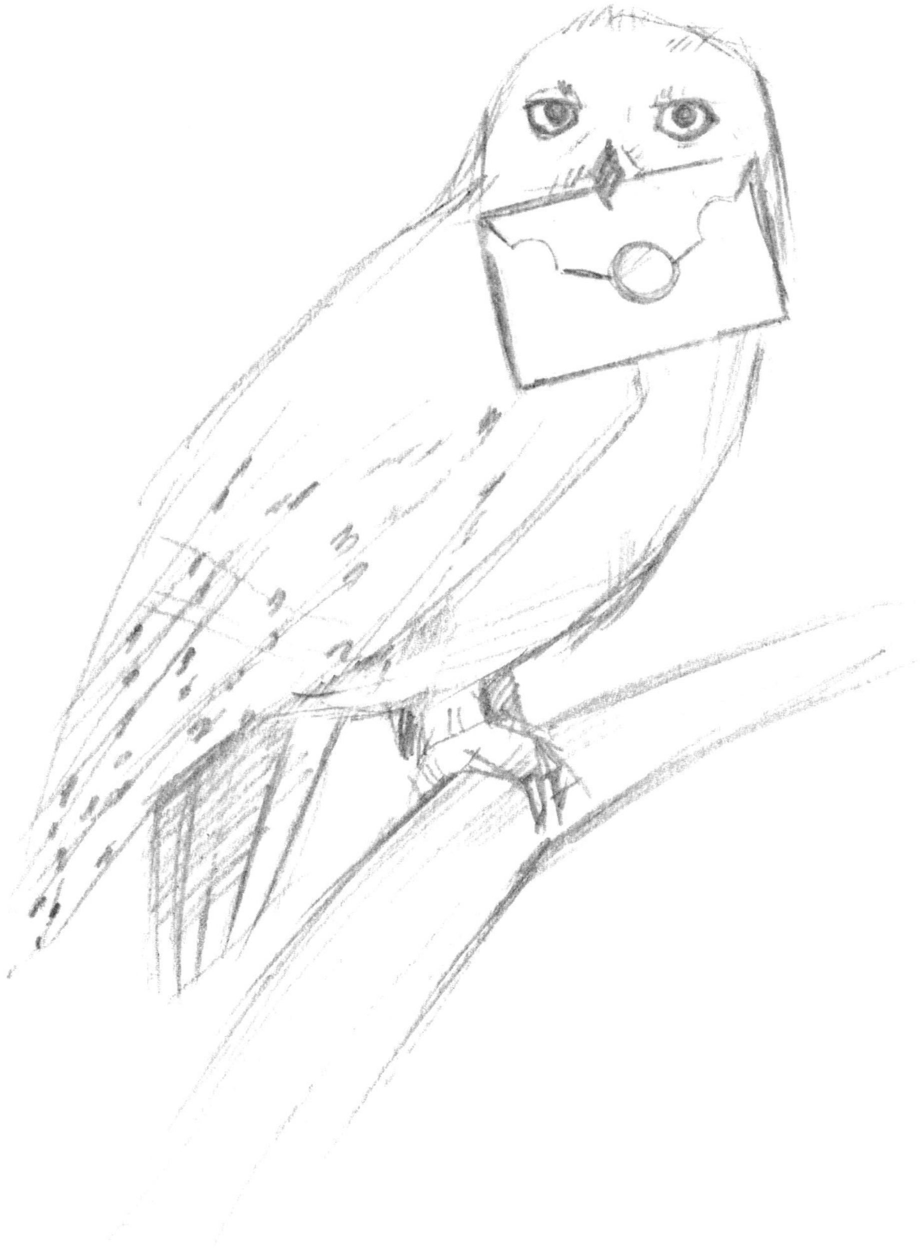

Hogwarts Crest

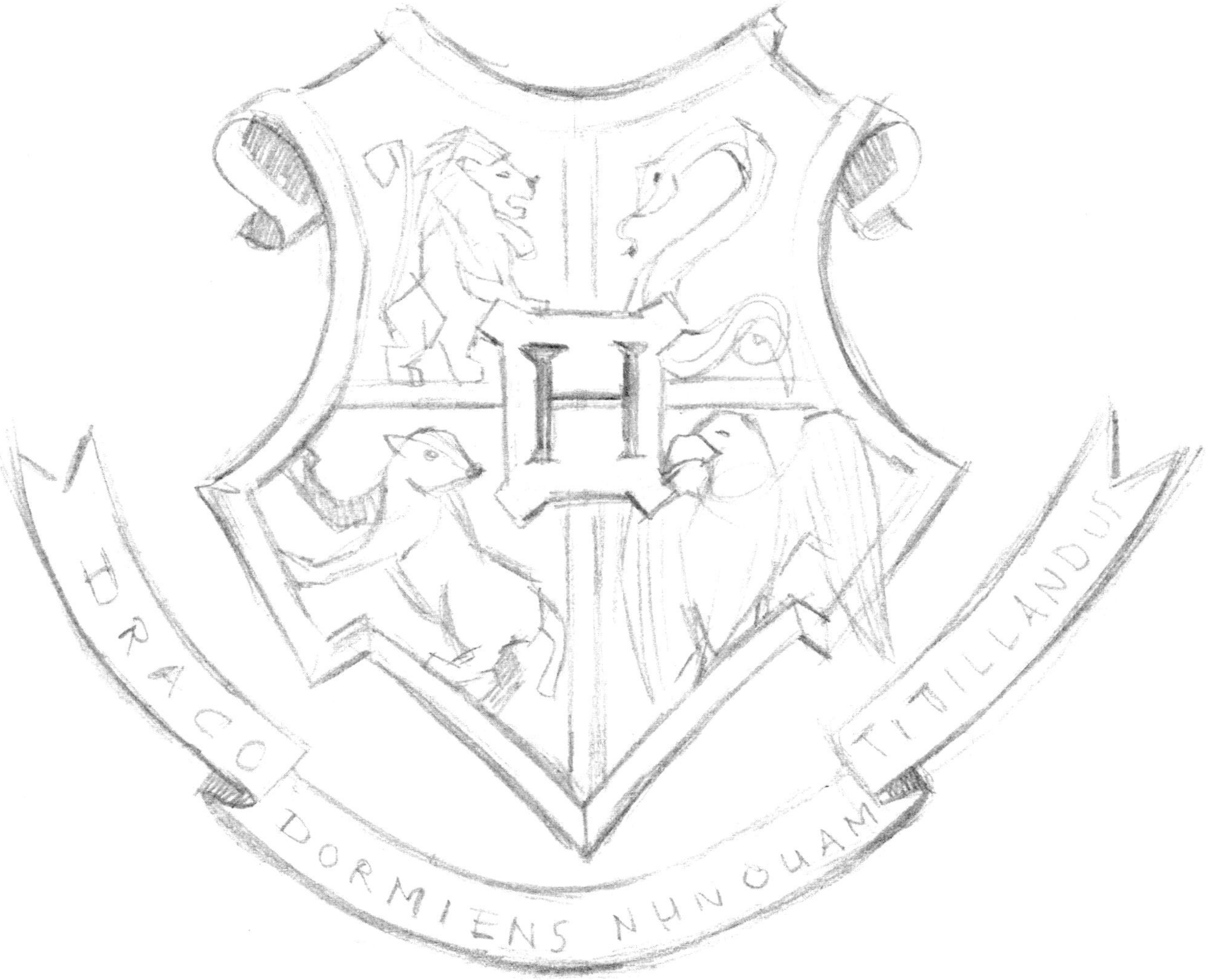

H
DRACO DORMIENS NUNQUAM TITILLANDUS

Gryffindor Crest

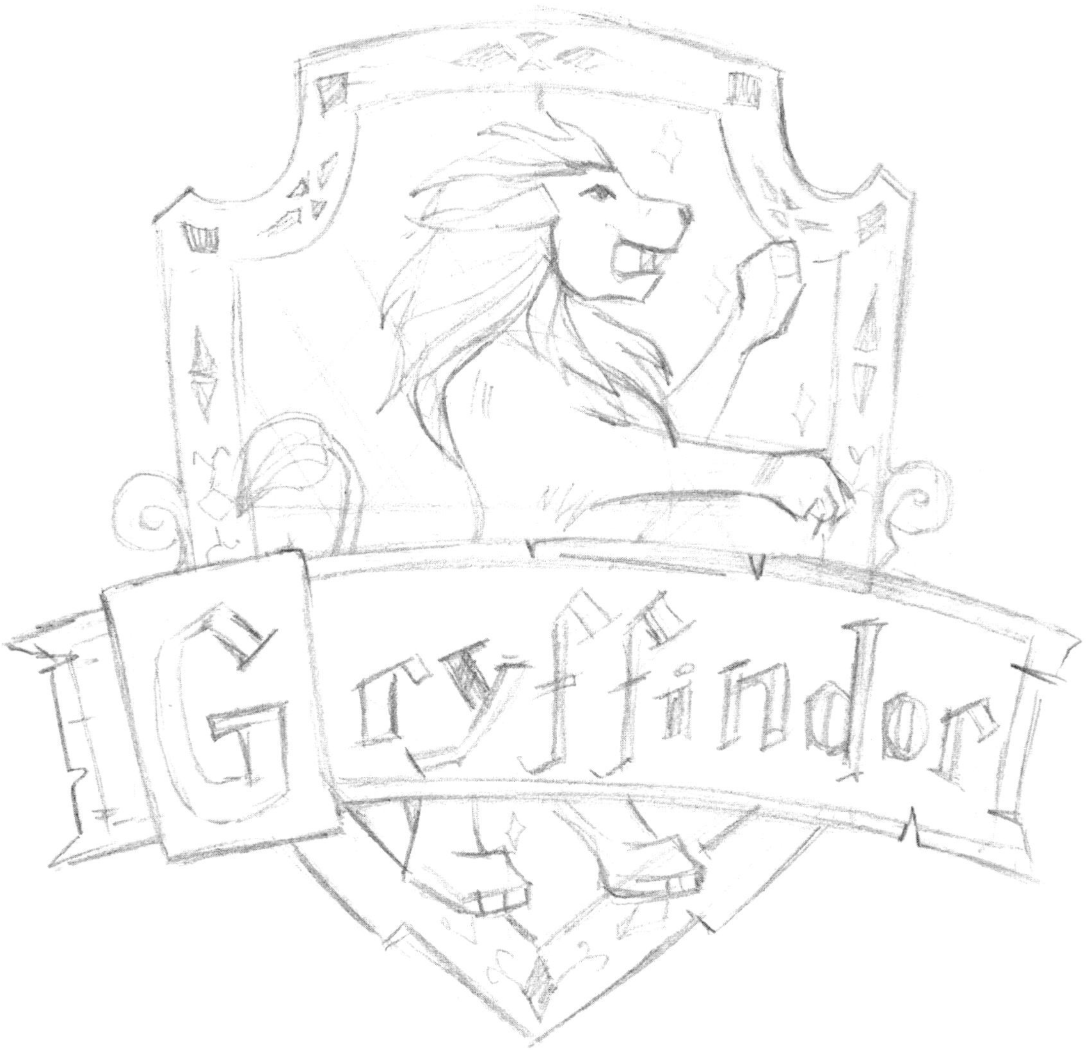
Gryffindor

Slytherin Crest

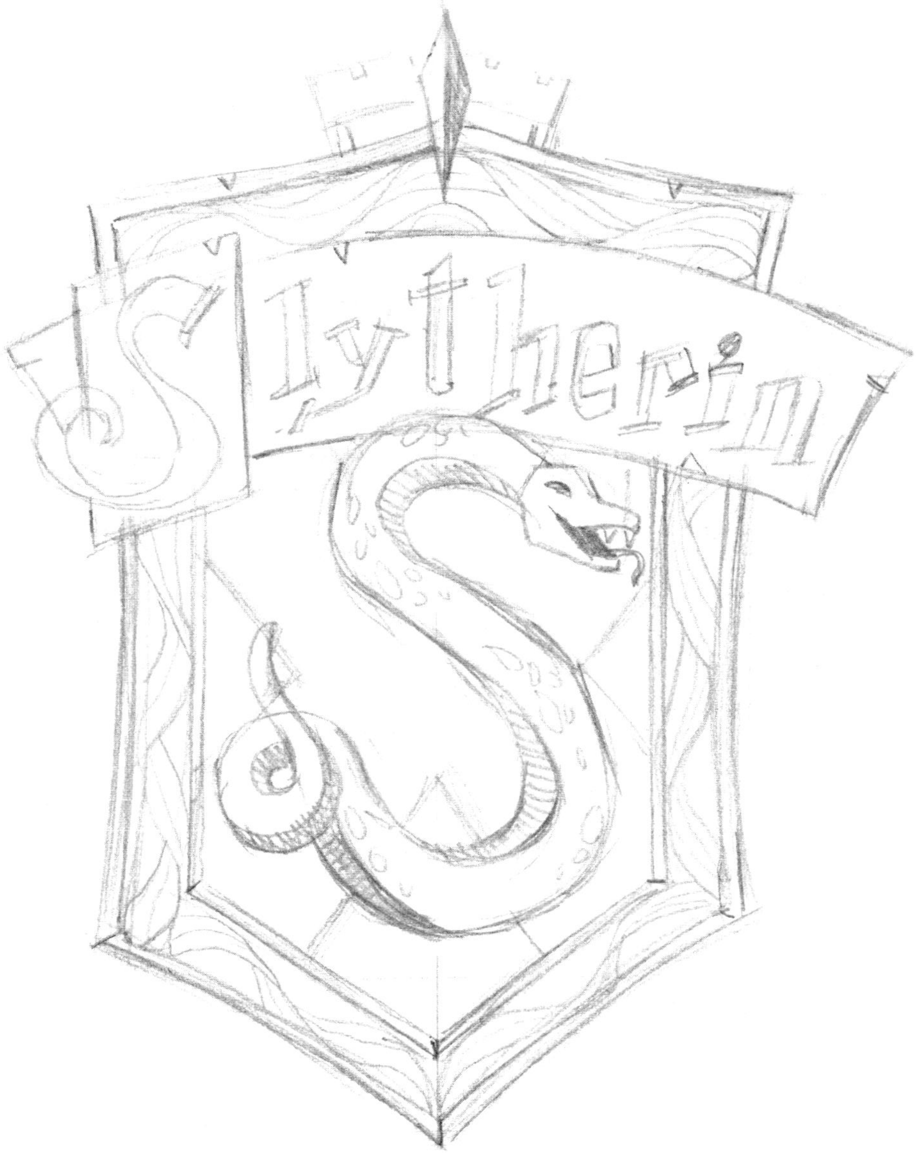
Slytherin

Ravenclaw Crest

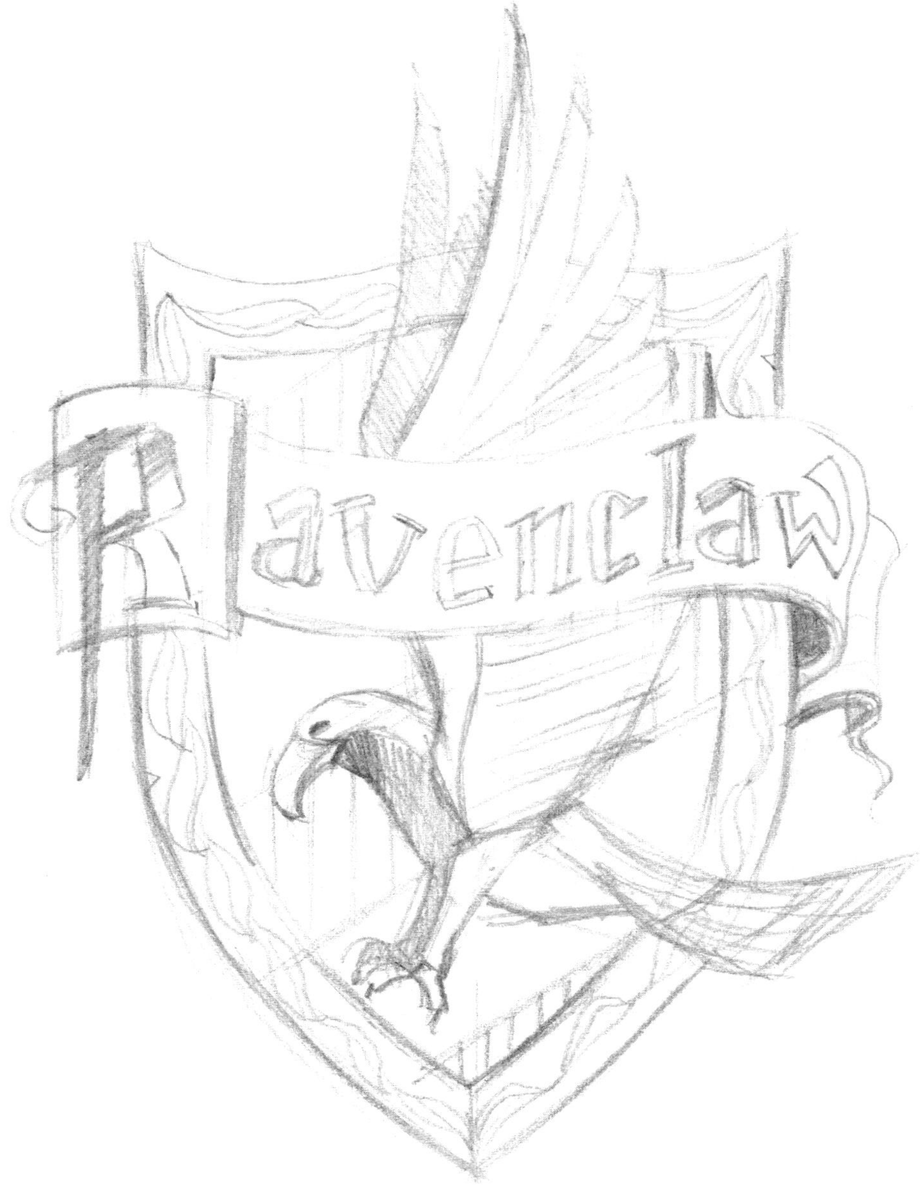
Ravenclaw

Hufflepuff Crest

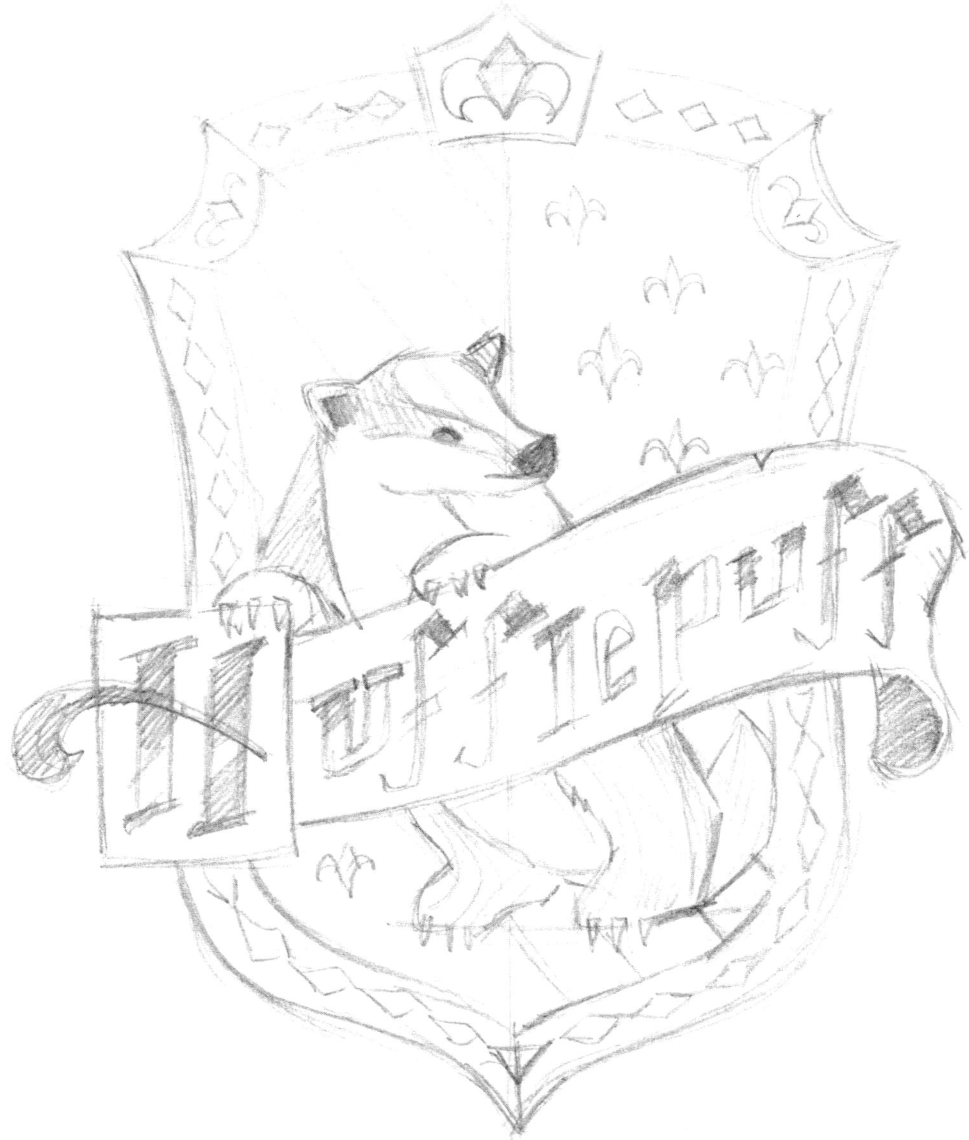
Hufflepuff

Nimbus 2000

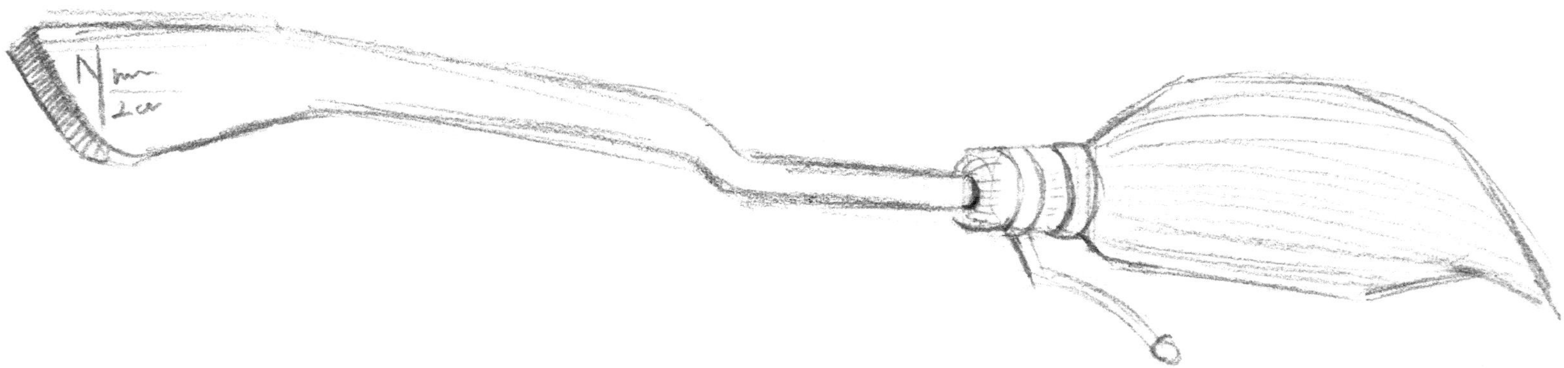

The Golden Snitch

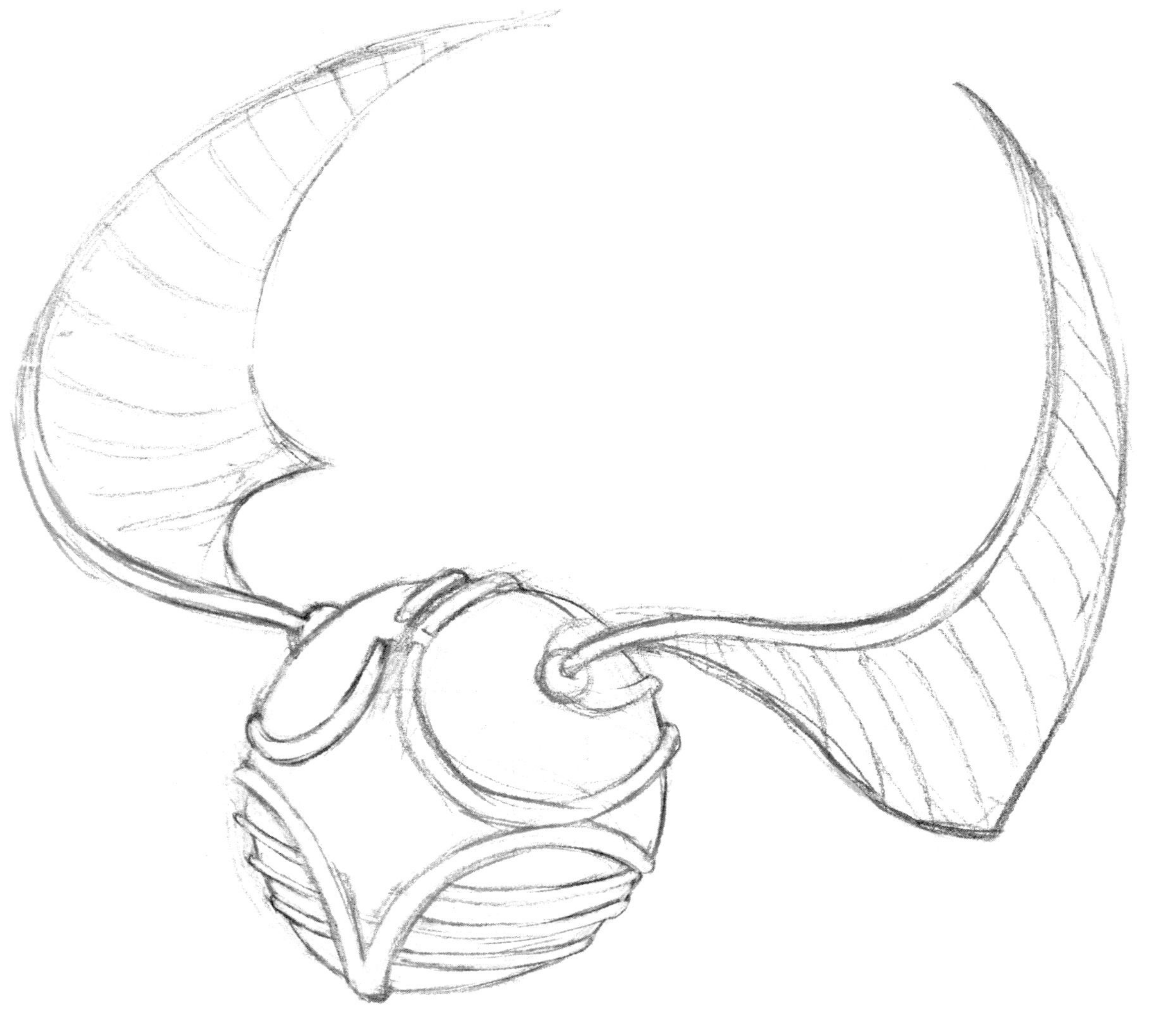

Hagrid's Hut

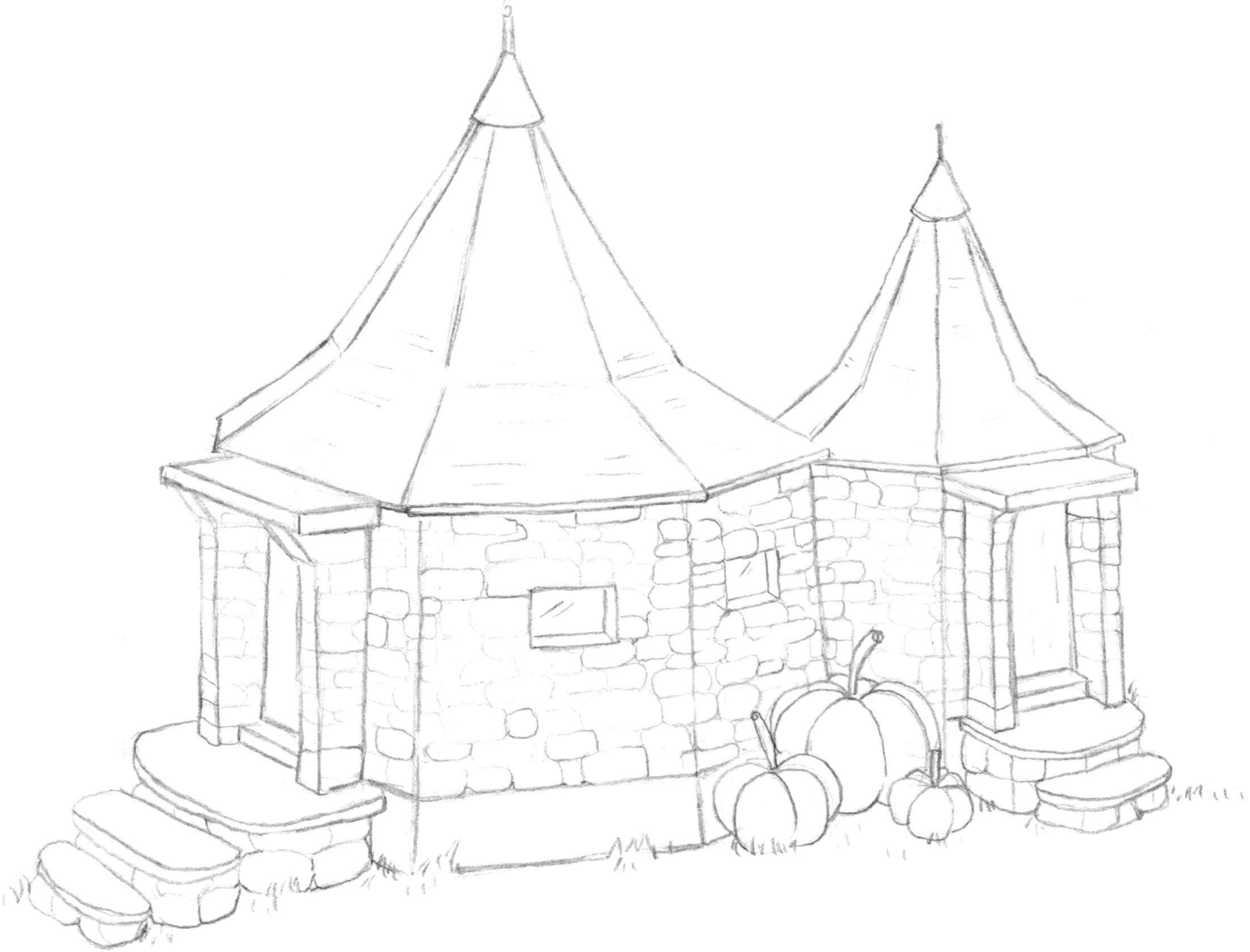

Golden Egg

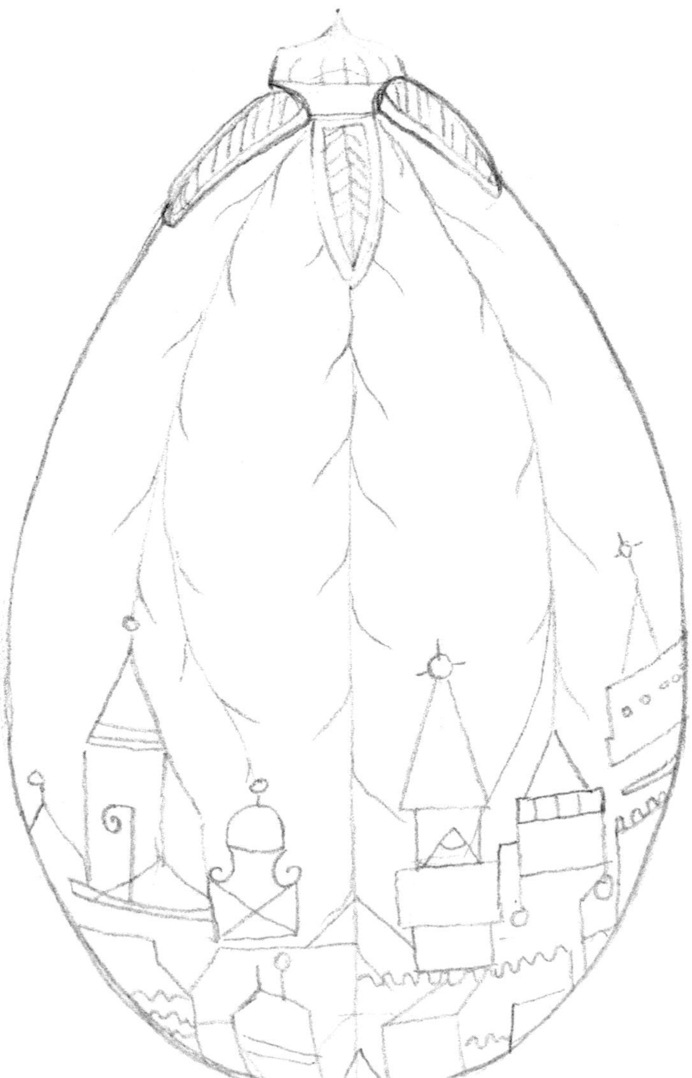

Dobby

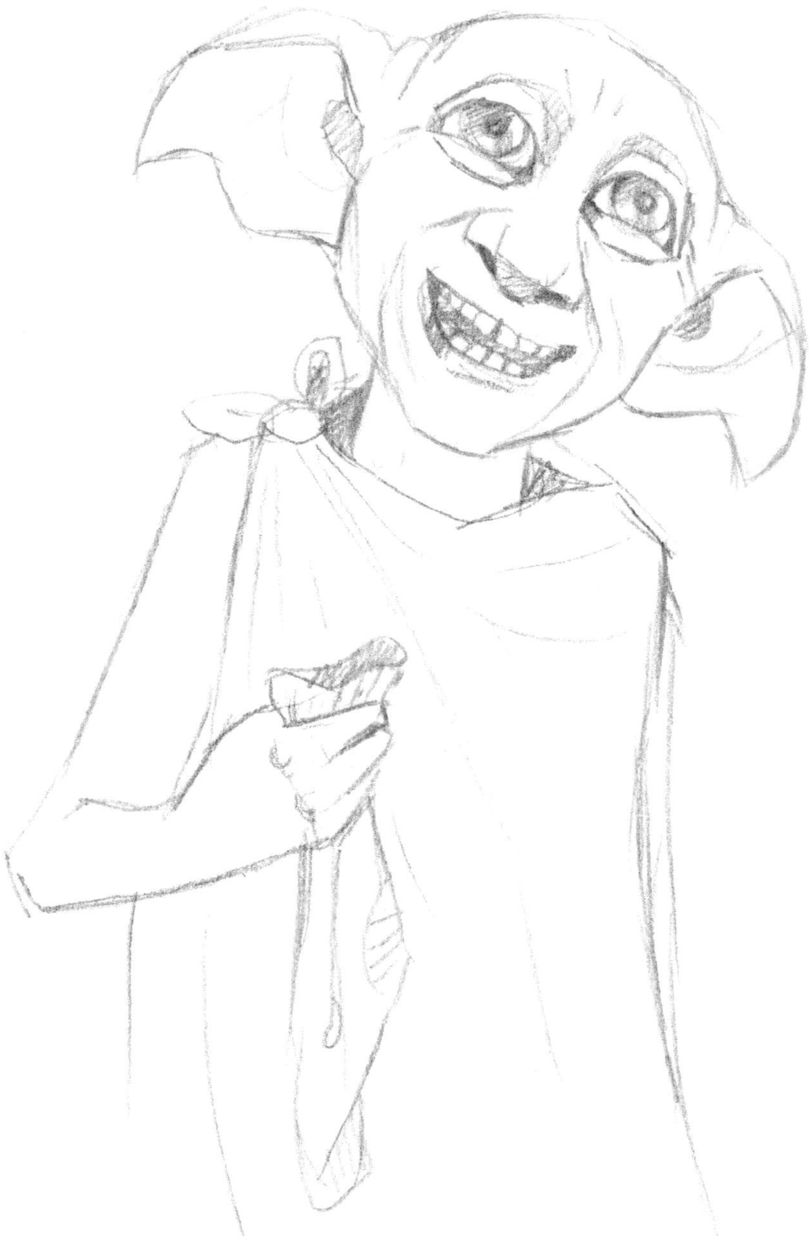

The Marauder's Map

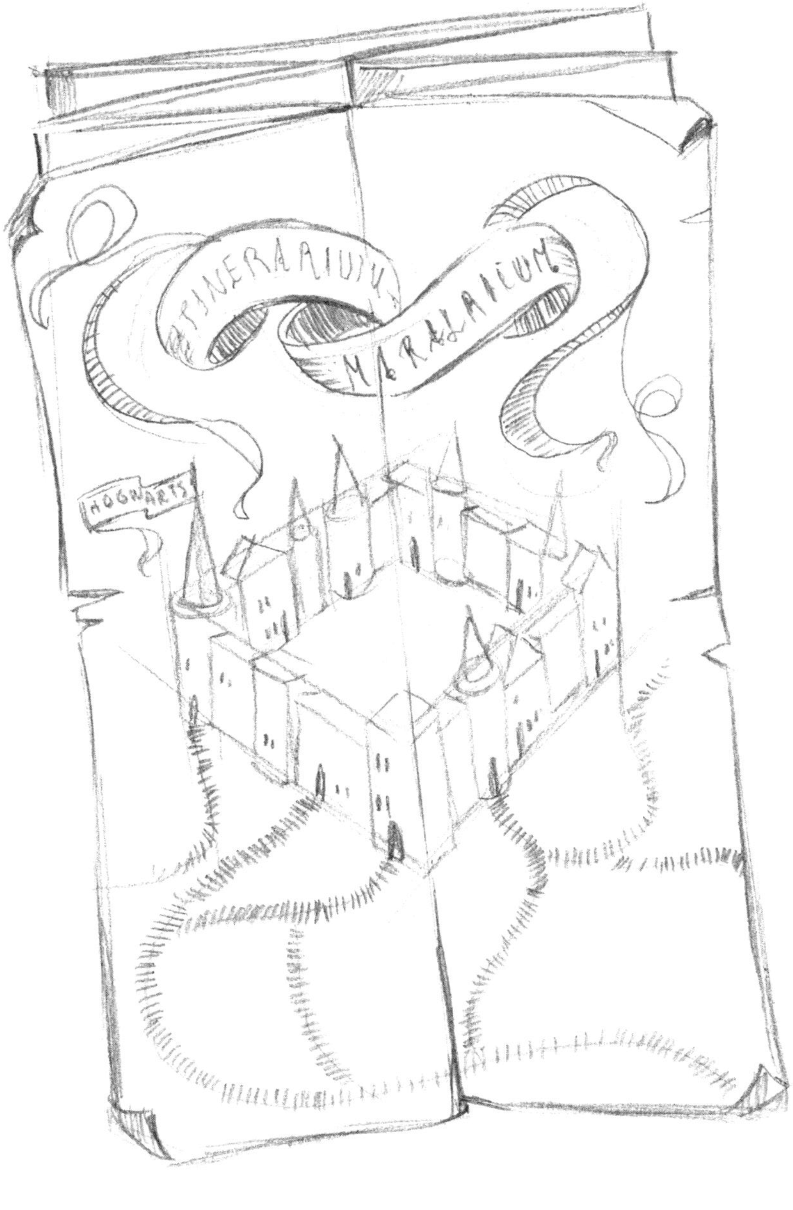
HOGWARTS

Love Potion

LOVE
POTION

Weasleys' Wizard Wheezes Logo

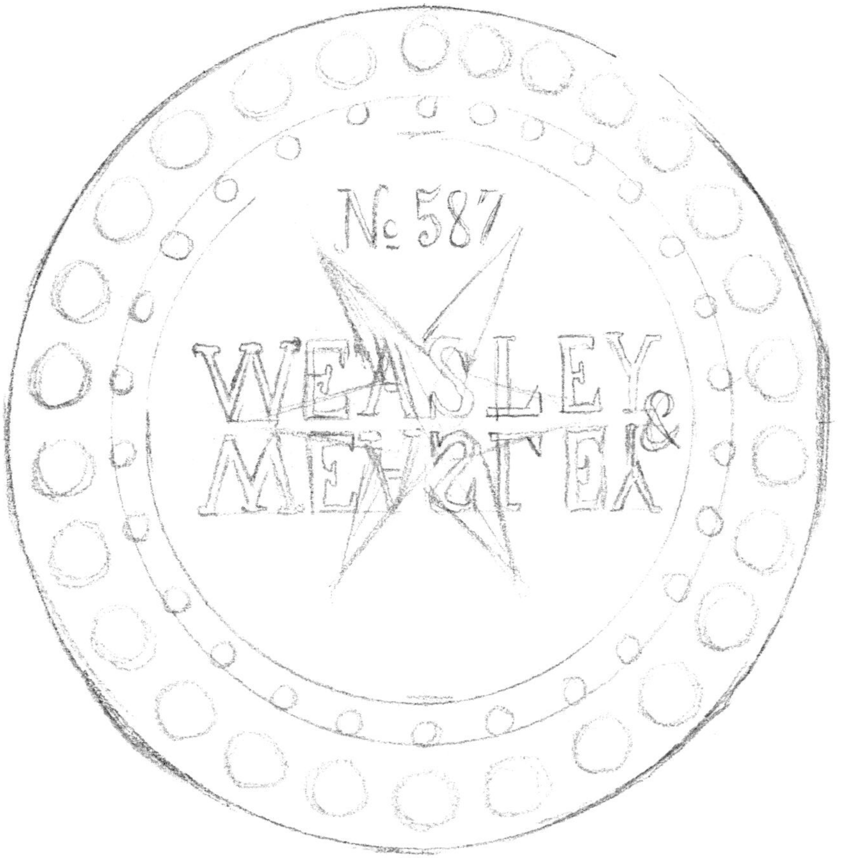
№ 587
WEASLEY
&

Stag Patronus

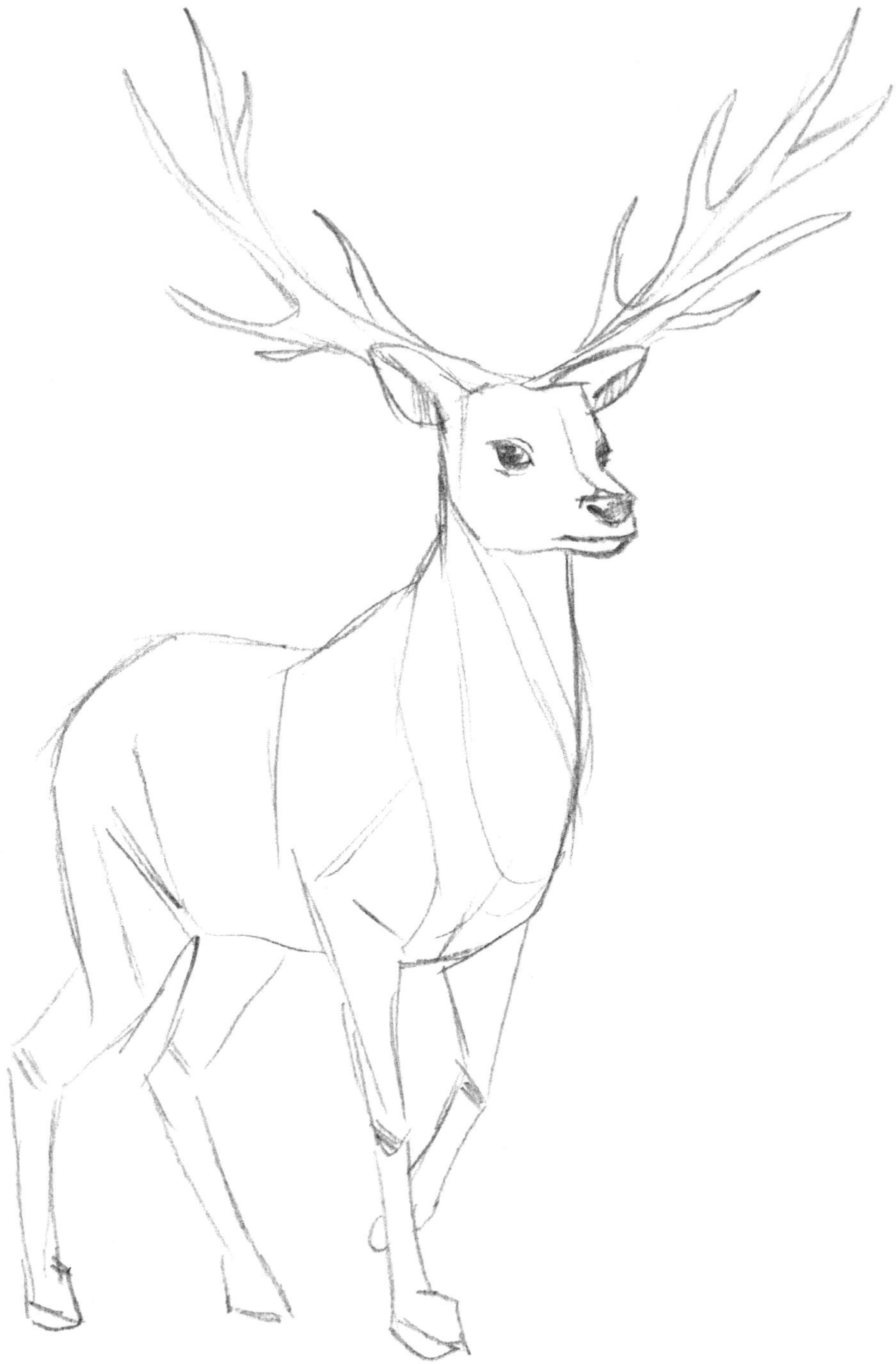

Death Eater Mask

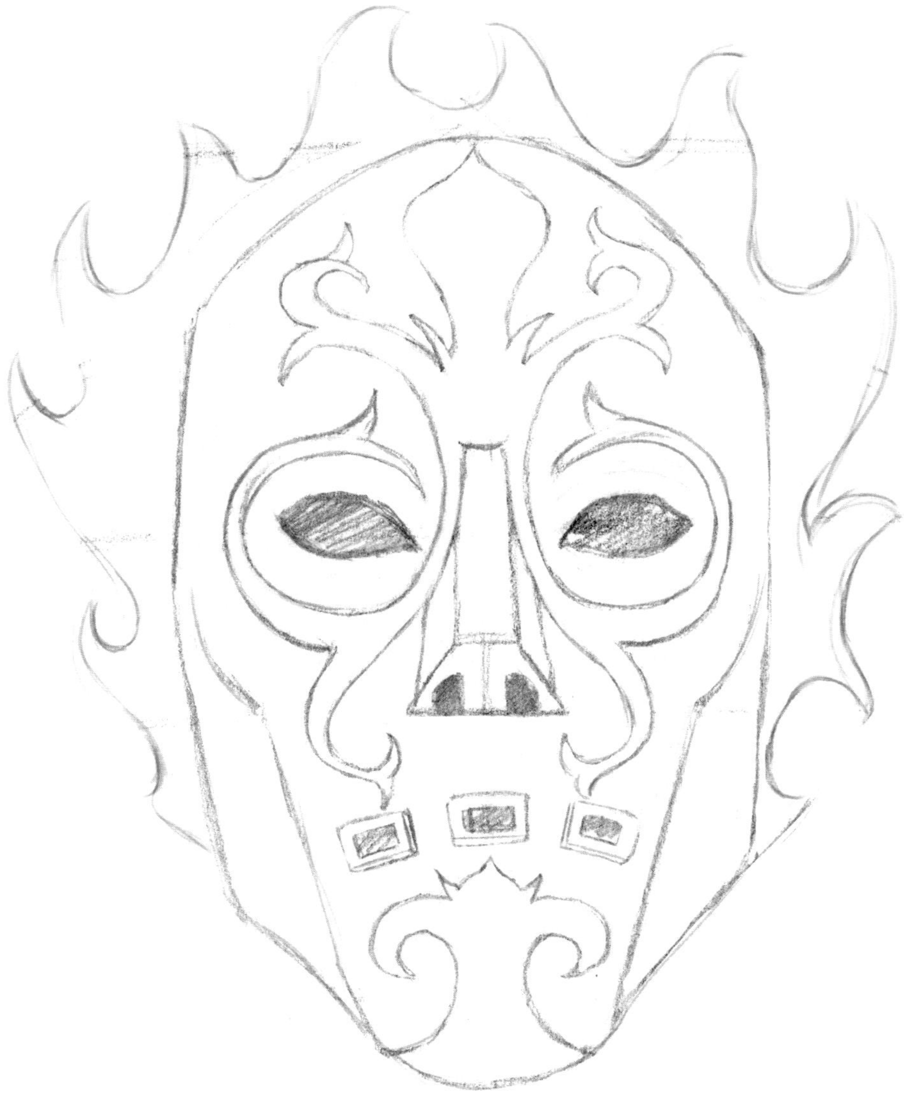

Tom Riddle's Diary and Basilisk Fang

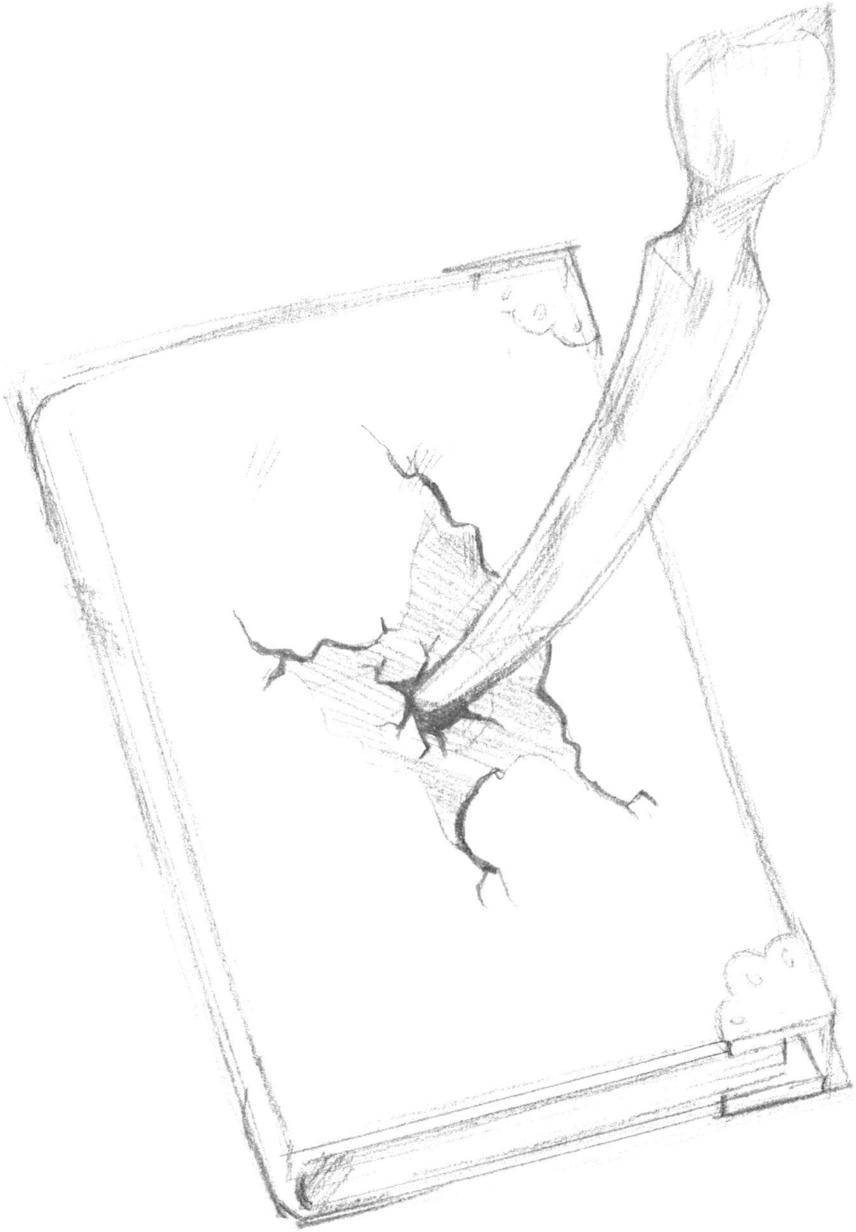

Bertie Bott's Every-Flavour Beans

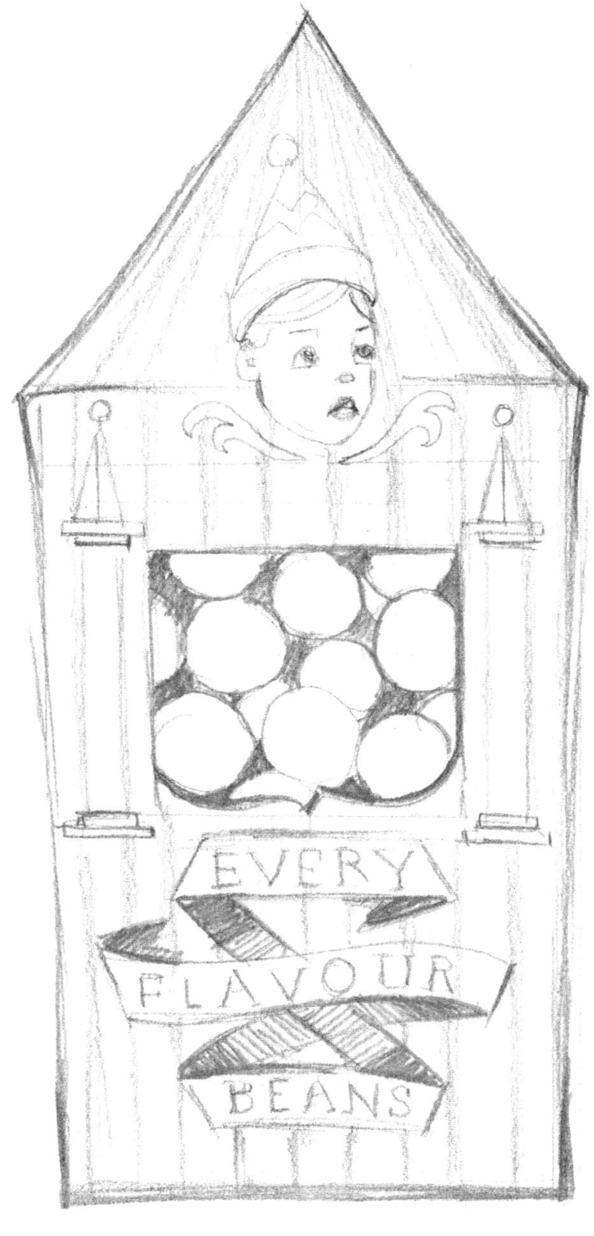
EVERY
FLAVOUR
BEANS

The Monster Book of Monsters

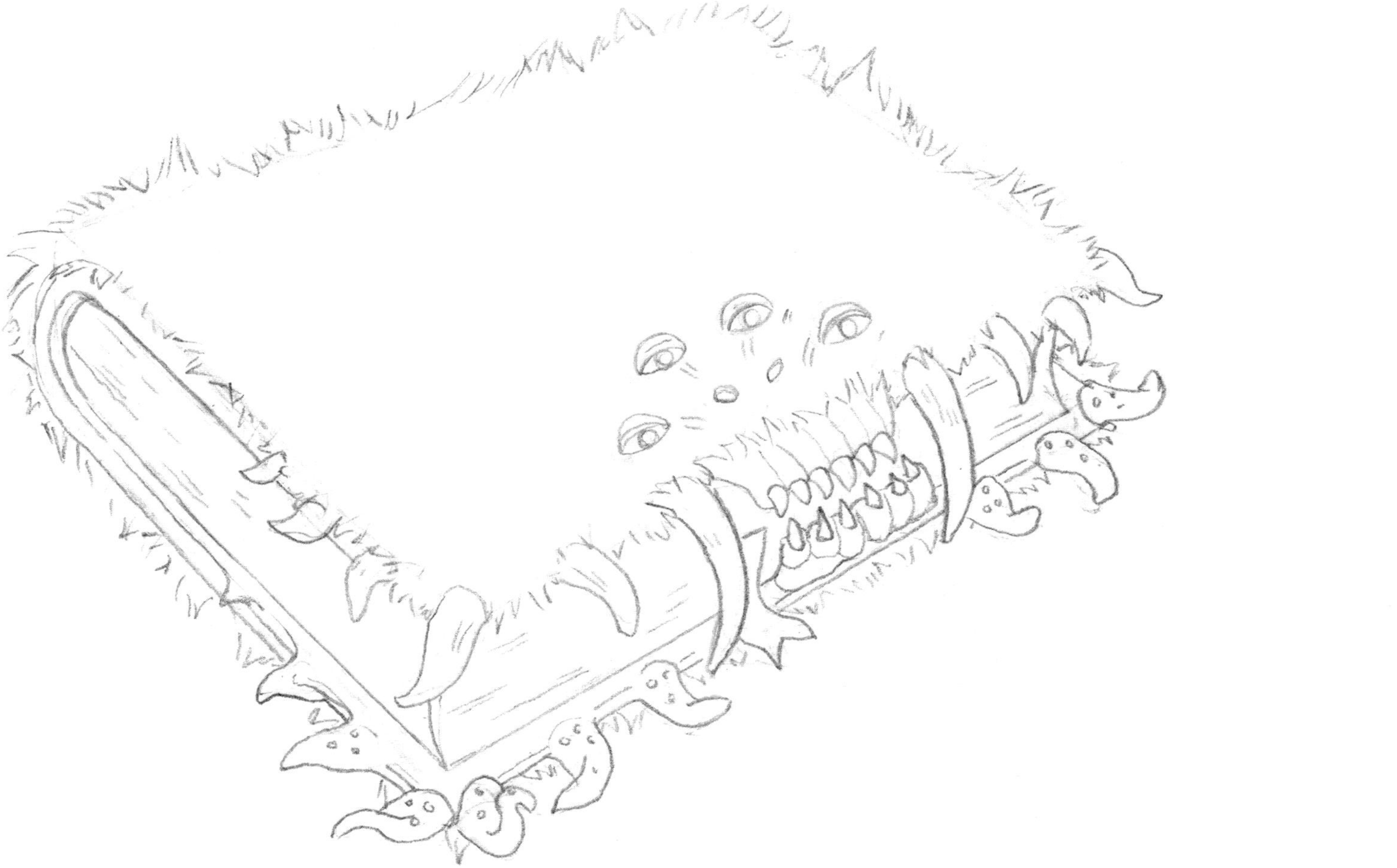

Chocolate Frog

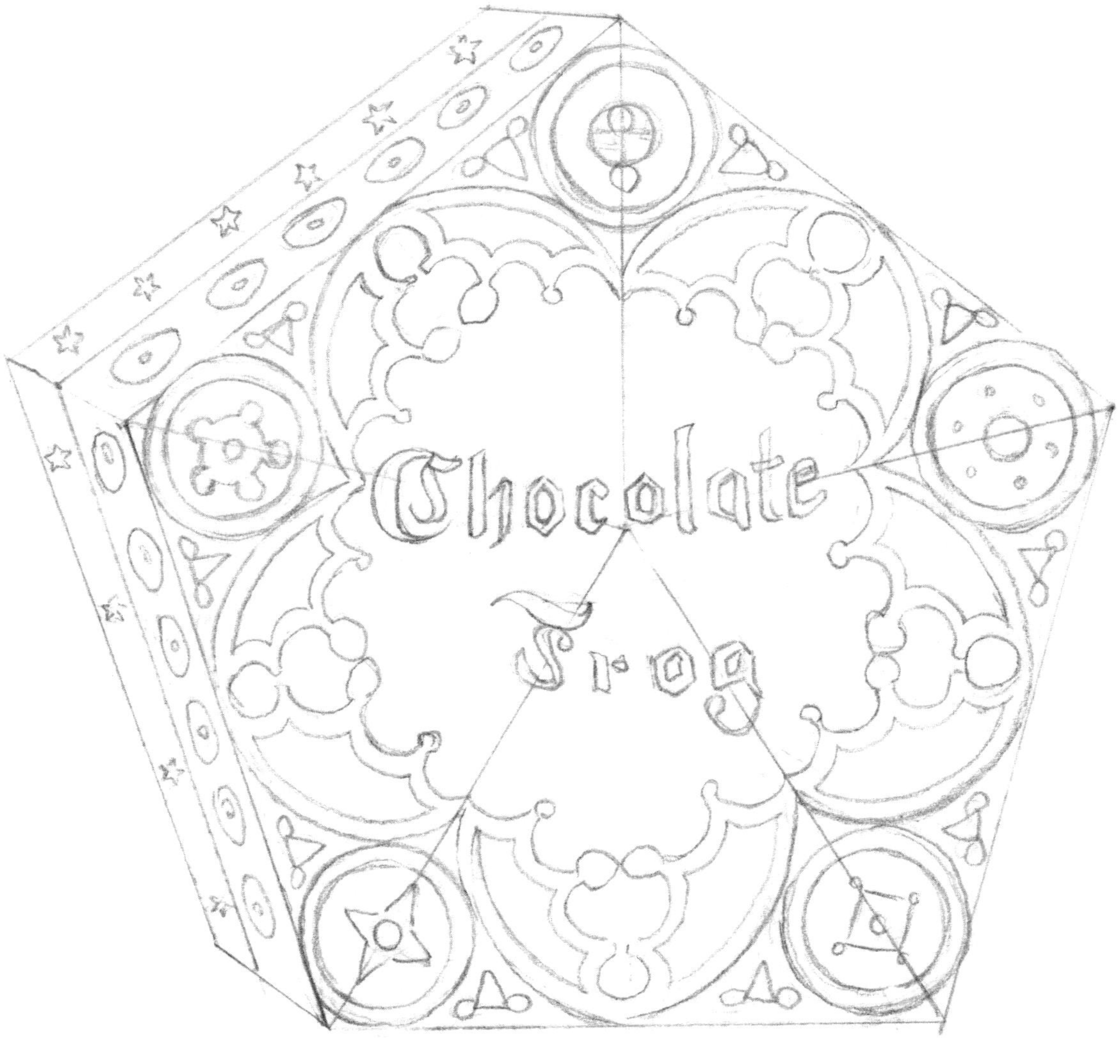
Chocolate
Frog

Hogwarts Castle

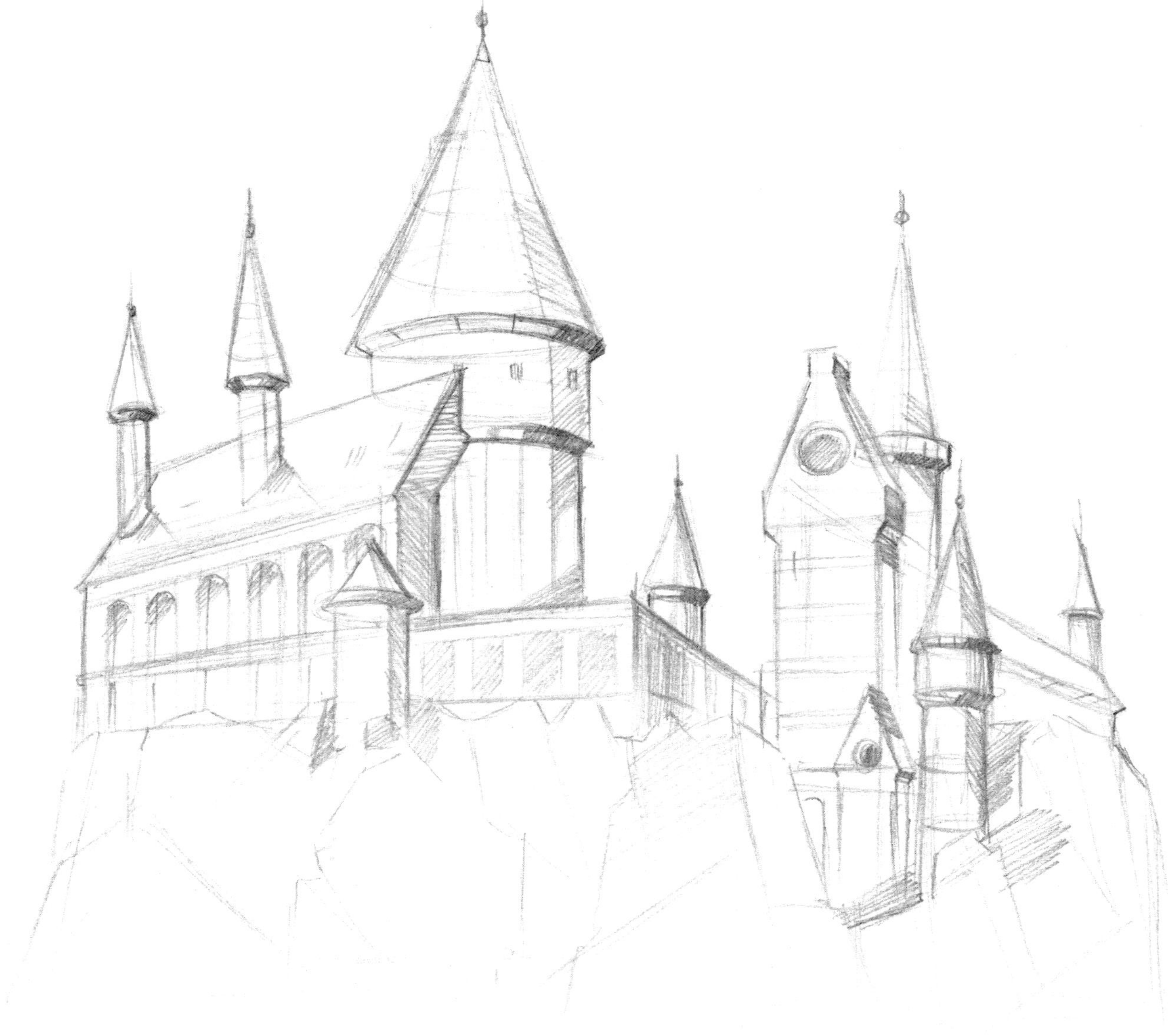

Howler

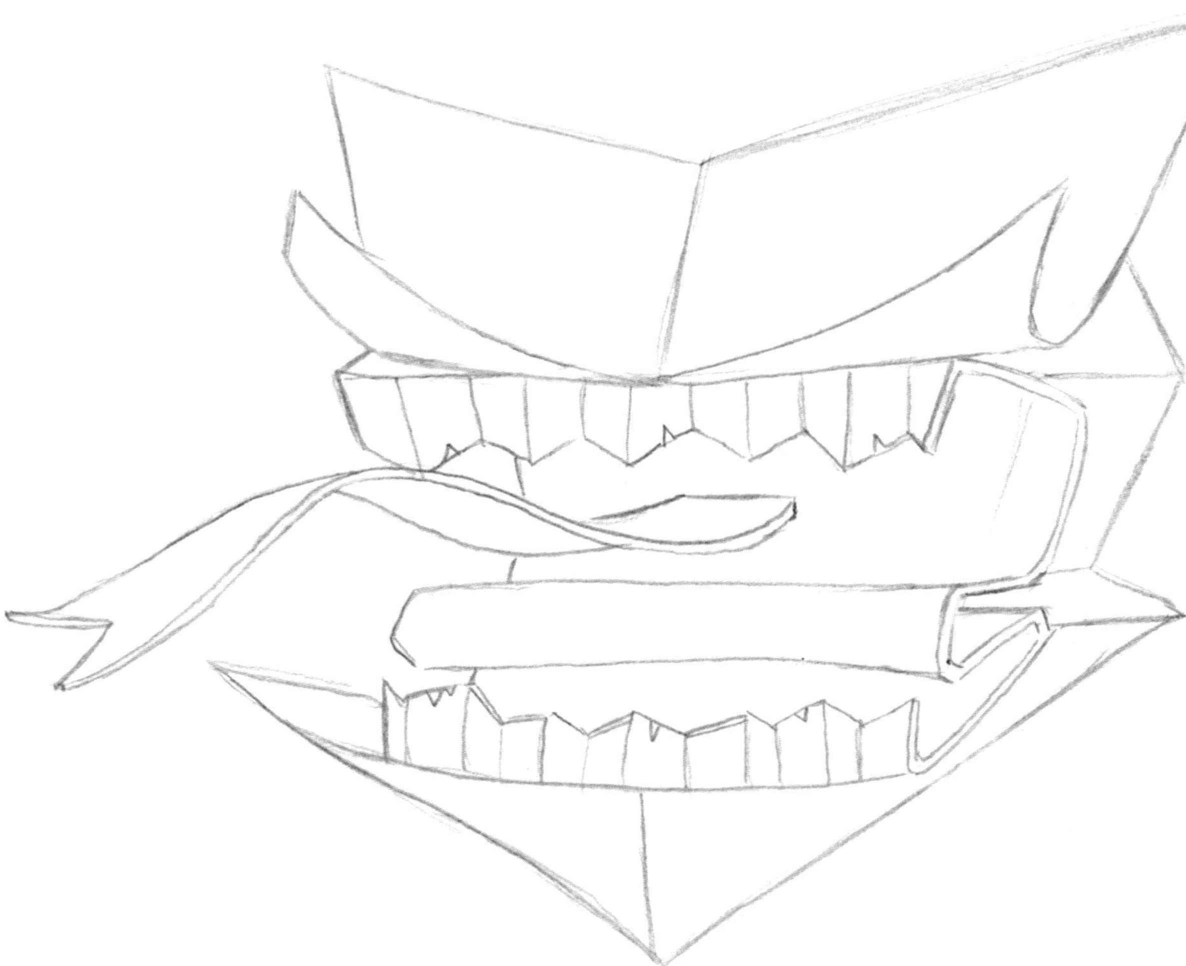

Time-Turner

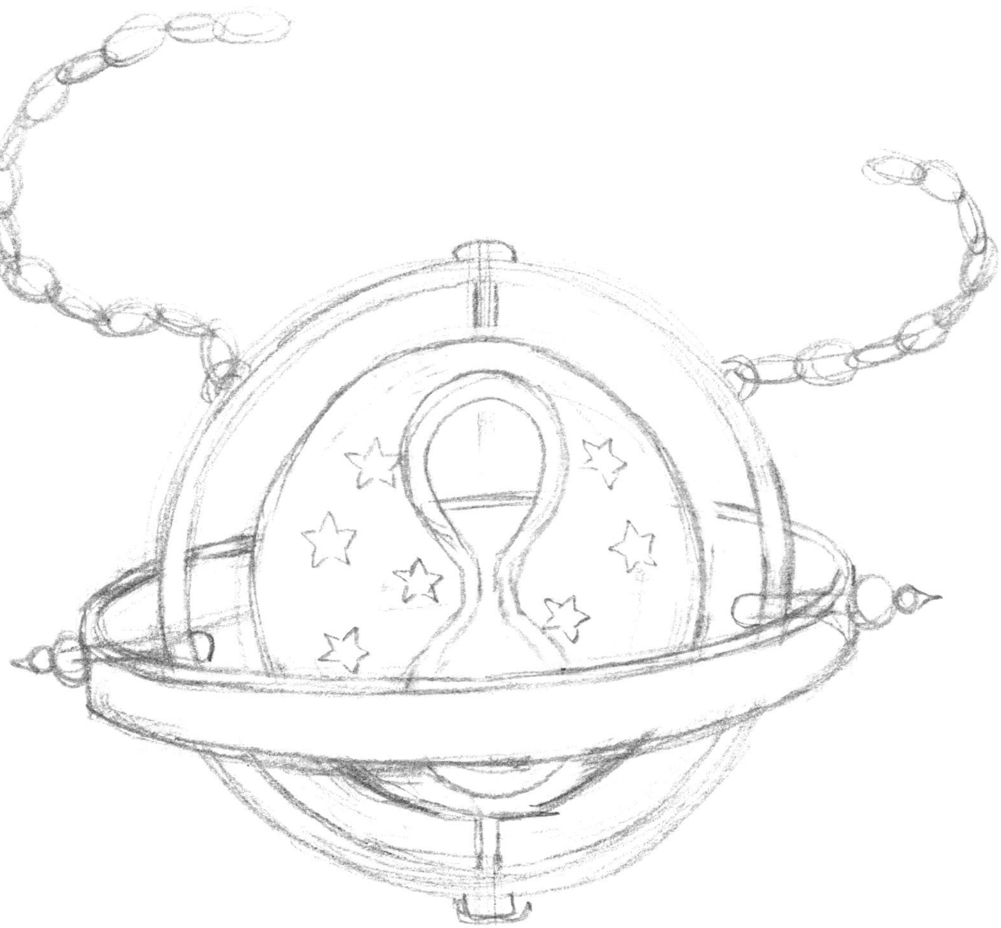

The Dark Mark

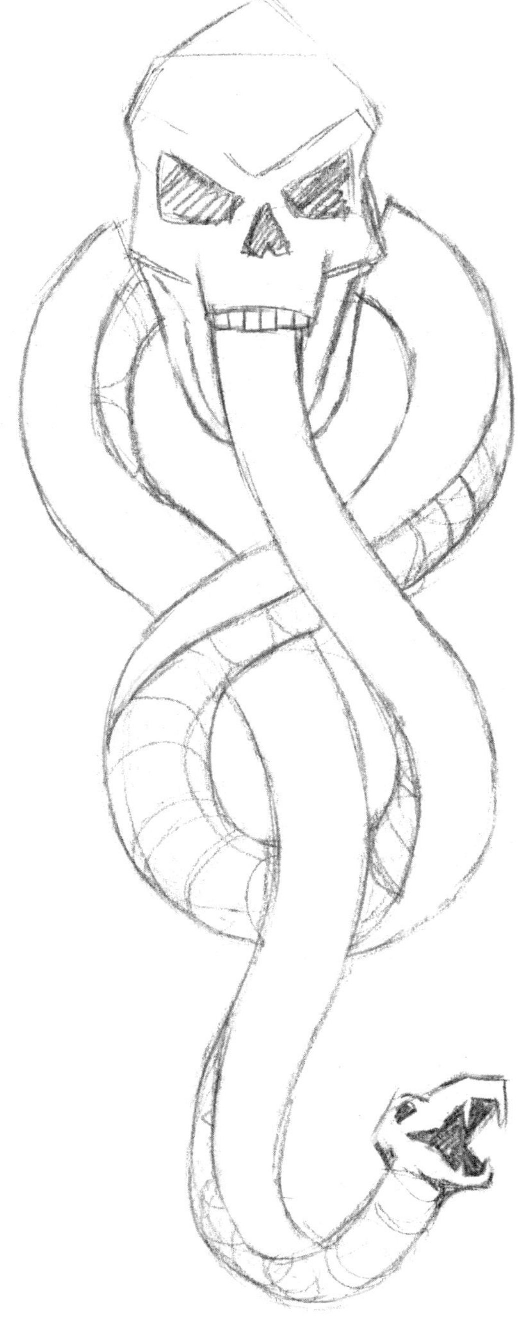

The Whomping Willow

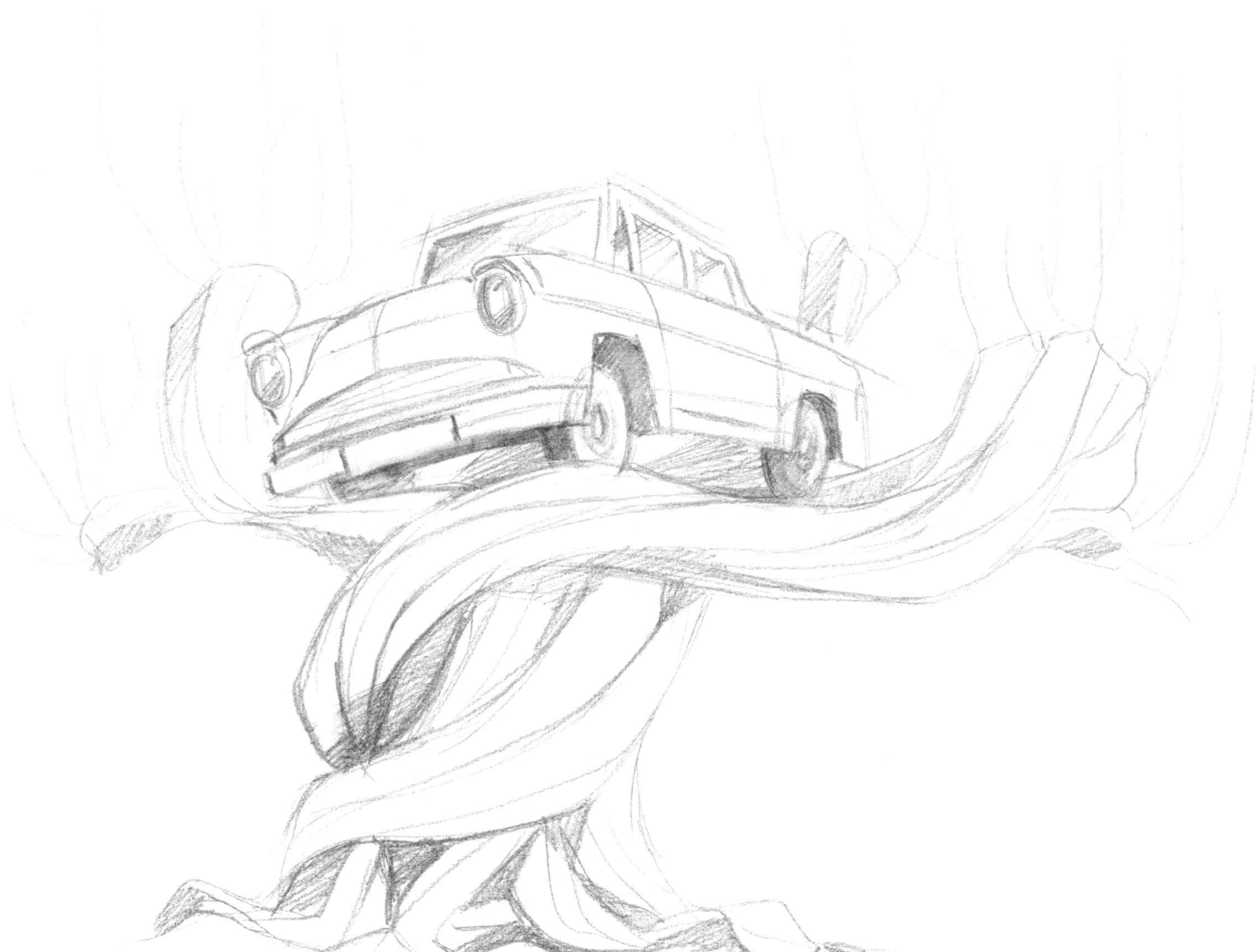

The Knight Bus

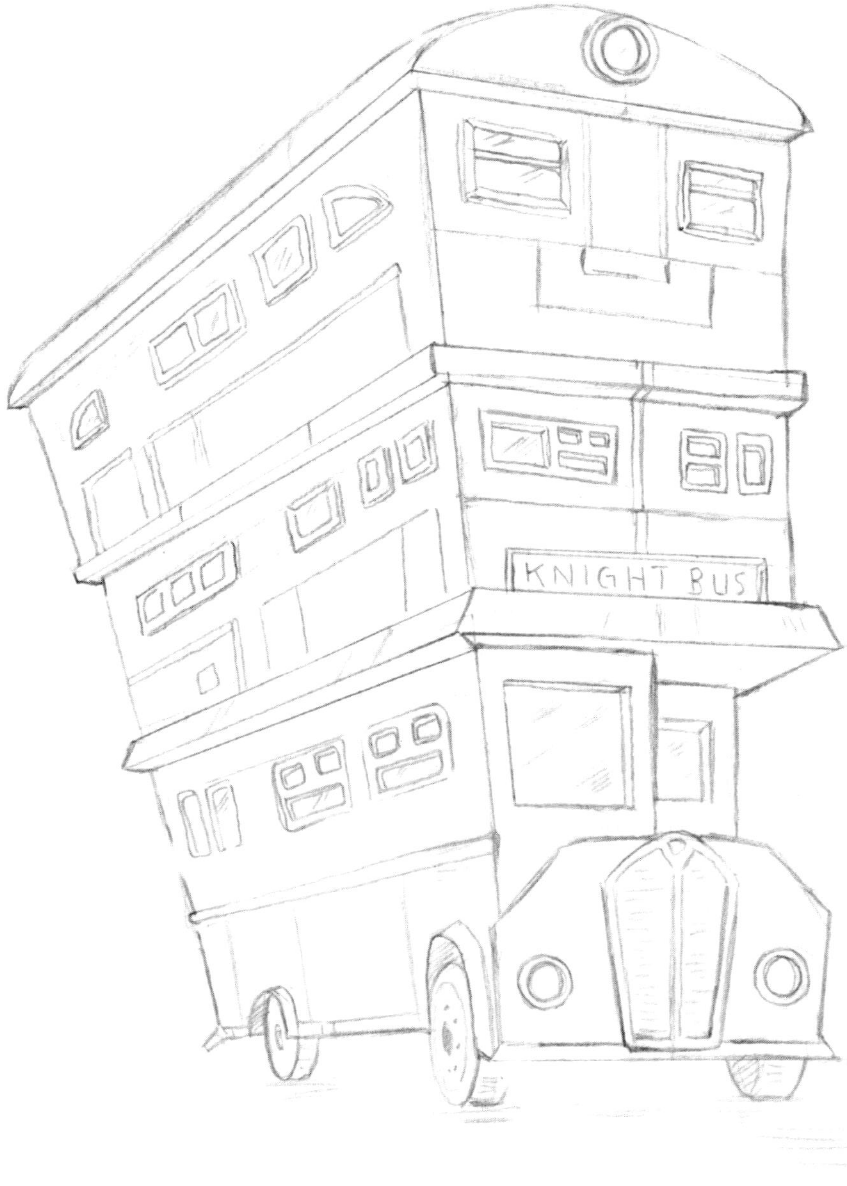
KNIGHT BUS

Hogwarts Express

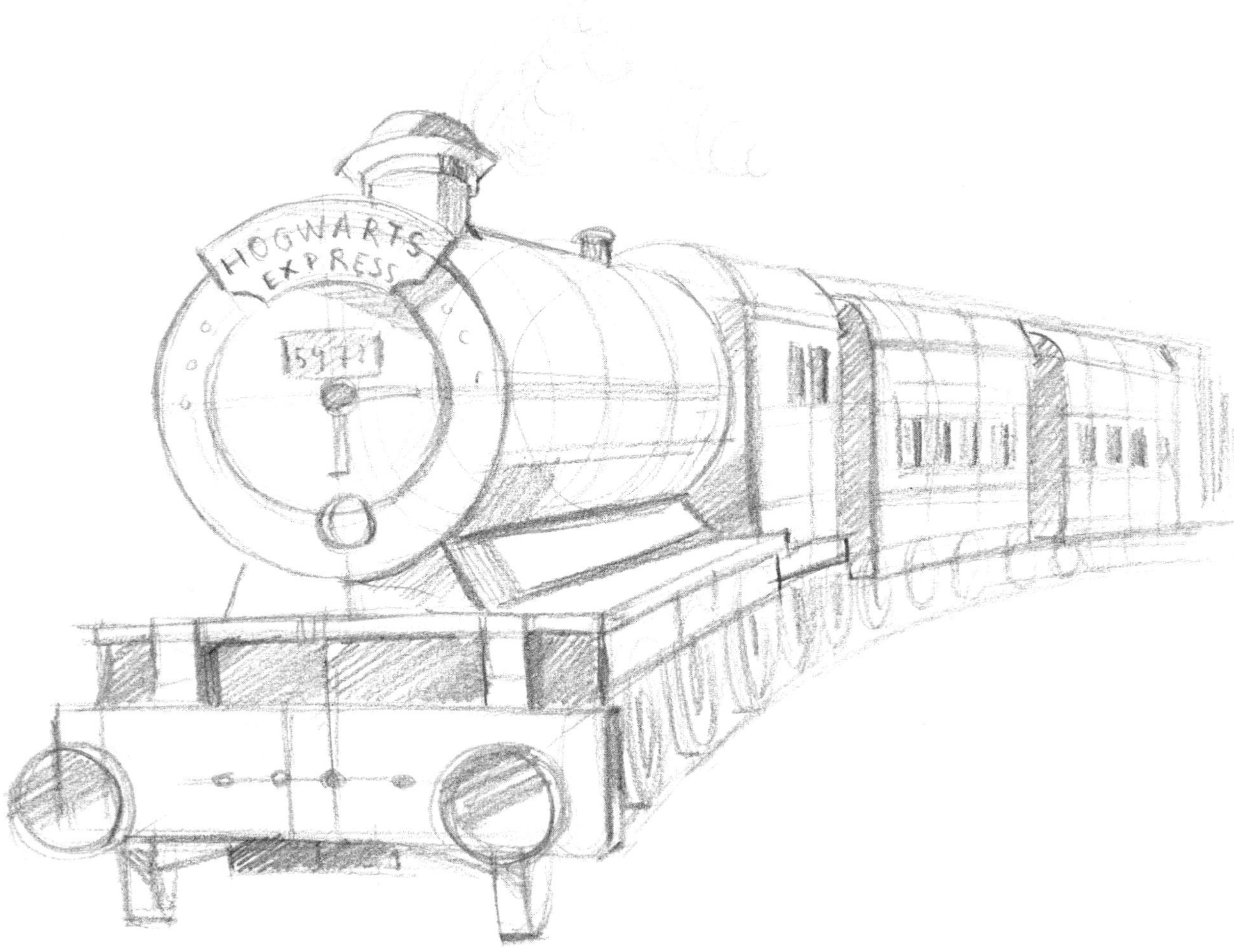
HOGWARTS
EXPRESS
5972

The Forbidden Forest